CHARMING CHISELER

Jenna Ross Thriller, Book 2

Judith A. Barrett

Wobbly Creek, LLC

CHARMING CHISELER

JENNA ROSS THRILLER BOOK 2

Published in the United States of America by Wobbly Creek, LLC

2025 Georgia

wobblycreek.com

Cover by Wobbly Creek, LLC

ISBN 978-1-953870-99-5 eBook

ISBN 978-1-967288-04-5 Paperback

DEDICATION

Charming Chiseler is dedicated to the colors peach and soft green and to hard-working farmers, especially those with peach, citrus, and pecan orchards.

PREVIOUSLY

My name is Jenna Ross. I'm an accountant and have been alone, except for my sweet Golden Retriever, Katy, since my husband was killed in action five years ago.

I have an unusual gift of touch. Sometimes when I touch people, I feel their joy, sorrow, or anger as if it were my own; my gift however, has an intense side of intuition so sharp that it manifests as visions when I touch certain objects, and it feels more like a burden.

Almost a year ago, I inherited a charming bed-and-breakfast in Georgia through my husband's family. I hoped having a renewed purpose in my life would help heal my grief as I threw all my energy into reviving the Peach Blossom Retreat.

To my surprise, the business flourished beyond what one person could manage, so I hired Morgan Farley, a former hotel manager, as my operations manager. Architect Shane Lawson and general contractor Clarence Moore updated the inn and installed an automated security system. Their work continued with repairing my cottage behind the inn and updating an old barn on my property to become an event center. Mr. Moore and his wife, Bobbie, leased the barn to establish the event center.

My only irritant was the grumpy landscaper, Ethan Bentley, who didn't have a good word to say about anything I did, but to be fair, the feeling was mutual.

When I heard about an embezzlement at a large bank, it sparked my curiosity as an accountant, but after I found the body of a guest who had ties to the bank, I was drawn to untangle the web of deceit.

Despite the ongoing tension between the irritable Ethan Bentley and me, I closed in on the truth thanks to my intuitive senses and with the help of the 1922 portrait of twenty-two-year-old Nettie Wyndham, the owner of the Wyndham estate in the 1920s, and Nettie's presence through her yellow chair.

Spoiler alert: I stopped the killer, and Ethan and I agreed on a tenuous truce.

CHAPTER ONE

Jenna stared at the phone as she hung up. "That was a surprise."

"What's that?" Morgan had entered their new, shared office from the dining room. Her hot pink shirt complemented her dark brown skin, and her crisp, navy blue trousers added to her always-professional look.

Katy, Jenna's golden retriever, stretched then rolled over for a belly rub.

Morgan chuckled as she set the file folder she carried on Jenna's sturdy oak desk and kneeled next to Katy. "I see you had the same idea I did, Jenna. You're chasing away the Monday blues with your pale pink floral shirt."

"Seemed like the thing to do." Jenna smiled as she twisted her long, dark blonde hair into a messy bun and fastened it with a pink clip. Her faded jeans and western boots rounded out her more casual style.

"One of my former college acquaintances, Renee Sabot, will be here this afternoon and is bringing her assistant. She also requested two additional rooms on Friday for her editor and her writing collaborator."

Morgan gave Katy one last pat before she rose. "*The Renee Sabot?* Famous, world-renowned investigative journalist?"

"I don't know about all that, but the word on campus was that she was a natural-born snoop. I think she took that to heart and seized on it as a career." Jenna rolled her eyes.

"It's a wonder she didn't pursue a career in law enforcement," Morgan said.

Jenna shrugged. "When one of her friends teased her about it in the dining hall, she said there were too many rules." Jenna tilted her head. "Do you know her too?"

"Not personally, only by reputation, but I do know she has made a lot of enemies in her career."

"That's the Renee I knew. She definitely enjoyed stepping on toes. Anyway, she asked me to maintain her privacy and keep her visit confidential."

"We can do that; I'll refer to her as your old friend from college, but why is she coming here?"

"She was looking for a secluded place to work on her latest high profile case, and one of our former classmates told her assistant I owned the Peach Blossom Retreat. When the assistant looked us up online, she discovered The Barn and suggested Renee may want to check it out too while she's here."

"Bobbie has been advertising The Barn to build up interest for June weddings, family reunions, and graduation parties; she'll be happy to hear her ads are working." Morgan pointed to the folder on Jenna's desk. "The folder is from Shane; he wants you to review his sketches."

Jenna narrowed her eyes. "What are you doing here? Monday is your day off, and you're wearing work clothes."

"I'm doing Shane a favor. The sketches, remember?"

Jenna snorted as she opened the folder then raised her eyebrows. "I expected the sketches to be for the cottage, but these are for The Barn."

When she picked up the first page, she gasped for a breath and dropped the paper on her desk. *Shane is suffocating.*

Jenna cleared her throat. "Is Shane okay?"

"Not really; working with Bobbie is taking a toll on him, but please don't tell him I said anything." Morgan bit her lip. "He has some ideas that will cut the time for The Barn to be ready for guests and increase the overall efficiency of the operation, but he's frustrated because Bobbie won't listen to him, and Ethan said to leave him out of it."

"Typical Ethan," Jenna muttered.

Morgan glared. "You're not giving Ethan much slack."

"I'm giving him the slack he deserves because it's true; he doesn't want to get involved in anything."

Morgan sighed. "Shane's thinking about resigning from the project, so I told him he should talk to you. Text him after you've looked over his plans. He left to go into town to pick up some paint swatches for the colors Bobbie wanted. After he drops them off at the barn, he could come here."

Jenna read the page that lay flat on her desk; she quickly flipped it over to read the back page. She gingerly picked up the next page and examined the sketch on the second sheet.

Morgan asked, "When will Renee and her party be leaving?"

Jenna glanced up at her. "Renee said the four of them will leave on Sunday unless there are any loose ends; in that case, her assistant will stay with us another day or two."

Morgan furrowed her brow. "It didn't occur to me they'd be here through the weekend; I'll grab the reservation book."

When Morgan returned with the book, she handed it to Jenna. "What do you think about this? We can put Renee and her party in four of the upstairs guestrooms. Two couples are arriving on Thursday. They're friends, so I can put them in the two downstairs guestrooms that face the front of the inn. Another couple is arriving on Friday, and they specifically requested a downstairs room, so they could have the guestroom next to yours. That leaves us one empty room upstairs."

Jenna nodded as she followed along. "That's good."

"As a hotelier, I appreciate that all the rooms have their own ensuite bathrooms because it makes assigning guestrooms so much easier. People aren't really interested in sharing bathrooms, even if it is a tradition of B&Bs." Morgan rubbed her forehead. "I thought this might be a slow weekend for a change."

Jenna sighed. "So did I."

"Should I let Darlene know we'll have two guests for happy hour, or is that a bad idea because she'll prepare enough appetizers for six people?"

Jenna nodded. "I don't think you'll want to leave Darlene in the dark unless you plan to bake the pastries for tomorrow's continental breakfast. Tell Darlene and Wendy about the guests. When we see Shane, let's invite him to help us eat appetizers."

"Good point; I'm not the chef type. Wasn't Wendy a magnificent find for a housekeeper? She is very thorough and loves to surprise guests with her towel art. Shane and I already made dinner plans, but I'll send him a quick text about coming here for happy hour. I'm sure he'll be here. Can you tell how excited I am about Renee Sabot coming to the inn?"

Jenna snickered. "I'm sensing a bit of nervous energy in the air."

Morgan paced. "I'm a little worried because we'll have only one room available for this weekend unless Mr. Moore can pull out a miracle so you can finally move into your new home. I thought it was a mistake to delay rebuilding your cottage until after all the updates for the inn were completed, but the cottage will be ready sooner than I expected, so I guess you were right."

Jenna raised her eyebrows. "I don't suppose you'd care to share that I was right with Ethan, our know-it-all landscaper. Mr. Moore's crew is close to completing the project, but I don't know when the inspector is available, so I haven't seen any reason to push. I can always get a cot and sleep in the office for a weekend."

"I'd love to argue with you, but I have to talk to Darlene and Wendy first; bickering with you is more fun with a glass of wine in my hand, anyway." Morgan went into the kitchen and closed the door behind her.

Jenna furrowed her brow as she jotted down suggestions for Shane on her notepad. *This is really an interesting project, but I can see why Bobbie and Shane are clashing.*

While she was deep in thought as she examined Shane's sketch for the third time, her phone rang and startled her.

She smiled as she answered. "Hey, Bobbie."

"Are you terribly busy, Jenna? Do you have time to come to The Barn for a few minutes? I need a common sense perspective on a minor issue that is driving me nuts."

"Sure; Katy and I could use the walk. We'll be there in fifteen minutes."

Jenna threw on her lightweight jacket. "How about a walk, Katy?"

Katy trotted to the door to the dining room and whined. After Jenna opened the door, Katy dashed to the back door. Jenna passed the kitchen and called out, "Katy and I are going for a walk."

Darlene grumbled in Spanish then asked, "Why doesn't she come into the kitchen if she wants to talk?"

"Katy and Jenna are going for a walk," Morgan shouted.

"Why didn't she say so?"

Jenna shook her head. *Darlene's hearing is getting worse.*

While Jenna hurried along the path to the barn, Katy dashed into the brush then grinned when she popped out on the path ahead of Jenna.

When they reached the barn and reception building, Bobbie was standing on the reception center porch. Her silver hair was twisted into her signature bun on the crown of her head. Bobbie's bright pink blouse matched her pink cane.

Her eyes twinkled. "I see you got the memo that the color of the day is pink. Come into my office, Bean Counter."

Jenna chuckled as she and Katy followed Bobbie inside.

Jenna examined the reception area. "This is much larger than I thought it would be. The wood floor is nice. Are you going to move the arm chairs that are against the wall into a conversation grouping?"

Bobbie said, "I was thinking the space should be more of a waiting room, not a sitting room. Let's go into my office."

After they were seated, Bobbie continued, "Shane and I are having trouble agreeing on anything. I know I'm a stubborn woman, but I can't get him to understand he's the architect, and I'm the designer. I need a fresh approach to deal with him. What would you suggest?"

"Does he have any valid points?"

Bobbie stared at her. "That's a different perspective; I don't know because after I tell him for the third time what I want, his face gets red, and then he leaves."

Jenna raised her eyebrows.

Bobbie exhaled. "When I'm online with my groups, I pay attention to the nuances of not only what people say but also what they don't say. I'll try it with Shane."

Jenna nodded. "You might be surprised how well it works for you."

Bobbie sniffed. "I suppose I can try to be civil. That's not my strong suit when dealing with the bull-headed, know-it-alls like Shane and Ethan."

"I understand exactly what you're saying; Ethan must thrive on being annoying."

Bobbie tapped her fingers on her desk and then rose with the help of her pink cane.

Jenna watched as Bobbie paced.

Bobbie sighed. "I've kept a diary of my online groups, but the information might be too sensitive to leave it where just anyone might find it. I call it my diary of secrets, and I have to arrange for it to be in safer hands. Is that paranoid?"

"Without knowing what I'm talking about, I would guess it would depend on how easily identified the people could be in your notes and how compromising the information might be. You have a reputation for fighting for the underdog, so I would assume you wouldn't have written anything hurtful about the people in your groups."

As Jenna rose to leave, her fingertips brushed against a dark green hardcover book on the corner of Bobbie's desk that was on top of a spiral notebook. Her fingers tingled. *Secrets.*

Jenna stared at the book.

Bobbie was already in the doorway and glanced back at Jenna. "Are you coming? You were a big help; thanks."

Jenna smiled as she followed Bobbie to the front door. "Anytime."

On the way back to the inn, Jenna frowned. *There was much more to that conversation than Bobbie let on. Her diary of secrets was on her desk. What was the spiral notebook?*

Jenna returned to her office and then went into the kitchen. "Where's Morgan?" she asked.

"I don't know. If she's not in the office, she must be upstairs. I can't keep track of either of you," Darlene grumbled.

Jenna called Shane.

"Oh, good; a friendly voice." Shane chuckled as he answered.

"And I have news for you that will make you happy. I went over your plans for the barn, and you've nailed it. I'm ready to discuss them so we can finalize your plans whenever you're available."

"That's great news. I'll be there in thirty minutes."

After Jenna reviewed the month to date expenses and compared them to the prior year, she made a few changes to her budget to reflect the updated expenses.

While she jotted down notes for Morgan, Darlene shouted from the kitchen, "Boss Lady, come tell me what you think."

Jenna finished her note for Morgan and sighed. *Two entrances to the office aren't as convenient as I thought they would be.*

Jenna went into the kitchen and joined her wiry chef who stood at the commercial-sized stove. Darlene pushed back her gray hair from her forehead with the back of her arm and pointed at a small bowl on the counter behind her. "Try that."

Jenna examined the bowl and spoke loudly so Darlene would hear her. "Corn salad?"

Darlene smiled. "Mexican street corn salad. It's my special recipe; tell me if it's too spicy."

Jenna took a small bite, and then a larger bite. "Mmm; tasty, and just enough spice to give me a mouth buzz but not a mouth burn. It's perfect."

"What's perfect?" Morgan came into the kitchen.

"Try this." Darlene served up another small portion of the corn salad.

Morgan took a bite. "Mmm. I like it."

When Shane strode into the kitchen wearing a navy blue shirt with a bright yellow tie, he smiled at Morgan. "Hello, stranger; long time, no see."

Morgan giggled, and Jenna rolled her eyes.

Darlene pulled out another small bowl with Mexican street corn and set it on the counter. "You look like a fancy lawyer on your way to a courtroom."

Shane frowned. "That doesn't sound good."

"It's very good; you're always professional," Darlene said. "Here. Your taste buds are more delicate than Boss Lady's. Is this too spicy?"

Shane peered over his glasses to examine the appetizer then took a bite. After he finished the corn salad with his next bite, Shane stared at the small bowl. "I'm not sure; I might need another sample."

Darlene chuckled as she pulled out a larger serving and handed it to Shane. "It must not be too bad."

Jenna smiled. "Bring your bowl with you so we can go over your plan."

"I have a few more things to do upstairs. I'll be down soon." Morgan finger-waved at Shane then left.

Shane ate his corn salad while he followed Jenna to the office. He stopped in the doorway as he scanned the room. "Does the shared large office still work?"

"It's perfect for collaboration, and both of us micro-focus on our tasks, so there's no distraction."

After they sat at the wooden work table that had developed a soft patina from years of service, Shane smacked his lips as he opened his briefcase. "The heat of Darlene's appetizer sneaks up on you, doesn't it? I have a more recent draft to show you."

He put a sketch of the reception center building on the table and pointed with his pencil. "Bobbie originally wanted shelves lining the wall opposite the wide porch for storage in the barn, but I convinced her we'd have more room and flexibility for events if we expand the storage room at the reception center."

Jenna peered at the sketch. "It looks like you're taking space from Bobbie's office and the reception area; is that right?"

"Yes, and Bobbie was okay with it; what she didn't like was adding the second, wider door with a ramp at the back of the building. She thought it would detract from the overall high-end ambiance of The Barn."

"Shouldn't we have a ramp anyway, for wheelchairs? Maybe the reception center needs to be more rustic rather than elegant."

Shane pointed at the sketch with his pencil as he talked. "Our blueprint includes the ramp for wheelchairs at the entrance. I added double doors and a ramp to the back of the building. It's wide enough to move tables and chairs from the reception center to the barn. She said a second ramp would be an eyesore. Our discussion turned into an argument, and she threw this at me."

He pulled out a dark green hardcover book from his briefcase. "She told me to give it to you because I didn't understand women. I didn't look at it, but I think it must be her design notes. She gave me a pamphlet for furniture too."

Jenna raised her eyebrows. *Bobbie's diary of secrets.*

Shane's phone buzzed a text. When he glanced at it, he set the book and the pamphlet on top of Jenna's file cabinet and snorted. "I just now got a strange text from Bobbie in response to a text I sent her yesterday. I left the barn less than thirty minutes ago. Her text just said help. Do you suppose it's just a pocket text?"

Shane handed Jenna his phone. Jenna frowned. "Could be, or something might have happened. Is she still at her office in the reception center?"

"As far as I know. She might yell at me for hovering, but I'm going to check on her. Can we continue our discussion later?"

"Of course; can I go with you?" Jenna handed back his phone.

"Let's go," Shane said.

Jenna grabbed her coat on the way out, and Katy followed them as they rushed outside.

Shane held his car's back door open for Katy while Jenna climbed into the passenger seat. As he roared down the road toward the barn, he said, "Bobbie's more bossy than dramatic."

"That's true, but I hope this is an accidental call."

On their way to The Barn, a car sped past them as it headed toward town. Jenna caught a brief glimpse of the driver, but the windows were darkly tinted, so all she could tell was the driver was tall.

Jenna exhaled. *Darlene would say I think everybody is tall.*

Shane whipped into The Barn's driveway and sped up the driveway, spewing gravel on the way. After he slammed on the brakes in front of the reception center, Jenna hopped out and opened the door for Katy. As Shane ran toward the building, Jenna raced to The Barn with Katy alongside her.

When she reached the barn, Jenna's chest tightened at the sight of Bobbie who was sprawled on her stomach in the middle of the floor.

Katy growled then barked.

Jenna yelled, "Shane, she's here!"

Katy dashed to Bobbie and nudged her as Jenna dropped to her knees; when Bobbie didn't respond, Katy whined.

Jenna put her face close to Bobbie's and lightly placed her fingers on Bobbie's neck.

Jenna exhaled in relief as Shane rushed in. "Her breathing is rapid and shallow, and her pulse is weak, but at least she's breathing."

"I'll call for help." While Shane was on his phone, Jenna examined the wooden ladder on the floor; one side of the top step had broken loose and was resting on the step below it. The ladder lay on a side rail with its legs locked open, and next to it was a broken light bulb with shards of glass surrounding it. Jenna leaned close to Bobbie again. *Still breathing.*

"Keep breathing, Bobbie," she whispered.

Jenna was so focused on watching Bobbie breathe Shane startled her when he spoke. "I called nine-one-one and Ethan."

Jenna grit her teeth. "Ethan? Why didn't you call Morgan?"

"She's busy, and Ethan will bring Mr. Moore here. Did you and Ethan have another falling out?"

When she glared at him, Shane walked out.

Bobbie's so pale. As Jenna smoothed Bobbie's hair away from her face, Jenna's fingertips stung like she'd been zapped by static electricity. A gust of wind blew through the barn. *My cane. Hit me with my cane.*

"I'm so sorry, Bobbie; Shane called for help." She scanned the room. *Where's Bobbie's pink cane?*

Jenna craned her neck to stare up at the bare rafters. She frowned at the bare lightbulb that dangled from a cord overhead. *None of this makes sense.*

Jenna leaned close to Bobbie and whispered, "The ambulance will be here soon."

In a few minutes that seemed like an eternity, the muffled sound of a siren in the distance soon pierced the air with its howling tones.

"They're almost here, Bobbie. Can you hear them?" Jenna held her breath as she waited for a reaction from Bobbie.

Jenna stiffened her back when she heard Ethan's truck roar up the driveway, followed by a car and the ambulance.

"Do you know what happened?" Mr. Moore asked as he hurried into The Barn with Shane at his side. A deputy sheriff followed them in.

"It looked like she might have fallen off the ladder," Shane said. "We didn't move her."

Ethan led the ambulance crew inside as they rushed to Bobbie with their cot. Shane offered Jenna a hand to help her to her feet. She furrowed her brow when Ethan glared at Shane. *What's he so cranky about?*

The paramedic assessed Bobbie. "Let's load and go."

The crew rolled her to a backboard so they could lift her without causing her any more injury, and then strapped the board onto the cot.

Ethan took Mr. Moore's arm, and they followed the crew as they rolled the cot to the ambulance. Shane walked along behind them.

Jenna strode to the barn door and flipped the light switch. The bare bulb hanging from the rafter and all the newly installed inset lights came on. She turned off the switch.

After the ambulance left with sirens blaring, Shane, the deputy, and Ethan returned to the barn.

Ethan asked, "Is there anything else we need to do here?"

"Bobbie will want her purse; it's probably in her office." Jenna avoided Ethan's icy blue eyes and his new mustache as she scanned the area around the heavy barn door, but before she and Katy headed toward the reception center, the deputy stopped her.

"Miss Jenna, did you see Mrs. Moore fall?" the deputy asked.

Jenna shook her head.

"It's best if you don't remove anything until after the investigators have inspected the scene," the deputy said.

"That makes sense," Jenna said.

Ethan and Shane caught up with Jenna at the reception center door as she continued inside.

Shane said, "I thought the deputy said..."

Jenna interrupted him. "He said don't remove anything; I won't. I need to use the restroom, and the ones in the barn don't have any supplies."

She scanned the reception area then checked the office. Bobbie's purse was open and on her office chair, and her cell phone was on the floor under her desk. Jenna furrowed her brow. *Where's her cane?*

"Are you looking for something?" Ethan joined her at the door to Bobbie's office.

Jenna stuck her nose in the air and pushed past him. She checked the restrooms. *Nothing.*

Jenna headed toward the front door.

Shane asked, "Do we postpone our discussion about The Barn until later, Jenna?"

Jenna rubbed her forehead. "I don't know."

Shane said, "Maybe we could have a brief conversation, so the project won't be delayed."

"Should I be included in the discussion?" Ethan asked.

Jenna forced her face to stay neutral as she side-glanced at Shane. *I think I understand how irritating it must have been for Bobbie to be in the middle of these two.*

"You've already said you weren't interested, but you're welcome to join us if you've changed your mind," Shane said.

"I think I have," Ethan said.

Shane nodded.

They really are irritating. Jenna stormed out of the building. On her way to Shane's car, Jenna stopped at Bobbie's car and peered inside. *Locked, and no cane.*

Jenna opened the back door of Shane's car for Katy then climbed into the passenger seat.

On their way back to the house, Shane asked, "What's the problem between you and Ethan now? Does Morgan know?"

Jenna grit her teeth. "It's nothing worth talking about."

Shane side-glanced at Jenna. "That's nice; then why do I feel like I'm in trouble for asking?"

Jenna sighed. "If you're in trouble, it's not with me."

Shane exhaled in relief. "Thanks. I'm always in hot water with Bobbie and sometimes Darlene, but I don't think I'm in trouble with Morgan. Maybe I'd better check. There is something going on with you, though. What is it?"

Jenna gazed at him. "I've been a little overwhelmed, and it's made me edgy. Let's talk about your plans for The Barn."

"You should tell Ethan that."

"Why? He doesn't care about the barn or how overwhelmed I am, and now you're sounding as bossy as Darlene," Jenna grumbled as Shane parked.

She opened the back door and Katy jumped out. After Jenna slammed the door with all her strength, she stretched her stride to walk away from Shane, but he kept up and walked alongside her.

"Do you mind?" she growled. "I'd like some time alone."

Shane stopped and raised both hands. When he took a sideways step away from her, Jenna side-glanced at him.

"Oh, come on," she said.

After they went into her office and sat at the work table, Jenna said, "I'm sorry I snapped at you."

Shane cleared his throat then shook his head. "Let's look at my draft for the reception center."

"Is the work on the barn finished?" Jenna asked.

"We still haven't decided if the walls will stay as-is, which are too rustic for my taste, or if we want a more finished look. The chandelier in the middle of the room is another open item. Do you have any ideas?"

"Not really; I was just curious. Let's look at the draft."

While Shane reviewed his plan, Ethan joined them.

Jenna glared at Ethan then returned her attention to Shane's plan. "I agree that the reception area is too big and needs to be scaled back. It looks like a warehouse when it should have a more cozy, friendly feel. Expanding the storage room makes sense, but I wouldn't take any space away from Bobbie's office."

Shane furrowed his brow as he examined his sketch then grabbed his pencil and drew some lines. "If we make the storage room this big, Bobbie's office can stay the same as it is, and the reception center will still be twice as big as Bobbie's office. Half of the storage area could be for storing tables and chairs."

Jenna and Ethan leaned over the paper on the table to scrutinize the sketch.

Jenna straightened her back and crossed her arms. "I can't see; you're in my way."

Ethan side-glanced at her then sat back. "Have you thought about a back door, so you aren't moving tables and chairs through the reception area?"

Shane nodded. "Bobbie and I talked about it earlier, but she vetoed it because she thought it would ruin the look of the building. She agreed it wasn't logical to store the tables and chairs in the barn, but now, how to store them in the building and move them to the barn is our top unresolved issue."

"How many tables and chairs has Bobbie ordered?" Jenna asked.

Shane his pencil tapped on the page. "She told me she planned to order enough for medium-sized parties, but I didn't get a straightforward answer about how many tables and chairs that would be. She said if she placed her order by Tuesday or Wednesday this week, they'd be delivered next week, so she had plenty of time to make sure she found what she wanted. Maybe I'm looking at this wrong. I'll focus on my estimate of tables and chairs and how we could store and move them in and out of storage. One of Bobbie's first designs was for a farmhouse-style reception center, but I thought it should be more upscale to appeal to the more affluent crowd. She told me I was wrong, and now I'm thinking I might have been. If I follow her design and put up temporary dividers, we'll have the reception and storage areas ready before the end of the week. She can always change the décor later."

"The driveway is finished, and the parking lot is waiting for the paint contractor. I planted chrysanthemums and snapdragons. If you decide to go with a back door, I'll put in a ramp and a service path to The Barn. Let me know if there's anything I can do to help you." Ethan rose and left.

When Shane's phone rang, he frowned as he glanced at it. "Excuse me; I have to take this."

Jenna nodded as she examined the draft more closely while Shane strode out of the office as he answered the phone.

A few minutes later, Shane returned and sat down at the table. "That was Mr. Moore. Bobbie has a serious head injury and is on her way to the trauma hospital in Atlanta. An old friend is driving Mr. Moore there. He doesn't have any idea how long he'll be gone. I told him not to worry about the projects because we'd step in."

"We, like you and me?" Jenna asked.

"Yes, except mostly you." Shane peered at Jenna. "Now, you can be mad at me."

Jenna shrugged. "Okay, but I would have told him the same thing. How do we split up the work?"

"The Barn project is at a point where I can finish it up; Ethan has a few minor tasks, but he's self-sufficient. I think we should ask Morgan to manage the reservations and to coordinate the subcontractors for food, decorations, and other stuff I don't know anything about."

"I can handle the billing and Adrienne, my lawyer's paralegal, can take care of any contracts. You talk to Morgan," Jenna said.

"I could, but it would be better if you talk to her."

"You're right, so we'll talk to her together. What about the cottage? Will that have to go on hold?"

"It's a completely separate project from the barn. There are workers who are counting on the income from the construction, but I'm sure Mr. Moore and his lawyer are looking at that. If I have a clear roadmap, I can manage the barn project, but I'm not qualified to tackle the cottage," Shane said.

"Taking care of the accounting is right up my alley. Payroll is the most important, but I'll have to talk to Mr. Moore about that."

Shane said, "I asked him about payroll, and he said we should talk to his lawyer."

"That helps."

Morgan came into the office. "Is this a private party?"

Morgan's eyes twinkled as she and Shane exchanged a look.

When Jenna fluttered her eyelashes, Morgan scowled at her.

While Jenna and Shane caught her up on what had happened, Morgan scribbled quick notes on a pad.

She asked, "Do we know how Bobbie planned to track reservations?"

"She hadn't decided," Shane said.

Morgan raised her eyebrows. "That makes it easy, then. I think I can add The Barn as a subset of the reservations for the B&B. I'll call our tech support at the reservation system to walk me through it. Shane, can you give me an overall concept of what we expect for The Barn and reservations?"

"Sure can. Do you want to be included, Jenna?"

"I don't have to be. Do you have the farmhouse style plan for the reception area, Shane? Morgan might have another perspective, and she can order what we need. Are we set?" Jenna asked.

"Not quite," Shane said. "We need clear direction. Jenna, we need you to be the boss. I've been through the team leadership scenario, and it didn't work."

Jenna gazed at the two of them then exhaled. "Okay, as long as the two of you have my back, I'll do it. What about Mr. Moore's other projects besides the cottage?"

"I thought there was another project, but I'll check with Terrell. As Mr. Moore's senior electrician, he would know whether we should offer to help with any other projects." Shane rose. "Are you ready for a walk through of The Barn and the reception building, Morgan?"

"That's a good idea."

After they left, Jenna called Adrienne to give her an update and to ask her to contact Mr. Moore's lawyer.

When she hung up, Jenna reviewed the notes she took while Adrienne talked. *I'm glad I called her. I wouldn't have thought of half the things she brought up.*

She stared at her phone. *I should let Ethan know Mr. Moore went to Atlanta.*

She sent a text. "Bobbie's condition is serious. She was transferred to a hospital in Atlanta. Mr. Moore left to stay with her."

Her phone rang. *Why couldn't he have just texted?*

When she answered, Ethan said, "What about the cottage?"

"I guess that will have to wait while Shane concentrates on the barn and the reception center."

"I have a general contractor's license, and I can step in for Mr. Moore. There isn't much more work to do, and it would take just as much effort and time for his workmen to shut down the project as it would to finish it."

Be civil. Jenna bit her lip. "I'll talk to my lawyer's paralegal."

"Adrienne is fast. Let me know when we're official." Ethan hung up.

Jenna called Shane. When he answered, she said, "Ethan offered to take over the work on the cottage."

"That's a tremendous relief. He's an experienced contractor, and the guys like working with him. Nobody was saying anything, but Mr. Moore's crew have been worried about their jobs. I know you'll be happy to have your cottage back."

Jenna hung up then called Adrienne. "Ethan's a licensed general contractor and has offered to take over completion of the cottage, but I'm not crazy about the idea because isn't that changing horses midstream? How do I tell him that without sounding like I don't trust him to do a good job?"

"I think it's an excellent idea for him to step in. I'll contact Mr. Moore's lawyer, and we'll whip up a contract for Ethan before the end of the day, so he will have it for the county inspections."

After she hung up, Jenna sighed. Katy laid her chin on Jenna's knee.

Jenna stroked Katy's neck. "I thought Shane and Adrienne were on my side, but neither one of them flinched at the idea of Ethan working on my house."

Jenna's phone buzzed a text from Morgan. "On our way back."

"They weren't gone very long. I wonder if something's wrong."

CHAPTER TWO

Morgan came into the office and shifted her office chair so she could face Jenna. "Shane dropped me off so he could work on his plan for the reception center. The deputy sheriff wouldn't let us go into the barn or the reception building. He claimed it was just precautionary until an investigator could examine the property. He said the sheriff will be here later to talk to you."

"Investigator? Do they think someone pushed Bobbie off the ladder?"

"I asked the same thing, and he told me it was routine because it was an unwitnessed fall. Shane and I chatted about some of the design issues he and Bobbie have run into. I suggested we go with rustic glam."

Jenna raised her eyebrows. "I love it; what did he say?"

Morgan chuckled. "He said he didn't have a clue of what that would look like, but if I did, he loved it."

Morgan turned back to her computer. "I can create a list of the changes for the barn reservations for you to review it before I ask for any modifications to our system."

"Updating our current reservation system to include reservations for events at the barn was an excellent idea; hopefully our requested changes are as simple as I think they should be. I'm on hold as far as starting anything new for a while until I hear more from Adrienne, so I'm feeling a little restless. Let's go for a walk, Katy."

Jenna grabbed a sweater on her way out. When they were outside, Katy bounded for the cottage, but Jenna headed for the driveway.

"Come on, Katy."

As Jenna sauntered down the driveway, Katy explored the ditch and the nearby brush. When they were near the end of the driveway, Jenna's phone rang.

The sheriff said, "I'll be there in a few minutes to chat. Is that convenient for you?"

"Katy and I are headed back to the inn from our walk. We'll be outside."

The sheriff chuckled. "You and Katy are living right."

After she hung up, she said, "Let's head back, Katy; Sheriff Jenkins is on his way here."

When Jenna broke into a jog, Katy raced up the driveway. Jenna was out of breath when she reached the inn. Katy grinned as she waited at the back door.

After she caught her breath, Jenna said, "I need to do that more often, except I should run down the driveway, not up. I used to love to run in college, Katy, but it was a mistake to start with an uphill run after a long break."

Jenna heard a car turn in the inn's driveway. "Sheriff's here, Katy."

The sheriff climbed out of his cruiser. He was in his forties, but his brown hair, graceful movements despite a few extra pounds, and infectious grin gave him a more youthful aura. "I need to pay you a social visit sometime instead of official interrogations. Can we talk in your office?"

As they strolled together and went inside, Jenna said, "Morgan and I share an office. We can sit in the living room if you'd like to have a little privacy. We'll have to stop by the kitchen, though, because Darlene has a new appetizer, and she's doing her version of a taste survey."

Jenna opened the kitchen door and spoke loudly. "Darlene, the sheriff is here; we're going to be in the living room."

"One minute; Sheriff, I need your opinion." She stuck a spoon into a bowl of corn salad. "Try this and tell me if it's too spicy."

The sheriff took a bite. "This is delicious, Darlene. Is it your recipe?"

Darlene beamed as she nodded. "Thank you."

The sheriff finished his appetizer then set his bowl on the counter.

After Jenna sat in her favorite pale yellow chair with Katy at her feet, the sheriff sat on the oversized sage green sofa that faced Jenna and the wood-burning fireplace. He pulled out a small notebook from his shirt pocket. "Why did you go to the barn?"

Jenna told him about the text Shane received from Bobbie.

The sheriff nodded. "Tell me exactly what you saw."

"Bobbie was on her stomach, and the ladder and a broken light bulb were next to her. Katy nudged her, but Bobbie didn't move. When I kneeled next to her, she was breathing and had a pulse, but she didn't respond to me. Shane came inside the barn; after he called nine-one-one, he called Ethan. The ambulance arrived shortly before Ethan and Mr. Moore did."

"What were you looking for when you went into the reception center?"

"I went into the reception center to visit the restroom."

The sheriff chuckled. "Sure you did. So, what did you see?"

"Her cell phone was under her desk, and her purse was on her office chair and open."

Tell him about the cane. Jenna glanced up at Nettie's portrait that hung over the sofa. Nettie's eyes were shrouded by a shadow cast by a passing cloud.

"I was looking for Bobbie's cane."

The sheriff nodded. "Something was gnawing at me; I knew I'd figure it out if I talked to you. Bobbie would never admit it, but she couldn't take two steps without falling if she didn't have her pink cane."

"That's what I was thinking," Jenna said.

The sheriff continued, "The whole thing stinks, doesn't it? She couldn't have sent the text to Shane in her office then walked out to the barn without her cane. If she took her cane with her, then where is it? Bobbie has always been fearless, but I don't think she would have climbed a ladder to change a light bulb that was working."

"Did you find her cane?" Jenna asked.

The sheriff raised an eyebrow. "That's police business." He gazed at her and shook his head.

"The whole ladder thing had to have been staged; somebody pulled her away from her office, took her into the barn, and hit her hard enough to..." Jenna cleared her throat.

"Sure looks like it. You're off the case now. It's mine, not yours. Deal?"

"Yes, sir."

The sheriff examined her face. "You're not that great a liar, Mrs. Ross. Is there anything else?"

Jenna shook her head.

"Call me if you think of anything."

He rose and stopped at the doorway. "Anything. Any time."

After the sheriff left, a tear slipped down Jenna's face. She brushed it away and took three deep breaths to compose herself.

"I hope Bobbie will be all right. The sheriff doesn't need to worry about us, does he, Katy? We've got plenty to keep us busy."

Jenna's phone buzzed; she sighed as she read the text from Renee. "We received the confirmation from the Peach Blossom Retreat. We're thirty minutes away."

Jenna strolled through the kitchen. Katy flopped down next to Darlene while Jenna continued to her office.

"I received a text from Renee. She'll be here in thirty minutes."

Morgan grinned. "I have this urge to polish the banister and dust all the chandeliers. This is the closest

I've ever been to a genuine celebrity. If I get all gushy, push me down. Oh wait; that won't work. I outweigh you by thirty pounds. Knock me down with one of your glares. That would do it."

Jenna laughed. "You've been hanging around Shane too much."

"Oh, you've got that wrong. It hasn't been nearly enough." Morgan winked.

Jenna furrowed her brow. "I think I've caught your case of nerves. I want to run upstairs to check the guestrooms, but Wendy would think I don't trust her."

"You don't have to because I already did, and Wendy laughed at me."

Jenna smiled. "Thanks for taking one for the team. Adrienne sent me a long list of tasks she wants completed by tomorrow."

"I looked at the online ads for the barn and discovered Bobbie has been using a promotions company. I researched the company, and they charge more than I would have expected for generic ads. When I was in college, I was an intern at an ad company for a few months and enjoyed it. I'd like to create some of my own. Do you mind reviewing them before they go live?" Morgan asked.

"I'd love to. What about the company that's doing the ads for the inn?"

"I'd forgotten about them. They're great, and their price is reasonable. Maybe we should give them the barn ads. I'll call them for a quote; we may get a discount for a second account." Morgan frowned. "Are we making too many changes? I don't want Bobbie to feel like we tossed out everything she had in place and ruined all her plans."

Jenna forced the sadness out of her mind before she spoke. "She might be in the hospital for a while; I'm sure she'll be grateful for our help."

While Jenna gathered the data for Adrienne's task list, Morgan hummed under her breath while she worked on her computer. Jenna smiled. *I wonder if Morgan even knows she hums when she's in deep concentration.*

After Jenna sent the data to Adrienne, she stretched. "I hear a car."

Morgan snapped her laptop closed and rushed out the dining room door. Jenna shut down her system and followed her, but hung back so Morgan could greet the guests.

After the car parked, Morgan bounced on her toes while she gave Renee and her assistant time to approach the house. When their guests were near the porch, Morgan opened the door. "Welcome, Renee and Sophia. I'm Morgan."

Renee was slender, tanned, and an inch taller than Morgan; her dark brown hair skimmed her shoulders. She wore jeans, a red plaid long-sleeved shirt, and suede fashion boots. Sophia was almost as tall as Renee, but was curvier. She wore a white blouse, a black pencil skirt, and red heels. Her blue-tinted hair was cut in a short, stylish bob with bangs and was a perfect match for her blue eyes. Both women carried large suitcases and computer bags.

"Hey, Renee," Jenna said. "Nice to meet you, Sophia."

Renee dropped her suitcase and bag and rushed toward Jenna with her arms wide to prepare for a hug.

Morgan stepped in front of Jenna and grabbed Renee's right hand and shook it. "I'm a big fan of yours, Ms. Sabot."

"Of course you are." Renee patted her hair then stepped back as she turned to Jenna. "How do you keep getting younger, girl? I love this old house, and the grounds are beautiful. Tell me what time your shirtless hottie mows, so I can sit on the front porch and watch."

Morgan blinked, and Jenna snorted. "You're a topnotch investigative journalist. Wouldn't you be insulted if I told you?"

"Of course not. Snitches are my secret investigating weapon."

Morgan strode to the registration desk, and Sophia followed her.

After Renee and Sophia signed in, Morgan gave them their room keys. "As part of our recent renovation and upgrade to the inn, we added top of the line automated security. Our front door is always locked for everyone's safety. The door at the end of this hall is the guest entrance and is also always locked. You can push on the bar to exit, but you will need your room key to enter."

"So, all the exterior doors are always locked? Isn't that inconvenient for you?" Renee asked.

"Not really. There isn't any reason for anyone to come to the inn unless they have a reservation, and we are always here to greet new guests."

Jenna wandered to the living room so she wouldn't look like she was hovering while Morgan continued her welcome spiel.

Morgan led Renee and Sophia past the guest restroom to the dining room. "The continental breakfast begins at seven every morning and goes until eight, and on Saturday and Sunday mornings we have a breakfast buffet from eight until ten."

When they joined Jenna in the living room, Sophia stared at Nettie Wyndham's portrait. "She looks delicate, but I'll bet she was a force. Is she one of your ancestors?"

Jenna smiled at the twinkle in Nettie's eyes when a sunbeam streamed in through the window.

"Nettie Wyndham saved the estate and most of the surrounding farms and homes from foreclosure in the 1920s when small banks began failing. She was my husband's great-great grandmother, but I feel directly related to her."

Renee ran her hand over the smooth wooden fireplace mantel. "Are you going to have a full house this weekend? I know guests are expected to leave a bed-and-breakfast for the day, but is there somewhere my team and I could work and not be in anyone's way?"

"We'll be close to full, but you could certainly work in here. If your work is sensitive or confidential, I'd recommend working in your rooms where you'd have more privacy than in the living room," Jenna said.

Morgan added, "We vacuum and dust the living room and dining room every morning and prepare the dining room for happy hour every afternoon, beginning at four."

"Sounds like we could work in the dining room for several hours, which is perfect," Renee said.

Sophia side-glanced at Renee. "You won't have to clean up behind us; we'll leave it tidy."

Morgan side-glanced at Jenna. "I'll show you to your rooms."

Jenna waited at the bottom of the stairs.

Renee said, "Oh my, these rooms are beautiful, and look how spacious they are, Sophia."

Why do I think Renee put her hand over her heart at the sight of the precious rooms? Jenna snorted and returned to the kitchen.

"I saw the two women coming up the walk." Darlene pointed to the sheet of paper on the counter as she hung up her apron. "Here are the instructions for your appetizers tonight and tomorrow night and for the continental breakfast in the morning. I'll see you on Wednesday. If you talk to Mr. Moore, tell him we're all praying for Bobbie."

"I will. Thanks for coming in."

Darlene grunted and motioned her hand in annoyance to hide the red spots that grew on her cheeks. "Just don't leave a big mess in my kitchen."

While Jenna reviewed Adrienne's list to be sure she had covered everything, Morgan came into the office. Morgan was engrossed in a phone conversation with their reservation system support when Jenna's phone buzzed a text from Renee.

"Is there anywhere we can talk uninterrupted?"

Jenna furrowed her brow then replied, "Care to go for a walk?"

"I'll meet you on the front porch."

When Jenna rose, so did Katy. "Are you ready for a walk, girl?"

Katy grinned as Jenna put on her lightweight jacket. Jenna unlocked the front door with her electronic key, and the two of them went out.

Renee rose from a rocker and smiled. "I knew you and Katy would be interested in a walk. When we were in college, I heard you went for your walks no matter what the weather was. I should have picked up the habit, but I'm too busy. Where are we going?"

Katy trotted to the driveway then turned and stared at Jenna.

Jenna chuckled. "Katy suggests a walk down the driveway. Our long walk is down the driveway and back, then we take the path to The Barn or the much longer walk to the peach orchard and back."

As they walked, Renee said, "I got a call from a woman named Bobbie Moore, who is the executive director of The Barn. I assume you know her."

Jenna nodded. *I didn't know Bobbie was the Executive Director; what an impressive title. I like it.*

"Sophia said she sounded like an older woman on the phone. I hope this doesn't sound judgmental, but we have to know if she is reliable and relatively stable, mentally, I mean?"

Jenna side-glanced at Renee. "Yes, she is. She has a reputation for being stubborn."

"Sophia said the same thing." Renee smiled. "So, if she told you something about what she perceived as criminal activity, even if it sounded a little farfetched, you would believe her?"

"Absolutely. What did she tell you?"

"Not much, but enough to pique my interest. Is it possible for you to arrange a meeting with her? If she agrees you can hear what she has to say, then I'd like for you to come with me."

Jenna exhaled and turned to Renee. "She was badly injured earlier today and is in a trauma hospital in Atlanta."

Renee gaped at Jenna. "Injured how?"

"It appears that she fell off a ladder at the barn; she was unconscious when we found her and as far as we know, still is. Because no one witnessed the fall, it's being investigated. What did she say when she called you?"

Renee exhaled. "Actually, she talked to Sophia, not me. Sophia said it might be worth our while to come here to check her out, so I'm kind of humoring her. She said it might help her research. Is it okay if I invite Sophia to join us?"

"Sure."

Renee sent a text. While they waited for Sophia, Renee checked her phone.

"I'm terribly sorry, but do you mind talking to Sophia without me? She'll fill me in later."

Jenna shrugged.

"I knew you'd understand." Renee hurried around the house and disappeared.

When Sophia came outside, she joined Jenna and Katy in the back of the house.

"I'm sorry, Jenna. Renee decided if our whole reason for coming here was to talk to Bobbie Moore, and Mrs. Moore will be in the hospital for a while, then we should wait until she was well enough for visitors. But I'd really like to talk to you about her."

"Do you want to go inside or take a walk?"

"A walk sounds wonderful; I don't get many opportunities to be outdoors."

As they strolled down the driveway, Jenna said, "Renee asked me if Bobbie Moore was mentally sharp. She said that's why you two came here."

"That's the thing. When I talked to her, I couldn't decide if she was terribly confused or talking in code. She started off by saying little pitchers have big ears. Do you know what that means?"

Jenna smiled. "I have not heard that since I was four or five years old. When the adults talked about adult stuff, I was always interested. My grandma would shush them by saying little pitchers have big ears. It meant that somebody, basically me, who shouldn't hear the conversation was listening."

"Okay. I'm not sure I ever heard that before."

Sophia gazed at Jenna. "I'll quote Bobbie verbatim. 'Mark my words, there is a sheik with a badminton racket that would make a car's knee turn copper.' I didn't know or even care if cars had knees, but I couldn't just brush her off because she was so sincere. I told her I'd have to see if I could find a place to stay because I thought that would be the kindest way to close the conversation. She told me about the Peach Blossom Retreat and the brilliant owner, Jenna Ross. When I told Renee about Jenna Ross and the Peach Blossom Retreat, she said she went to school with you."

Sophia grinned. "Little pitchers have big ears. I'll have to remember that. What about the rest of it?"

"I've been studying the slang and language of the jazz age, so I might have a different take on what Bobbie said. A sheik was a boyfriend, and I think she may have said badminton so she could say racket. The car knee is probably carnie, which was a term for a traveling carnival worker, and copper is a police officer."

Sophia's eyes narrowed. "Someone who is pretending to be a boyfriend has a carnie racket going, right? So what's the racket?"

"I don't know, but if I was going to guess it would be one where the house wins. So if I charge you two dollars to play a game, and you win, I give you a one dollar prize. If ten people play, and two win, I'm still up eighteen dollars, right?"

Sophia nodded. "If all ten win, you only have five dollars, so the game is at least challenging but not rigged."

"Right, but if a carnival was caught with a rigged game, it was shut down. Even though carnies were notoriously crooked, no carnie wanted to be stuck in some town in the middle of nowhere with no way to get home."

Sophia gazed at Jenna. "What about mark my word? That just means pay attention, right?"

Jenna met Sophia's gaze. "Yes, but in the carnival world, a mark would be the victim, and that's it for me because I don't have a clue what she meant by that."

As they turned back to the inn, Sophia said, "Renee might cancel the rest of the team. If she does, I assume she will want to leave after breakfast in the morning, but she hasn't said anything; I'm just speculating. You said sometimes you walk to the barn. I'd love to take that walk and get a peek at it."

"I'm not sure if the investigation is finished, so we might not get very close to it. You'll get an idea of how spacious it is, though. Talk to Morgan if you're interested in more details about the barn, because she is taking over while Bobbie is in the hospital."

"How serious are Bobbie's injuries?"

"We haven't heard anything yet, so I don't know."

As they strolled along the path Ethan had cleared, Sophia said, "Renee may have a need for the barn for a private event."

Jenna smiled. "Morgan will love to host her event, and we can promise you we'll be discreet."

Sophia chuckled. "Renee claimed a reporter tracked her to a swanky hotel in New York City this afternoon, and the hotel staff is frantically trying to figure out which name she's registered under. I don't know if that's just another one of her stories, but she's decided she's a genuine celebrity."

"That sounds more like the Renee I knew in college." Jenna stopped and pointed. "That's the barn."

"Wow, it's huge and secluded. Will Morgan be at happy hour?"

"She sure will, and so will Shane, the architect for the barn. Ready to go back?"

As they strolled along the path, Sophia asked, "Do you know when The Barn will be ready for an event?"

"Talk to Morgan at happy hour; the building may be ready soon, but I don't know enough about events to guess what else might have to be done. Morgan's our events expert; she'd be happy to work with you."

Sophia scanned the backyard as they continued to the guest entrance. "Your groundskeeping crew must be expensive, but they are worth every penny."

"I'll let them know you appreciate their work."

Sophia cocked her head. "You don't sound very enthusiastic."

Jenna shrugged as she opened the side door. "I don't know. I've always thrived on meeting obstacles head on, but the least little thing irritates me now."

Renee met them at the door. "Like what? Sounds like something has definitely got your shorts in a wad, so to speak."

"Fancy talk for a tabloid writer."

Renee laughed. "You'll find all my articles at the grocery store checkout along with the gossip and aliens landed magazines, and you always have been a master at changing the subject."

Sophia nodded. "Man trouble."

"No, there's no man in my life; just a stack of problems that gets higher every day," Jenna said.

"It's all work, then? Your staff is excellent; could you lean on them more for help?" Sophia asked.

Jenna nodded. "You're right; I'll have to look into it."

Renee snorted as she headed toward the stairs. "I'll see you at happy hour, Pinocchio."

Jenna huffed as she headed toward the dining room. When she went into her office, she slammed the door.

Morgan jumped and stared at Jenna. "What on earth is wrong? Are you mad at me?"

"No," Jenna grumbled.

Morgan left for the kitchen then returned. "Come have a cup of tea with me. We deserve a cookie break."

They sipped their tea and ate a cookie in silence. When Morgan reached for her second cookie, she asked, "Is there something about Renee I should know? Do you want to talk?"

"Thank you for blocking that phony hug Renee tried when she came in the door. Everything about her irritates me and always has. Thanks for the tea and cookies. I feel better."

"Any time." After they drank their tea, Morgan asked, "Do you want more?"

"No, I've had plenty. Where'd you get the cookies?"

"From Darlene's stash in the freezer." Morgan whispered, "We'll tell her Shane took them."

Jenna snickered. "Poor Shane. Thanks for the cookies; I can work now."

Morgan handed her the last cookie. "Here you go. One for the road."

Morgan said, "Here's the list of the changes for our system so it will include the barn's reservations. Read over them and tell me if you have anything to add, so I can send them for changes to our system."

Jenna read the list. "You'll want to manage partial payments; for example, we require a nonrefundable deposit for the rooms, so we probably want something similar for the barn."

While Morgan was on the phone with the reservation system customer support, Jenna opened the email from

Adrienne with the contract listing Mr. Moore, Ethan, and her for completion of the cottage.

Jenna read the contract then added her electronic signature. Adrienne sent a text to her. "All parties signed. Contract is approved."

Adrienne called. Jenna frowned at her phone. "Is there a problem, Adrienne?"

"I just wanted to remind you it is common courtesy to welcome a new contractor. Be nice."

"I will."

"You'll know if you're not doing your job if the construction workers grumble. They'll pick up your attitude."

"Okay, I'll have a wonderful attitude."

"That wasn't so bad, was it?" Adrienne hung up.

Jenna picked up her jacket. "Want to go for a walk, Katy? Everybody's getting on my case about Ethan."

When Jenna and Katy went out the back door, Jenna's eyes widened at Sophia who was snapping photos of the grounds.

"Hi, Sophia. How are you doing?"

"Great. Just getting a few pictures of the landscaping and the old inn. Its architecture is so unique."

Jenna cocked her head and gazed at the house. "I've never thought about it before; I guess it is."

"If I understood Morgan correctly, the inn is always locked, but our room keys open the side door. Is it alarmed?"

"If the door is opened by the panic bar after ten o'clock the alarm sounds, but if it's unlocked from the outside by a room key, the alarm doesn't go off. We do have a log of the time, date, and room key when the door is opened."

"Thanks." Sophia hurried to the side door then rushed inside.

Jenna stared at her. "Want to walk to the barn for a change, Katy? I don't think I'm the problem after all; it's everybody else."

Katy barked then trotted to the path to the old barn. When they were close to the barn, Jenna heard a man's voice. "Okay, that's it. I'll call the sheriff. Lock the buildings, and we can go. I'll drop off the keys at the Peach Blossom Retreat."

Jenna motioned for Katy to head back toward the inn.

As they got close, Jenna said, "I'll wait until we get the official news from the sheriff, but getting The Barn and reception center back will be an enormous relief."

Katy yipped and raced ahead. Jenna jogged along the path behind her. When they reached the inn, Jenna grinned. "That wasn't bad after all. I just have to jog every day until I can run up the driveway without collapsing."

Jenna heard a car turn in the driveway. "We'll wait here for whoever is returning the keys to the reception center and the barn."

A cruiser with the Georgia Bureau of Investigation logo on its passenger door parked behind the work trucks. A tall young man who wore a long-sleeved navy shirt with the GBI patch and khaki pants climbed out of the car and scanned the area. As he strode to Jenna, he smiled.

She returned his smile. *He has cute dimples.*

He held out his hand. "I'm Clint."

Jenna noticed the black ring with an inlay of blue stones on the ring finger of his left hand. *Of course, he's married.*

"Jenna." They shook hands.

He handed a key ring to Jenna then held his hand for Katy to sniff. After she gave her approval, he stroked her chin. "These are the keys to the barn and the building. The sheriff said you were particularly interested in Mrs. Moore's pink cane, and so is he."

He pulled a business card out of his top shirt pocket. "The sheriff said if anyone could find the cane, it would be you. My cell phone is on the back of the card. Text me anytime."

Jenna nodded and dropped the card into her jacket pocket.

Clint chuckled, and the dimples reappeared. "Don't worry about disturbing me; we have a newborn at our house, and this is our first week without a grandma around. We sleep in shifts."

Jenna smiled as she turned back toward the inn.

Clint strolled along with her. "My father-in-law said no child should grow up without a dog, so we have a one-year-old rescue pup too."

"Makes sense to me." Jenna slipped on a twig and turned her ankle when it rolled. Clint caught her mid-fall.

As she regained her balance, Clint peered at her. "Are you okay?"

Jenna exhaled. "Thanks to you, I am; I just stepped wrong."

"Do you want me to help you to the door?"

Jenna put her weight on her ankle. "No, I can make it."

Clint strode to his cruiser and left. Jenna stared at the ground as she cautiously made her way to the back door. Katy limped alongside Jenna.

When Jenna looked up, Morgan waited outside the door with her arms crossed and her eyes twinkling. "So, who was that hunk? Where did you find him?"

Morgan scanned the yard behind Jenna. "Shane said Ethan was at the cottage and was on his way here to talk to you about something. I thought I saw Ethan when you launched into your flailing tumble, but I must have been mistaken." She cocked her head. "And what's wrong with Katy?"

CHAPTER THREE

Morgan stared as Katy trotted past her and went inside. "Never mind. I think she was limping in sympathy. Now, nothing's wrong."

Jenna glared as she passed Morgan. "He's the GBI investigator, and for your information, Miss Nosy, he's a new father."

Morgan sniffed. "My story is much more interesting; so, what color flowers do you want at your wedding?"

Jenna side-glanced at Morgan. "Same color you're having at yours."

"Oh, good; your prickly nerves are gone. What did the GBI investigator say?"

Jenna handed her the key ring. "These are for you; we're back in business."

"That's great news! As soon as Shane's available, he can show me what he has in mind for the reception center. I'll pester you later to help me with some new design decisions, because I've changed my mind again. I love the idea of rustic glam, but I'm having trouble narrowing down what that looks like."

"You'll figure it out. I'm excited about the barn and the reception center having a style distinct from the inn. Does that make sense?" Jenna asked.

Morgan nodded. "It does to me."

After they were in the office, Morgan said, "I had a long talk with Renee and Sophia. Renee would like to stay through Sunday after all because they have the privacy to work here."

"What about Darlene and Wendy?"

"I talked to Wendy so she could plan on what she calls a quick tidy for their rooms instead of the thorough cleaning she does after a guest leaves. I sent Darlene a text. Shane told me the fastest way to get on Darlene's bad side was to leave her out of the loop. If you're ready for a surprise, Darlene and I agreed to reduce the happy hour appetizers on Monday through Thursday to chips with a homemade dip and one other appetizer."

Jenna's eyebrows rose. "How did you do that? I've been begging her to cut back on the selection of appetizers she made so she wouldn't have to work so many extra hours."

Morgan smirked. "It was tricky especially since you had talked her into switching to the continental breakfast instead of the full breakfast buffet Mondays through Fridays. I'm actually sorry I missed that conversation."

Jenna snorted. "It was definitely loud. I went so far as to claim I could be put in jail because I required her to be here every day of the week."

Morgan shook her head. "I thought I pulled out the big guns. I took the more subtle route and casually mentioned that you were cranky because you were worried about rising food costs, so we tossed around a few ideas."

"You and casually don't fit in the same sentence, but I'm glad my cranky reputation helped."

Morgan headed toward the back door. "I texted Shane to let him know I have the keys. He's on his way here so he can show me what he has in mind. I'll be back in time to put the appetizers in the oven and start a pot of coffee. I reminded Renee that we didn't serve alcohol, but she told me she read that on our website, so she brought her own."

Jenna's neck felt prickly; she grumbled. "Ethan's at the back door."

Morgan cocked her head. "I didn't hear anything, but I'll let him in since I was on my way out, anyway."

"Tell him I'm busy."

"Oh, no. You're not putting me in the middle. Tell him yourself; I have enough…"

Morgan was interrupted by a knock at the back door. "I must have missed the first knock."

Morgan picked up her sweater from the back of her desk chair and headed toward the back door. "Come in, Ethan. Shane and I are going to The Barn, but we'll be right back. We'll see you at happy hour."

Ethan snorted. "I'm not staying that long. Where's Jenna?"

"In the office."

Ethan strode into the office and stood in the doorway with his arms crossed. "You should sit down."

He is so bossy. Jenna jutted her jaw. "I'll stand."

Ethan exhaled. "Mr. Moore's lawyer called me. Bobbie took a turn for the worst, and they rushed her into surgery."

His voice softened as he stepped closer to her. "Jenna, she didn't make it."

Jenna stared at Ethan in disbelieve. When her knees buckled, Ethan reached for her, but she jerked away her arm and grabbed onto her desk.

When she dropped into her chair, a tear trickled down her face. "That's horrible."

Ethan nodded then cleared his throat as he pulled out a chair at the work table and sat. "Mr. Moore told his lawyer he wants the barn project to move forward because Bobbie was so proud of her first real project. Mr. Moore doesn't want to have anything to do with the barn because he feels like that's where Bobbie died. The lawyer told me he didn't understand what Mr. Moore meant, but I do. Anyway, Mr. Moore wants someone to buy out Bobbie's share of the barn; I told the lawyer I'm not interested, and he can talk to Shane, but I don't think he will be interested, either. The logical choice would be you, but would that work?"

Jenna brushed away the tears. "Why wouldn't it? Do you think I'm not experienced enough? Morgan can take over the operations."

"Do you expect Morgan to stay when you leave?"

Jenna slammed her hands on her desk as she rose. "What does that mean? Why would I leave? This is my home."

Ethan glowered as he rose from his chair. "For how long?"

"What is wrong..." Jenna inhaled and examined his face.

She exhaled then gritted her teeth. "I have no clue what you're talking about, but I can't imagine if you're the only one competent enough to take over the barn project that you'd let Mr. Moore down."

Ethan narrowed his eyes. "Would you?"

Jenna glowered as she strode to him. His chest was at her eye level. She raised her head and stared at his neck.

Ethan cleared his throat.

Jenna snickered. "This wasn't as intimidating as I intended."

Ethan smiled. "Oh, I'm definitely intimidated. Let's sit at the table and start over."

After they sat across from each other, Jenna said, "I wouldn't let Mr. Moore down, and I'm not going anywhere. Why did you think I was?"

"I might have jumped to the worst-case scenario when I was coming here from the cottage and saw something that maybe was none of my business," Ethan mumbled.

Jenna nodded. "If Mr. Moore wants us to take over for him and Bobbie, we should figure out how to do that."

"That's what I wanted to say, but it came out wrong."

"No kidding. Mr. Moore has a long-term lease agreement with me to use the barn as an event center, and his general contractor business paid for the upgrades to the barn and to the reception center. Does he want you to buy out his lease or his entire business? Maybe you need a lawyer to clarify that with Mr. Moore's lawyer."

Ethan nodded. "I'll call my lawyer."

Jenna continued, "I'd like to turn over the design decisions and operations to Morgan. She worked with an event coordinator as an intern for a year, so she has experience that I don't have. She has already set up the barn on our reservation system, but maybe we jumped the gun. Is all of this okay with you?"

"See, that's the thing. I don't want to have anything to do with the operations for the barn, but I don't mind taking on Mr. Moore's general contracting work. So, now what do we do?"

Jenna rubbed her forehead. "Why don't you talk to your lawyer, and I'll talk to Adrienne. Maybe the two of them can come up with a reasonable plan to present to Mr. Moore's lawyer."

She cocked her head as she gazed at Ethan. "If you're taking on Mr. Moore's contracting work, I don't see what that has to do with the business operations of the barn."

Ethan furrowed his brow. "I'm getting myself confused because I definitely can't take on a different type of business, like events management. You aren't interested in the general contracting business, are you?"

"You're right; I don't want anything to do with general contracting." Jenna lifted an eyebrow as she side-glanced at Ethan. "I'll deny I ever said that."

Ethan chuckled as he rose and headed to the door. "I wouldn't have expected anything else from you."

Before he left, Jenna said, "This might work after all, Ethan."

His blue eyes twinkled. "I think you're right."

After Jenna called Adrienne and told her about the discussion with Ethan and their conclusion, a wave of sadness rolled over her and tears rolled down her face.

She hurried to the living room and sat in the yellow chair.

"Nettie, this is all just so unbelievable. Bobbie and Mr. Moore are wonderful people. They don't deserve this."

Jenna felt a light touch on her shoulder and closed her eyes. "Thanks," she whispered. "It's so hard because it reminds me that Tom is gone."

You'll always remember Tom. Read her diary.

Jenna patted the chair's arm. "I will."

"Will what?" Sophia strolled into the living room.

Jenna smiled. "I rarely get caught talking to myself."

"Nothing beats a good pep talk, does it?" Sophia returned her smile then gazed at the fireplace.

Listen to her.

Jenna nodded.

"We just heard Bobbie Moore died from injuries from a fall. I know she was a friend of yours, and I'm so sorry for your loss."

"Thank you; it was a terrible shock."

Sophia pulled the straw-filled leather hassock close to the sofa. "I was intrigued by Bobbie Moore because what she said tied into one of Renee's articles I had been working on six months ago until Renee dropped it and moved on to another topic."

Jenna nodded. "When we were in college, Renee frequently bounced from one thing to the next."

After Sophia sat down, she put up her feet. "I know, but I didn't blame her for once. I was hitting one dead end after another, literally. After receiving a tip, I'd follow up, but my contacts disappeared, had dementia, or died. I thought it was just bad timing because most of them were elderly. Now, I'm not so sure."

"I've never been much of a believer of coincidences, either."

"When Bobbie Moore first called Renee over two months ago, Renee pushed her off onto me. Mrs. Moore told me a young girl had joined an online group she was in, and the group had kind of adopted her. When I asked whether the girl was asking for money, she said no, but after one of the snoopier women discovered the girl's birthday was coming up, over half of the group joined a private group and dropped the original group. Bobbie told me she'd have more for me soon because she had wangled an invitation to join the private group."

"That sounds exactly like something Bobbie would do," Jenna said.

Sophia stared out the window and exhaled. "Renee came up with yet another case that was more interesting to her, and my attention was diverted. I'd forgotten all about Bobbie until last week when I was in a restaurant and overheard a woman talking about their mother who was a member of an online knitting group, and a young girl joined the group. When I called Bobbie and reminded her of her earlier call, she complained about the problems she was having with tables, chairs, and a Nigerian Prince. Was it hard for you to break in and ask a question when you talked to Bobbie?"

Jenna nodded. "Bobbie could definitely be single-minded sometimes."

Sophia returned to the sofa. "When I asked her what I could do, she told me Renee would have a pleasant stay at the Peach Blossom Retreat. I told Renee Bobbie Moore might have a story after all. She thought about it for a few days then told me she decided it might be worth talking to Bobbie Moore after all and called you."

"Bobbie's mind was always working; it was just a little hard to follow her thought processes sometimes. I know about her tables and chairs problem, and my mom told me about an old email phishing scam that involved a Nigerian Prince."

Sophia groaned. "I thought Bobbie Moore was confused when she threw in the Nigerian Prince. I barely listened to her after that. How could I have forgotten such a classic scam? From what I remember, the Nigerian Prince's email was an urgent plea for help to get money out of Nigeria. In exchange for a sizeable good faith deposit on your part along with your bank information so the con man could deposit his supposedly vast wealth into your bank account, and he'd give you an unbelievably enormous sum of money for your kindness."

Jenna nodded. "And only a few seconds after he had your deposit and bank information, he'd empty your account and disappear. If you didn't remember the scam, the mention of a Nigerian Prince would definitely leave you questioning her mental status."

Sophia cocked her head. "She was definitely sharper than I realized."

"Mom said the problem with the Nigerian Prince was that people were embarrassed they had been duped, so they didn't report it to anyone even though they had lost their life savings and were completely destitute."

"I'll do some digging to see if there are any reports about an updated Nigerian Prince scam, but it seems unlikely, doesn't it?" Sophia rose. "I'll see you at six for happy hour. I made dinner reservations for us at seven. Renee didn't believe me when I told her it's only ten minutes from here to the restaurant in town. We're used to allowing two hours to travel to a restaurant."

After Jenna sat at her desk, she turned on her computer. While she browsed the addition of reservations for the barn, a movement on the front lawn caught her attention. Katy whined then dashed out of the office to the back door.

When Katy's whine became more urgent and she yipped, Jenna hurried to open the back door for her. Katy snatched up her tennis ball as she dashed outside. Jenna chuckled at the sound of a lawnmower as it headed toward the backyard. *I wonder if Renee is peeking out her window. She'll be disappointed because Ethan is definitely no nonsense and would never be a no-shirt kind of guy.*

Katy yipped in excitement, and the lawnmower engine was quiet.

Jenna heard a child laugh as she rounded the corner. Her eyes widened at a pre-teen boy with blond hair and the most out-of-control cowlick she'd ever seen. He pitched Katy's ball high into the air, and she waited for the first bounce before she raced toward it.

"Hi, Miss Jenna. I knew who you were right away because Uncle Ethan said you were the prettiest lady he'd ever seen. I'm Ryan. What's her name?" He pointed at Katy.

Ethan said what?

Jenna cleared her throat. "That's Katy."

"Katy." Ryan grinned when Katy trotted to him, dropped the tennis ball at his feet, and gazed at him expectantly. Ryan picked up the ball and threw it higher and farther. Katy raced after the ball.

"I'm staying with Uncle Ethan for two days. Mom and Dad went to Grandma's house to help her clean out her attic. They've been afraid Grandma would climb into the attic herself, so Dad's going to empty everything out of the attic then come home. Mom's staying to help Grandma sort through things. Uncle Ethan and I think Mom will be home this weekend."

When Katy trotted back, she dropped the ball at Ryan's feet, and he picked it up. "This has to be the last time, Katy. I'm sorry, but I have to finish mowing because we're leaving soon. Can I visit Katy tomorrow, Miss Jenna? Uncle Ethan has another meeting with Mr. Shane at the barn after I get out of school."

"She'd love it. If we're not outside, knock on the door, so we know you're here."

Ryan grinned as he hopped on the mower and started the engine.

"Come on, Katy. Ryan will visit us tomorrow."

Katy turned to watch Ryan.

Jenna rolled her eyes then used her firm voice. "Come, girl."

Katy trudged into the house behind Jenna.

On their way to the office, they met Sophia as she raced down the stairs.

Sophia slid to a stop. "What's wrong with Katy?"

"She has a new boyfriend, but she had to come inside so he could finish mowing."

Sophia smiled. "I saw him mowing. You have great taste, Katy; he is cute. See you later."

After Sophia rushed out the side door, Jenna stopped in the kitchen and put on a pot of coffee while Katy continued to mope. When the coffee was ready, Jenna carried her cup into the office and set it on her desk. Katy followed her, flopped down next to Jenna's chair, and stared at her.

Jenna kneeled next to her and stroked her neck. "He said he'd be back tomorrow."

Katy closed her eyes.

When Jenna rose, she spied Bobbie's book Shane had given her. When she picked it up, it glowed. *Diary of secrets.* She stood next to the file cabinet and read the first page, and then sat in her chair.

After the fourth page, she furrowed her brow. "This is Bobbie's diary of her online groups, Katy."

Katy whimpered in her sleep.

Jenna continued, "These pages have lists with a title that must be a shortened name for the group. She tried to hide the members' identities because all the names on the list look more like passwords."

She flipped through the pages until she found another type of list. "Each password is listed with a dollar amount next to each one, and the smallest amount on the first page is twenty thousand dollars for one password."

Jenna carefully went through the diary and read each page. "Bobbie would have a list somewhere of the real names or at least the online names for all the passwords. It's not here."

Jenna furrowed her brow. 'I can scan this in then strip off the first seven numbers and letters then put them in numeric order. I just need the key."

A knock at the back door interrupted her. She grabbed the furniture pamphlet to mark her place, slammed the diary shut, and stuck it into the middle drawer of her desk. After she rose to answer the door, she locked the drawer and put the key in her jeans watch pocket.

When she opened the door, Jenna flinched at the seriousness of Ethan's face. "What's wrong? Is someone else hurt? Come inside."

Ethan stared at her then followed her into the kitchen.

"Coffee?" Jenna asked.

"Maybe half a cup, if it's made. I apologize for not telling you earlier Ryan would be here after school. Shane and I were deep in discussion at the barn, and Ryan decided he'd help me out by mowing your yard. I didn't miss him until just a few minutes ago. It's really my fault because I mentioned your yard had to be mowed before the weekend."

"It wasn't a problem at all; Katy adores him."

Ethan's smile was weak. "He loves mowing and dogs. My brother has always said Ryan has grass and dirt in his veins, just like I do."

"He certainly did a wonderful job."

Ethan finished his coffee then set down his cup. "My brother and his wife went to her mother's house to help her clean out her attic. The original plan was for them to go to her house over the weekend, but my sister-in-law's mother said she'd empty the attic herself."

Jenna smiled. "That would definitely turn it into a family emergency."

Ethan chuckled. "My brother called it something else, but he took the time off work so it wouldn't be his fault if she fell. He'll be home the day after tomorrow, but his wife will stay for a few days to help her mother sort through the items that have been in the attic for at least forty years. My brother and his family live twenty-five miles west of here, so it's simple for me to take Ryan to school and pick him up at the end of the day."

Ethan has a soft side? "I'm sure Ryan is enjoying his time with you."

Ethan exhaled. "Anyway, I'll try to keep closer tabs on him."

"You don't have to do that on our account. He's welcome here. Katy would love to have him around, and if he has schoolwork, he's can study in my office or in the kitchen when Darlene is here."

Ethan's shoulders relaxed. "He'd like that."

"Katy and I would too."

Ethan rose. "Thank you. I wasn't sure how you'd take to a rambunctious boy underfoot."

Jenna stared at him. *What do you mean by that? I put up with you, don't I?*

After he left, Jenna exhaled. "Am I mistaken, or was Ethan almost human when he talked about Ryan except for that parting jab at me? I didn't say what I was thinking because it might have started another argument. The good news is Ryan will be around after school for two days, Katy."

Katy grinned.

"Jenna?" Renee called out from the dining room as she tapped on the office door.

Katy stayed in the kitchen when Jenna left.

"Katy and I were in the kitchen," Jenna said as she entered the dining room from the hallway.

Renee turned and smiled. "I love this old house with all its doors. I'll bet there's a secret passageway somewhere."

Jenna chuckled. "I don't know of any, but that doesn't mean there couldn't be. What can I do for you?"

"The deadline for an article my editor is working on was moved up. Is it possible for her and my collaborator to come here Wednesday instead of Friday?" Renee glanced to the left and pushed her hair behind her ear.

Jenna raised an eyebrow. *That's not why they're coming, and I'm not sure they're really the editor and collaborator.*

She nodded. "I'm sure it is, but I'll verify with Morgan. Give me a few minutes."

"Thank you; I'll wait in the living room."

Jenna went into the office and checked the reservation system before she called Morgan.

Morgan answered almost immediately. "Hi, we're on our way back."

"Renee wants to move her other two reservations from Friday to Wednesday. The system shows they're available."

"They are. I'll lock them in for her when I get there. Did she say why? Not that it matters; I'm just curious."

Jenna rose and peered out the window. *I wonder why Sophia was taking photos of the house.* "Evidently, a deadline moved."

Morgan snorted. "You aren't convinced, either, are you? Seems to me for a journalist she's lousy at time management with all the changes she's made, and she hasn't even been here a full day. Was she always like that? We just turned at the driveway; I'll be there soon."

When Jenna went into the living room, Renee was standing at the front window. "It's so peaceful here. Do you have security cameras?"

Jenna put her hand on the back of the yellow chair. *Beware.*

"Of course. Our offsite security team monitors the grounds for us around the clock."

Jenna glanced toward Nettie, who winked at her.

Renee turned and furrowed her brow. "I suppose I shouldn't be surprised you'd have the latest technology."

"Just seemed like common sense." Jenna glanced at the clock. "I'll see you at six. Morgan's coming up the driveway."

After Jenna hurried to the kitchen, she heard Renee go upstairs.

When Morgan came into the kitchen, she sat at the counter. "Ready for my news?"

"Sure am." Jenna looked up from the instruction sheet Darlene had left.

"We figured out what rustic glam is. It's warm and natural with touches of sophistication and luxury. We'll take advantage of the rustic wood walls of the barn as a backdrop and have metallic accents and soft textures. Our colors will be pastels with deep-toned accents."

"I can't wait to see it."

"I'll be ordering a few things this evening. My priority is the barn. Speaking of which, what do you think about giving the barn an actual name, like the Vintage Peach Barn, Vintage Barn, or Peach Blossom Barn?"

Jenna's eyes twinkled. "I like Vintage Peach Barn. It's simple and you could use peach blossoms in the logo as a nod to the Peach Blossom Retreat. Could we call the reception center the Peach Pit?"

Morgan burst out laughing. "I think we should. Rustic glam with a touch of whimsy can be our tagline for the Vintage Peach Barn."

"Anything else?" Jenna asked.

"That's it; I have to change the name on our system, but that will be easy. What about you?"

"Ethan's nephew is staying with him, so he'll be around. Ryan and Katy really hit it off."

Morgan said, "That's great."

"On the business side, I told Renee we have security cameras all over the property and an offsite team that monitors the cameras around the clock. I think my hackles were raised when I discovered Sophia taking photos of the house from all angles. She asked if there were any alarms on the guest entrance other than the one that goes off after ten o'clock. I told her we have security logs that include the date, time, and the room key used to unlock the door, and we received alerts on our phones. So when Renee quizzed me about security cameras, I heard alarm bells in my head that were so loud, I almost covered my ears." Jenna shrugged. "Just so you know."

"You think Renee and Sophia will verify with me, don't you?" Morgan asked.

"I wouldn't be surprised; it's what I would do."

"Anything else?"

"Ethan has a soft spot when it comes to Ryan. Ryan's dad will be back in two days, and we can expect Katy to mope after he leaves."

"I don't blame her. I'll bet Ryan is a fun guy."

Chapter Four

Morgan washed her hands so she could begin preparing for happy hour. "Shane's bringing pizza and tacos for us to enjoy after happy hour is over."

"Good; it will be nice to relax with friends."

"Shane wants to invite Ethan and Ryan to have supper with us. What do you think?"

Katy's ears perked up, and she whined.

Jenna chuckled. "She already knows his name. We enjoy Ryan's company, but I don't want to interfere with his homework."

After Morgan sent the text and went into the dining room to set up, Jenna sat at the counter and studied Darlene's instructions.

When Morgan returned, she said, "Shane ran with your suggestion that we don't interfere with Ryan's homework. He suggested to Ethan that we eat at six. What do you think? You and Katy can eat with Ryan and Ethan while Shane and I cover happy hour. After happy hour, you can join Shane and me while we eat, and we'll celebrate the end of the day with wine. What do you think?"

"Seems like a set up to me, but it makes sense."

"Good. I already told him that was what you would say, including the set up part."

Jenna said, "I've been thinking..."

Morgan put her hands up to her face with a pretense of being shocked. "Oh, no. Now it's my turn to be railroaded, isn't it?"

Jenna snickered. "Absolutely. We can warm the appetizer, make coffee and iced tea, and set up for two guests in less than twenty minutes."

Morgan joined her at the counter. "I know you're going somewhere with this."

Jenna exhaled. "We used to lock the door to the dining room after breakfast and didn't unlock it until happy hour, so we could keep a supply of plates, cups, silverware, and napkins in the cabinets without worrying about the temptation of pilfering."

"It was definitely more efficient than what we're doing now because we're carrying what we need to the dining room twice a day. Our guests knew the living room was always open to them, so there was no reason for them to wander around the house." Morgan furrowed our brow. "But after we moved the office, we left the dining room door unlocked in case a guest needed our attention."

"Renee's security camera question started me thinking."

Morgan interrupted. "Uh oh."

Jenna snorted. "Why can't we have an intercom system with a buzzer or bell at the registration desk, so our guests don't have to wander around or stand in the hallway and yell for us."

Morgan raised her eyebrows and nodded. "That's a good idea. We can talk to Shane; I'm sure he'll come up with something."

Jenna smiled. "He always does."

Morgan beamed. "Since I have some free time I didn't expect, I'll jump online for some ideas for the barn. I'm planning to make the tables and chairs rustic glam with tablecloths and slipcovers because wooden tables and chairs would be too cumbersome to move from the Peach Pit to the Vintage Peach and then back again."

"I can't wait to see what you come up with."

After Morgan left the kitchen for the office, Jenna wandered into the living room and sat in the yellow chair.

She relaxed as she stroke the right arm of the chair. "Bobbie gave her diary of secrets to Shane. They argued, but she trusted him. The spiral notebook must have the list of names to go with the passwords. She gave the spiral notebook to someone else."

Yes.

"Who would it be?"

Jenna smiled. "Either Foster or the Sergeant of Arms. I'll bet it was Foster."

Yes.

Jenna called Foster. "Is now a good time to talk?"

"Sure is; is everything okay?"

"Yes. I wondered if you know anything about a spiral-bound notebook that belonged to Bobbie Moore."

"It's funny because she dropped by my office two weeks ago and asked me to put a spiral-bound notebook in my safe. I had forgotten all about it, but I just remembered it a few minutes ago. I'm sure you understand."

Nettie reminded him. Jenna nodded. "Nettie's portrait was with you for a long time."

"She was, but she belonged at home." Foster's voice cracked. He cleared his throat. "I'm supposed to give the notebook to you. Would it be okay if I dropped by tomorrow, and if you don't mind, could I spend a little time with Nettie?"

"Certainly. I know she'll enjoy the visit too."

"Good. I'll text you before I leave so you can let me know if another time would be better."

"Perfect."

Foster knows I understand how he feels about Nettie. He stole her portrait years ago when the estate manager was selling off all the antiques so it wouldn't be sold to a stranger. He guarded her until he could return her to her home.

After she hung up, Jenna peered at Nettie's portrait. "Foster Kincaid will bring me the spiral-bound notebook he has been keeping for Bobbie. He plans to visit with you."

He's our good friend.

Jenna stared at Nettie's portrait. "You're right; I trust him."

Ethan's a good man too.

Jenna shook her head. "I don't see that."

You will.

Jenna narrowed her eyes. "Are you playing matchmaker?"

The wind chimes on the front porch jingled, and it sounded like a woman laughing.

Jenna exhaled as she rose from the chair. "Let's check the cottage, Katy. Maybe we can figure out how soon we can move back into our home."

On their short walk to the cottage, Jenna shuddered. "I have the strongest feeling someone's watching us, Katy. Let's go into the woods."

Jenna strolled into the shadow of the trees; when she was deeper into the woods, she stepped to the side so she'd be hidden behind a tree. After she turned and scanned the area between her and the house, a flash in a second-story window of the B&B caught her attention. *That's Sophia's room. I didn't know she was back.* She pulled out her phone to snap a photo, but nothing was there.

Katy barked and chased a squirrel up a tree. The squirrel chattered her complaints at Katy who searched the tree for a way to get to the squirrel.

When Jenna continued on her way to the cottage, Katy caught up with her.

Before she reached the cottage, Terrell called out to her. "Hey, Jenna. You have no business being here because you'll ruin the surprise."

Terrell strode from his truck and joined her in front of the cottage.

"What surprise?" she asked.

"The surprise you know nothing about. Just don't ruin it."

"I wanted to see how soon the cottage would be ready for me to move in."

"Soon, and I can't tell you any more except now you need to return to the B&B."

Jenna strolled back to the inn with Katy leading the way. "I'm not good at waiting for a surprise, and why is everybody so bossy these days? If I can find out what the surprise is, but don't tell anybody then I won't ruin the surprise, right Katy? We might have plans tonight for a stealthy visit after Morgan leaves."

After Jenna hung up her coat, she went into the office.

Morgan smiled. "You're just in time. You won't believe what I found. Look at these slip covers."

Jenna peered over Morgan's shoulder. "Those are beautiful. I love the pale cream slipcovers with the lower portion tied with wide bows in the back, and is that a peach blossom printed on the back of the seat? How many do you think we should order?"

"I guess we won't know until we have an idea of how many chairs we'll be ordering. I got ahead of myself, but the peach blossoms are perfect, aren't they? We should order at least two different styles of slipcovers, so we aren't stuck if we can't order additional slipcovers that match what we have."

"This is why you're in charge of design; I would order everything to match like a balance sheet."

"You have accounting principles running through your veins." Morgan grinned. "In the world of commerce, we want to tantalize and please our customer, so our target is emotions. We want people to swoon, laugh, or be surprised. Going with a blended style like rustic glam gives us the latitude to go after the feels."

Jenna rolled her eyes. "I think I'll just smile and nod at whatever you suggest because you lost me at tantalize. My version of a marketing campaign would be pictures of the barn with a 'Book Now' button."

Morgan laughed. "There is something to be said for the direct approach, except it's not for us."

While they looked at tablecloths and slipcovers for the chairs, Jenna asked, "Were you thinking about round, square, or rectangular tables?"

"Bobbie told Shane she wanted round tables for guests and rectangular tables for the buffet and drinks and a special rectangular table to serve as a head table for weddings and anniversaries. Shane and I decided we'd go with the decisions Bobbie had already made unless we come up with a compelling reason to change. Shane said Bobbie had a knack for understanding what worked best for entertaining groups."

While they scrolled through options for tablecloths, Jenna said, "A car is coming up the driveway."

"It's almost five o'clock, so it's probably Renee and Sophia. I don't expect to see Shane until closer to six. I'll pull together our happy hour appetizers."

"It's Monday; you aren't even supposed to be here, so it's my turn."

Morgan's eyes twinkled. "Okay, then I'll finish setting up the system for the barn reservations and work on some ads."

While Jenna was loading the utility tray with glasses, napkins, silverware, and plates, Renee and Sophia came into the B&B.

Renee's voice was whiny. "I don't understand why Nicci Dubois is coming here. She's only a senior developer at my fiancé's company."

Sophia said, "I thought she was a friend of yours, and you should probably stop referring to Orion as your fiancé. He hasn't proposed, and you don't want him to hear that from someone else."

"I'm sure he will any time now. Maybe if he hears it from someone else, he'll take the hint. Besides, we need to find a unique venue for our wedding."

"That has nothing to do with your project, and sometimes you overstep your boundaries."

Jenna heard footsteps running up the stairs then a door slam.

Jenna heard someone try the door to the locked dining room then footsteps going up the stairs.

Morgan opened the door from the office to the kitchen. "Did you call me?"

"No. Renee and Sophia came in; maybe you heard them in the foyer. I didn't hear much, but there seemed to be a little tension between them."

"It's probably related to their project." Morgan returned to the office.

Jenna rolled the cart into the dining room and set up for the two guests, and the two hosts, Morgan and Shane. She smiled as she put a tablecloth on the table closest to the sideboard. *I'll bet Shane will be torn between bailing and sticking close to Morgan.*

When Morgan joined her in the kitchen, Jenna pointed to the basket of tortilla chips and the bowl of salsa with individual bowls stacked next to the basket. "Those are ready for the sideboard. I'll take out the guacamole, sour cream, and the taquitos in a few minutes."

"We've never had guests on Monday and Tuesday since I've been here. Is this as unusual as I think?" Morgan asked.

Jenna furrowed her brow. "A few guests have arrived on Thursday and occasionally on Wednesday, but most weeks our rooms are filled from Friday afternoon through Monday morning. I hadn't thought about it, but Monday and Tuesday guests are rare."

"That's what I would have expected for a bed-and-breakfast. Do you think the Peach Blossom Barn will change that?" Morgan frowned. "I forgot we named it the Vintage Peach Barn."

Jenna put the taquitos, sour cream, and guacamole on a tray. "The Peach Blossom Barn sounded right when you said it. Maybe we shouldn't try to disengage the barn from the inn, except I still like the Peach Pit."

Morgan chuckled. "So do I."

Before Jenna carried her tray to the dining room, Morgan added the small bowls to the tray then followed Jenna with the chips and salsa bowl.

As they returned to the kitchen, Jenna said, "Let's skip making coffee. I've noticed almost no one drinks it at happy hour."

Renee and Sophia came down the stairs.

"You need to be more careful about what you say around people," Renee grumbled as they went into the living room.

"Me? I don't have a clue what you're talking about," Sophia said.

"You wouldn't."

Jenna frowned then side-glanced at Morgan, who was looking through the sideboard cabinets. *She didn't hear them.*

Morgan sighed. "I'd like to get a cold drink dispenser we could use for ice water."

Jenna furrowed her brow. "I think I saw one in a kitchen cabinet. I'll look."

While Jenna was in the kitchen, she heard a truck with a car following it up the driveway.

Jenna called out, "Morgan, they're here."

Katy whined.

Morgan hurried into the kitchen while Jenna pulled out a cold drink dispenser with peach blossoms painted on the side.

"Look what I found on the bottom shelf pushed way in the back." Jenna rose to her feet.

"That's perfect." Morgan ran her fingers lightly over the glass container. "I'll bet it has to be hand-washed. Did you hear that knock? I'll let them in."

Katy yipped and dashed ahead when Morgan opened the kitchen door to the hall.

Jenna nodded as she ran water into the sink to wash the glass dispenser.

"Katy," Ryan said; Katy yipped.

Ryan and Katy followed Morgan into the kitchen. "Hey, Miss Jenna. Are we too early? Uncle Ethan drove slow so we wouldn't get here too early. He said a man should never appear to be too eager."

Jenna suppressed a giggle when Morgan turned her back and coughed.

"You're welcome to come here early anytime, Ryan."

"You'll tell Uncle Ethan too?" Ryan asked.

"Yes, I will," Jenna said.

"Tell me what?" Ethan carried in three pizza boxes.

"Ryan is welcome to come here early anytime."

Morgan cleared her throat.

"And of course, you are too, Ethan."

Ethan peered at her. "Thank you."

"You're welcome." Jenna examined the tension in Ethan's arm muscles as he set the pizzas on the counter.

When he glanced at her, she smiled, and he returned her smile.

Shane came into the kitchen carrying two large sacks and a bottle of wine.

Jenna inhaled the enticing aroma of corn tortillas and chilies.

Morgan kissed Shane's cheek. "You smell wonderful."

Shane chuckled. "I'll bet you say that to all your taco delivery guys."

"No, just the cute ones." Morgan giggled when Shane's cheeks reddened.

Morgan reached for the water jug, but Shane picked it up before she could, and Ryan picked up the large bowl of ice.

Shane grinned. "Show us where you want this set up."

While the three of them went into the dining room, Jenna cleared her throat, and Ethan's back stiffened.

She said, "I'm sorry I've been so out of sorts, Ethan."

Ethan's face softened. "Is there anything I can do to help you?"

"Something has me on edge, but I'm not sure what it is." She peered at him. "Why did you decide to grow a mustache?"

Ethan stared at her. "It's kind of a family tradition when it's hunting season. My dad and uncles always did, so I did too as soon as I was old enough."

A family tradition. That was why Tom had a mustache until he went into the army. A tear escaped and slipped down her face.

"What's wrong, Jenna?"

Ethan took a step closer.

She sniffled. "I'm okay."

Jenna exhaled as she sat at the counter. "Maybe we can talk sometime like over coffee or something when we're not so busy."

Ethan smiled. "I'd like that."

Jenna's eyes twinkled. "Meanwhile, I apologize in advance for being snippy."

Ethan grinned. "And I'm sorry because I'll jump to the wrong conclusions when you're being snippy."

That cockeyed grin of his is contagious. Jenna smiled. "Tell me about your first mustache."

Ethan chuckled. "When I was thirteen, a few mustache hairs appeared at the corners of my mouth. I was highly offended when my grandmother told me I should wash my face before meals because I had a little dirt around my mouth."

"Oh, no," Jenna said. "What happened?"

"My dad told her it was a new fad, and he grabbed a handful of ashes from the fireplace and rubbed it at the corners of his mouth, and my grandmother was horrified but never said anything again."

Jenna smiled. "What a wonderful man."

"He really is. Dad and Mom will be here next month. You'll enjoy meeting them. They aren't anything like me."

Jenna laughed as Morgan, Shane, and Ryan returned to the kitchen.

"You have a nice laugh, Miss Jenna," Ryan said.

Ethan smiled. "She does, doesn't she?"

Morgan glanced at the clock. "It's six o'clock and time to unlock the dining room door. Are you helping me, Shane?"

"Sure am."

After they left, Jenna asked, "Tacos, pizza or both?"

"Both, please," Ryan said.

Jenna pulled out three plates from the cupboard. "Would you put a pizza on the table, Ryan? Is sweet tea okay with both of you?"

"That's great; I'll grab napkins and a sack of tacos," Ethan said.

While they ate, Ethan asked, "How was school?"

Jenna watched Ethan who smiled and nodded while Ryan talked about his classes, his friends, his lunch, and one particular girl who got on his nerves.

"I was telling one of my best jokes while I was getting off the school bus, and she interrupted me right before the funniest part and told me I'd left my backpack under my seat. Why does she have to be so bossy, Uncle Ethan?"

"Your dad's the expert when it comes to women, not me. What did your dad say?"

"He told me to ask Mom because he hasn't figured it out yet. I asked Mom, and she said I should appreciate a friend who had my back, but I don't need anybody watching my back."

"I don't know," Ethan said. "Sometimes it's kind of handy."

Ryan's eyes widened. "Would you let a girl watch your back?"

Jenna smiled as she raised her eyebrows and gazed at Ethan.

Ethan returned her smile. "It depends on the girl."

Ryan shrugged. "She has saved me from getting into trouble a couple of times, but I'd never tell her that."

Ethan met Jenna's gaze. "You might someday when you're a little older."

Ryan shuddered as he reached for another taco. "I'll never be that old."

"More tea, Ethan?" Jenna's eyes twinkled as she suppressed a smile.

"I'll get it." Ethan winked as he rose and then refilled their glasses.

After she finished eating, Jenna said, "I'll take over for Morgan, so she and Shane can eat while the food is still relatively warm."

"Do you want any help?" Ethan asked.

Jenna wrapped her long dark blonde hair into a tight bun then pulled her large pink hair clip from her back pocket and anchored it into place. "No, I won't be long. Don't leave, though. Maybe we can take Katy for a walk."

"Katy and I would like that," Ryan said.

When Jenna went into the dining room, Shane was standing near the doorway to the hall. Morgan and Renee were sitting at the table.

Morgan smiled as she rose. "Shift change. Are you coming with me, Shane?"

Shane nodded, and the two of them left. Jenna poured herself a glass of water and sat with Renee who sipped on her wine.

"How was your day?" Jenna asked.

"Not as productive as I had hoped."

Jenna nodded and sipped her water.

"Sophia took our bottle of wine upstairs. We'll leave for dinner as soon as she comes back down. I think the fresh air is too much for her; she's a city girl." Renee chuckled.

Jenna smiled. "Anything I can do to help you?"

Renee stared at Jenna. "I don't hear that very often these days."

Renee stared at her glass of wine. "Do you know if Bobbie had any particular friends or hobbies?"

Jenna furrowed her brow. "I really didn't know her all that well. I understand she had quite a few friends in town, which makes sense because she lived here all her life. What about you? Do you have any hobbies?"

Renee snorted. "I don't know how I could fit a hobby into my schedule. I'm double booked all the time. Do you have a hobby?"

"I love to read; my favorite time to read is early in the morning. It's a great way to start off the day. Weren't you on the archery team in college?"

Renee nodded. "I haven't thought about my bow in ages; I should take a little time off and go to an archery range to see how rusty I am."

"Rusty at what?" Sophia came into the dining room.

Renee winced. "Jenna remembered I was on the archery team in college."

"I didn't know that. I tried out for the Olympic archery team, but a car crash took me out of commission for a while, and that was the end of that. There's an archery range near here if you're interested; I always have my gear with me wherever I go. Are you ready to leave?"

Renee glanced at her half-full glass of wine.

"We have more wine for later. I left the bottle of wine in my room; we can get it when we return and relax in the living room. Did you want your jacket? I found it in the hall; you must have dropped it."

"I didn't want the jacket; I wanted my wine." Renee glanced at her half-full glass of wine.

Sophia draped Renee's jacket over the back of a chair and crossed her arms. "We can order wine with dinner."

Renee left her glass on the table as she rose. When she grabbed her jacket, a room key slipped to the floor.

Jenna narrowed her eyes as Renee headed to the door, and Sophia snatched up the key from the floor.

"I hate waste, and you know it," Renee grumbled as they left.

"Especially wine." Sophia's voice dripped with bitter sarcasm.

Jenna stacked the dishes on the utility cart and pushed it into the kitchen. Ethan sat at the kitchen table with Morgan and Shane while they ate, and Ryan sat on the floor with Katy.

Ethan rose from the table. "Can I help with that?"

"Leave the dishes," Morgan said. "Shane and I will take care of them. I suspect Katy and Ryan are ready for a run."

Ryan jumped up. "We sure are. Can we go now?"

"Let's go." Jenna said.

Ryan and Katy dashed out the back door with Ethan following them while Jenna grabbed her jacket.

When she went outside, Ethan smiled. "Ryan and Katy are running down the driveway to the road. Are you a runner?"

Jenna returned his smile. "I used to be; I'm slowly building back my stamina."

As they strolled toward the driveway, Ethan said, "I do my best thinking when I run, so I try to work in a short morning run two or three times a week."

Jenna stopped and pulled out her pink clip, and a light wind gust tossed her hair to the side.

As she smoothed it away from her face, Ethan asked, "Are you officially off duty now?"

"Yes; Morgan's in charge."

While they continued down the driveway, Jenna furrowed her brow. "I've been thinking about another project for us after the barn is in operation. The walk to the Paisley Peach Orchard is popular, but it's more than some guests can handle. Several guests have asked where they can go for a short walk."

Ethan nodded. "A shorter stroll that loops through the woods and back to the inn would be enjoyable for the guests who want to take a more leisurely walk and enjoy nature."

Jenna grabbed Ethan's arm. "Did you hear that? Katy just whined."

Katy yelped.

"She's hurt." Jenna raced toward the sound, but Ethan ran ahead of her.

"Uncle Ethan!" Ryan shouted.

CHAPTER FIVE

Before they reached the end of the driveway, Katy stopped yelping, and Jenna ran even faster to catch up with Ethan.

Jenna exhaled when she saw Ryan and Katy appear in the driveway near the road, and Ethan slowed to a walk so Jenna could join him. Katy had blackberry brambles tangled in her coat, and Ryan's arms and neck were scratched.

Ryan's face was wet with tears. "Katy chased a rabbit into a patch of blackberry bushes and got stuck. She fought to get loose, but she tangled herself up and got her collar caught in the branches. I finally got her collar off and convinced her to back out. Am I in trouble?"

Ethan hugged Ryan. "Not at all. You saved her from serious injury. She could have scratched her eyes in her panic to get loose. Let's go back to the inn and take care of those scratches, and I have clippers and leather gloves in my truck to remove those briars that are tangled in Katy's coat."

Katy trotted alongside Ryan as they headed up the driveway. She nudged his hand with her nose, and Ryan stroked her ears.

As they walked toward the inn, Jenna pulled out her phone and sent a text.

"Ethan, I asked Morgan to have dessert ready for Ryan and a treat for Katy."

Her phone buzzed a text.

She smiled. "And Morgan is on it."

"Will that cause a shortage for your guests?" Ethan asked.

"Not at all. Darlene always has desserts and snacks in case of emergencies. If nothing else, Morgan found a stash of cookies today; of course they might all be gone by now."

Katy glanced back over her shoulder at Jenna.

Jenna smiled. "Katy would like to hurry to the inn for her treat, Ryan."

"Is that okay?" he asked.

"It's up to you," Jenna said.

Ryan grinned. "Thanks. Let's go, Katy."

Ryan ran to the inn with Katy at his side.

Ethan chuckled. "Even I caught that look Katy gave you."

"I'd like to go find Katy's collar after you get the thorny sticks out of her coat."

"Okay, we can do that."

After they reached the inn, Ethan said, "I'll be right in."

When Jenna went into the kitchen, Ryan and Shane were sitting at the counter while Morgan dished up ice cream into bowls to go with their cookies. Katy rose from her spot at Ryan's feet and whined as Ethan came in the back door.

After Ethan carefully clipped and removed all the tangled branches from Katy, she licked his hand.

"You're welcome, Katy."

Ethan scratched her ears, and Katy grinned.

"Do you think I'll be able to find her collar, Ryan?" Jenna asked.

"Yes, ma'am. I smashed down all the brush around it so Katy could back out. It's close to the road and not too far from the driveway."

"You could get her another collar," Morgan said.

"Not really; I won't be long," Jenna said. "Can I borrow your clippers, Ethan?"

"I'll go with you." Ethan stuck the clippers into his back pocket.

After they were outside, Ethan said, "Give me a second to grab a flashlight. It will be dark by the time we get back to the inn."

As they strolled down the driveway, Ethan said, "You're not wearing boots, Jenna; you don't have to go into the brush."

"Thanks, but I have to find it."

"I got the feeling that Katy's collar is special."

Jenna pursed her lips and nodded. "It is."

They continued in silence until they neared the road.

"She's never worn any other collar," Jenna said.

Ethan nodded and turned on the flashlight as they walked a few yards down the road. He shined the light on the flattened brush.

"Ryan definitely smashed down the brush for Katy, didn't he?"

Jenna nodded. "He's really a kind-hearted kid."

"Ready to cross the ditch?" Ethan offered his hand.

Jenna furrowed her brow. *It's just to steady me on the uneven ground.*

She reached out, and when their hands touched, Jenna felt a wall between them. She hesitated before she took a step. *That's never been there before.*

After he helped her across the ditch and into the brush, Ethan released her hand as he walked farther into the brush and swept the area with the flashlight.

Jenna walked a few steps behind him as she concentrated on the brush ahead.

Jenna's foot suddenly slipped forward, and a flash of pink momentarily blinded her. She tried to regain her balance, but she sensed a heavy object overhead as it dropped toward her. She screamed and flung herself toward Ethan to avoid being hit. As she fell into the brush, Jenna raised her arms to protect her head.

Ethan snatched her off the ground and held her while she trembled. She felt the wall weakening.

"Did you see a snake? Did it strike you?" Ethan asked.

Jenna's eyes were wide and feral. "I saw pink, and something was going to hit me."

Jenna leaned against Ethan who brushed her hair away from her face, and the wall crumbled.

After she caught her breath, Jenna exhaled in relief. "I'm okay. I might have tripped over Bobbie's cane."

Ethan peered at her face. "You're serious."

She nodded.

Ethan kept one arm around her shoulders as he slowly scanned the area with the flashlight where Jenna had been standing.

After the second pass, he slightly shifted the light. "Wait. Right there. Do you see the pink?" he asked.

"Yes," Jenna whispered. "It's Bobbie's cane."

"Do you still have your phone?" Ethan asked.

"Yes, I'll text the sheriff." Jenna cleared her throat. "Excuse me. I'll need both hands to hold my phone and text."

Ethan sighed as he released her.

Jenna pulled out her phone from her back pocket. After she sent her text, her phone rang.

"Where are you?" the sheriff asked.

"Close to the road a few yards from the inn's driveway. The cane is in the brush."

"Has anybody picked it up?"

"No." Jenna told him about looking for Katy's collar.

"Do you mind waiting there for me? I'll be there in ten minutes."

After she hung up, she repeated what the sheriff had said.

Ethan reached for her hand. "Just in case."

Jenna gazed at her hand in his then at his face. *His eyes are such a clear blue.* She frowned as she examined at his mustache. *It's different from Tom's, but it still reminds me of him.*

"Is there something about my mustache that bothers you?" Ethan asked.

Jenna stiffened and pulled away her hand. Ethan said, "I didn't mean to upset you. Sorry."

Ethan turned the flashlight on the brush ahead. "I think I see it."

He pushed into the brush.

Jenna sighed with relief when she heard the snick-snick of the clippers.

Ethan came out of the brush holding Katy's collar high like a prize trophy.

After he gave the collar to Jenna, he said, "Are you okay?"

She put the collar on her arm like a bracelet and swallowed hard. "The sheriff's almost here."

Jenna took his hand as a car raced down the road toward the driveway. "You didn't upset me; we still need to have that coffee conversation."

"Will it include the flash of pink and when you thought something was falling on your head?"

"I can tell you now, but it's hard to process, so you might want to talk about it again later."

"I'd like to hear now."

"Sometimes when I touch things, I get very intense feelings, so when I slipped on Bobbie's cane, I saw pink and felt something come down on my head."

"Like a psychic?" he asked.

"Close. My understanding of a psychic is they predict or see future events. I sense feelings and sometimes circumstances. On very rare occasions, I've felt future events by touching things."

Ethan furrowed his brow. "You're right; I'll have to think about that. Does Morgan work tomorrow?"

"She's not supposed to, but she wasn't supposed to work today either."

"My brother is going to surprise Ryan after school tomorrow and pick him up. Ryan's mother will stay at her mother's, and my brother will join them this weekend. Why don't I pick up something for a quiet dinner we can eat in Darlene's kitchen?"

Jenna smiled. "That sounds nice, and thank you for not pointing out that a workaholic just complained to you about another workaholic."

Ethan chuckled. "You're welcome, and it was extremely difficult. I know you haven't noticed, but I have a hard time keeping my thoughts to myself."

Jenna laughed as the sheriff parked in the driveway. Before the sheriff climbed out of his cruiser, a deputy pulled in behind him.

"I never know what I'm going to see when I drive up to the Peach Blossom Retreat, but you two getting along is not what I would have ever expected. Where's the cane?" the sheriff asked as the deputy climbed out of his cruiser.

"Right there, Dan." Ethan pointed.

Sheriff Jenkins strode to them and peered at the pink cane nestled under the flattened weeds and brush. "You almost have to be on top of it to see it, don't you? As close as it is to the road, it must have been tossed out of a passing vehicle."

The sheriff motioned for the deputy to join them. "I'll call a team, but it will take them an hour to get here. Stay here."

The deputy nodded.

The sheriff turned to Jenna. "Do you have guests?"

"Yes, they've gone into town for dinner."

"Where can I park so I won't be in their way when they return?"

"You can park in the driveway near the back door."

The sheriff nodded. "I'll do that; it's become my usual parking place, anyway."

"Morgan can dish up dessert unless Shane and Ryan didn't leave us any," Jenna said.

"I'd never turn down a Darlene dessert." The sheriff pointed to his cruiser. "Want a ride to the back door?"

"The back seat of a cruiser? We'll walk." Jenna stuck her nose in the air. "I need the exercise."

The sheriff chuckled. "See you at the back door."

The sheriff waved as he drove past them and up the driveway.

Ethan squeezed Jenna's hand. "Run or walk?"

Jenna laughed. "Walk, but I don't think it's likely I'll fall. You don't have to hold on to me."

"Purely precautionary."

As they headed toward the inn, Ethan said, "Ryan and Katy bonded instantly, didn't they? My brother told me the original plan was for Ryan to go with him this weekend, but Ryan asked if he could stay with me. He found a dog park in Paisley that he said sounded perfect. According to Ryan, the weather is going to be mild on Saturday. He wanted me to ask if Katy would enjoy going to a dog park."

"I know she'd love it."

"Do you suppose you could get away?"

"I don't know; we'll be close to full capacity."

"In that case, you probably should go with us, so Morgan doesn't feel you're afraid to leave her in charge."

"That's true; she's imminently more qualified to run an inn than I am. In fact, I wonder if that's why she came in today. Maybe she's afraid to leave me in charge without supervision."

Ethan chuckled. "I'm sure that's not true, but it's still funny."

"It wasn't supposed to be funny," Jenna mumbled.

"What's your theory about Bobbie's cane?" Ethan asked.

"I think the bad guy approached Bobbie in her office then they went into the barn. They argued, and he grabbed Bobbie's cane away from her and repeatedly hit her with it. After she was unconscious, he staged the ladder. He took the cane with him because he was afraid it had his prints or because he was in a rage. He tossed the cane into the high grass because he didn't want to be caught with it, and he thought the high grass and brush would hide it for a long time."

"Do you think it's somebody local?"

Jenna shrugged. "Not necessarily, but definitely someone who knew Bobbie well enough to show up and pick a fight."

When they reached the inn, Jenna said, "That was a helpful talk and a pleasant walk, but."

Ethan's sudden stop threw Jenna off balance; she would have fallen if he hadn't caught her.

"Seems like I'm having trouble staying on my feet lately," she said.

"But what?" he growled as he continued to hold her in his arms.

"It was too short; what are you so mad about?"

Ethan glared at Jenna, but still hadn't released her.

Jenna peered up at him and giggled. "It was hilarious in my head."

Ethan lost control of his glare, and he laughed. "That was an ambush, and you won that round. Let's go inside for some dessert. I earned it."

Ethan slipped his arm around Jenna's shoulder; they headed to the back door where the sheriff waited in the shadows.

Ethen released Jenna when the sheriff cleared his throat. "The investigator is only twenty minutes away."

"Come inside; you can take your dessert with you if you have to," Jenna said.

While Ethan held the door, Jenna and the sheriff went inside together.

"That ambush was well-executed," the sheriff whispered.

Jenna side-glanced at him. "Your hearing is as good as mine."

"Convenient, isn't it?" he smiled.

Jenna returned his smile. "I've made good use of it."

When they went into the kitchen, Morgan said, "Hello, Sheriff Jenkins. How about a brownie with a side of ice cream? I can even make that to-go if that suits you better."

The sheriff sat at the counter. "Can you dish it up to-go just in case I get called away?"

"Sure thing." Morgan put a brownie into the microwave to give it a quick warm-up. After she scooped up a generous serving of vanilla ice cream and topped the warm brownie, the ice cream oozed over the sides.

After his first bite, the sheriff said, "This is delicious; is this another Darlene creation?"

Morgan smiled. "Of course."

The sheriff's phone buzzed a text. "The investigator is ten minutes out. I guess I'll have to eat and run."

He polished off his brownie and ice cream and scraped the paper bowl with his spoon. "Thanks. I'll probably drop by tomorrow sometime with more questions, Jenna."

Ethan gazed at Jenna. "We should probably get going too. Are you going to be okay?"

Jenna nodded.

Ryan kneeled next to Katy and stroked her face and back. "I'll see you this weekend, Katy."

Ethan awkwardly patted Jenna's shoulder. "See you in the morning."

She smiled. "Sounds good to me."

After Ethan and Ryan left, Morgan stared at Jenna. "I have questions. What investigator?"

"We found Bobbie's cane while we were looking for Katy's collar."

"Wow; I hope it helps their investigation. So, what was that pat on the shoulder all about? Was it a thank you for not hurting him?"

Jenna wrinkled her nose. "Oh hush. Open a bottle of wine, Shane, while I have a heart-to-heart with my Operations Manager."

Shane's eyes widened. "I can stay, right?"

Morgan raised her eyebrows. "Where would you go?"

"Oh, you know. I'd go visit one of my many girlfriends."

Morgan playfully punched his upper arm. "No. Stay here so we can blame you for everything."

Jenna pulled out three wine glasses while Morgan grabbed napkins.

Shane smirked as he pulled the cork and poured three glasses of wine. "As long as I'm being useful, I'll have to break hearts and stay."

After Shane joined them at the kitchen table, Jenna took her first sip of wine. "Excellent choice, Shane."

"Thank you; it's Morgan's favorite, so it was a logical choice."

"Morgan, does Renee have two room keys?"

"Not unless you gave her one too. Why?"

"There was an odd incident between Renee and Sophia over Renee's jacket that Renee claimed she didn't want, but when Renee picked up the jacket, a room key fell out. Renee didn't notice; Sophia picked it up, and the two of them bickered as they left, but there was no mention of the key. Am I just suspicious?"

"Maybe; there are other possibilities. You might have caught them in the middle of a long-running argument, for example."

"Could be; they seem to snipe at each other all the time. Let's talk about something else."

Morgan rose. "Okay, Shane, your turn. I'll grab chips and dip."

After Morgan handed out plates, she put the chips and dip on the table and sat down.

"I'd like to talk about the barn," Shane said.

Morgan and Jenna groaned.

"I need answers. Bobbie and I were all over the place with the design for the barn and the reception center from rustic to high end and back again. I finally realized I have to focus and get grounded. So, I'm back to the question, what will our guests be using the barn for and shouldn't the reception center be an auxiliary part of that?"

Morgan nodded as she pointed to her notepad. "Yes, the reception center should support the activities at the barn. I researched event centers like ours. I have my notes if you need more detail. They basically cater to weddings, anniversaries, adult birthdays, and family reunions."

"No corporate or children's events?" Jenna asked.

"Very few."

"Where do early arrivals wait while the staff is still setting up?" Shane asked.

"Some of them have a porch like we do, but the rest of them don't plan for early arrivals, and late arrivals are only a problem for sit-down, served meals, which we will not be hosting."

"What could we provide that would make us stand out?" Shane opened his briefcase and pulled out his sketchbook.

"If we expect a lot of weddings, we should have changing rooms for the bridal party," Jenna said.

"Two rooms with one room larger than the other," Morgan said.

Shane frowned as he sketched. "Which one is the bride's changing room?"

Morgan smirked. "We don't have to choose; we just make both of them comfortable with mirrors and lots of places to hang dresses."

"Do we really need the office?" Jenna asked.

"That's a good point, Boss Lady; everything's online now. The Peach Pit could have a comfortable reception area, two restrooms, two changing rooms, a storage closet and the large storage area, but we might have to come up with a different official name," Morgan said.

"It's nice to have direction; I can work with that and get you a draft. What about the barn?" Shane finished his rough sketch.

"I'd prefer leaving the barn rustic and using accessories to glam it up," Jenna said.

"Okay. Bobbie and I discussed two built-in sideboards to complement the huge dining table from the inn. What do you think about that?"

"Makes sense; I can't imagine we'd ever host an event with no food or drinks," Jenna said.

"Bobbie and I had picked out the built-ins for the barn, then she changed her mind because she decided we needed sideboards that would have more of an art déco look." Shane pulled out his phone. "This is what both of us liked, at least for a while."

"These are perfect; I love that they're in the style of the dining table but not an exact match," Jenna said.

Morgan peered at the photo then took Shane's phone and read the description. "I agree with Jenna."

"Good. I'll order them unless you want to place the order, then I'll send you the link. I'll bring you a draft of the reception center first thing in the morning.

If it's acceptable, the construction crew can start immediately."

"Place the order, if you don't mind, Shane; you already have the contacts and the links ready. Can I announce we're taking reservations for the Peach Blossom Barn event center for next month?" Morgan asked.

"After I check the shipping times for the sideboards in the morning, I can give you a firm date."

"That's great. I'm excited everything is pulling together. Jenna, your blogs are attracting attention, and I have ads ready to go."

"Speaking of which, are you ready to go, honey? I'd like to get to work on my draft," Shane said.

Morgan furrowed her brow. "Will you be okay, Jenna?"

Jenna rolled her eyes. "Of course; I have Katy. The doors are always locked, and in case you forgot, my brilliant security designer installed a keypad on the back door so it can stay locked and none of us will be locked out."

"See that? I've been telling you your designs are genius." Morgan put her hand on Shane's arm.

Shane grinned. "Talk about pressure. Now I have a reputation to keep up."

"You sure do." Morgan rose and pulled him up. "Let's go."

After they left, Jenna strolled into the living room and sat in the yellow chair. Katy followed her in and flopped down on Jenna's feet. When Jenna stroked the arm of the chair with her fingers, the fabric rustled. *Tell him.*

Jenna stared at Nettie's portrait on the wall and whispered, "Tell him?" Jenna furrowed her brow. "Tell who? Ethan? Tell him what?"

The lamp next to the chair flickered, and Nettie's usual playful demeanor was serious. The old house groaned as it sometimes did. *Mustache.*

"I don't see why. He'd just scoff at me."

When Jenna rose, Katy hopped up, and Nettie's face softened. *Wrong.*

"I'm not wrong; it's exactly what he would do."

Jenna flounced out of the living room and toward the back door. "Are you ready for one last stroll outside, Katy?"

While Katy patrolled the grounds between the inn and the cottage, Jenna listened to the buzz of cicadas. When she glanced at the sky, the incoming clouds obscured the moon and the stars.

"The cicadas say we're getting rain tonight; they might be right, Katy."

Katy trotted to Jenna, and after Jenna unlocked the back door with the keypad, they went inside.

Jenna went into her office and unlocked the middle drawer of her desk and pulled out Bobbie's diary of secrets.

She headed to her room. "Okay, diary. Let's see what Bobbie can tell me."

Katy followed her to her bedroom.

Jenna changed into sweatpants and a T-shirt and slipped on a sweatshirt and her fluffy slippers before she settled in her chair. Katy curled up close to Jenna and watched Jenna read.

After five pages, Jenna flipped through the rest of the book. "This is Bobbie's record of the groups she joined with gossipy details about the members. Maybe I'm reading it wrong."

Jenna rose and peered out her window. The tops of the trees behind the inn swayed with each gust of wind.

"The wind is making me restless. Let's go to the living room, Katy. I can put up my feet, and it's okay if I'm lounging in off-duty clothes, don't you think?"

Katy yipped, and they went to the kitchen. After Jenna brewed a cup of tea and gave Katy a treat, they went to the living room.

Jenna sat in her yellow chair and propped up her feet. Katy stared at her.

"I'm settled for a while," Jenna said.

Katy scratched at the rug and circled her favorite spot before she settled down.

Jenna stared at Nettie's portrait. "I thought Bobbie's diary was gossipy, but maybe it isn't."

Chatty.

"That's it; I'll read it as cozy, chatty details about her online friends because she does seem to care about them."

When Jenna imagined Bobbie's voice reading the diary to her, she understood how straightforward and without any judgment the details were.

After reading for an hour and enjoying getting to know Bobbie's online friends better, Jenna was interrupted by a car coming up the driveway. She stuck the pamphlet into the diary.

"I'm not interested in small talk right now, Katy. Should I hide in my office?"

No.

Jenna peered at Nettie and sighed. "I won't run away, but I will hope they go straight upstairs."

Katy raised her head and grinned.

When they came into the inn through the guest entrance, Sophia asked, "Aren't you concerned about Nicci coming here? Surely you know about the gossip."

"No, I don't know about any gossip," Renee said.

"I forget you aren't as plugged in at the company as I am. It's nothing."

"It must be something, or you wouldn't have brought it up."

As they started up the stairs, Sophia said, "Nicci almost lost her job after Orion broke up with her because she was so bitter."

Renee snorted. "That's nonsense. When was that supposed to have happened?"

"After you and Orion had been dating a while. She blamed you for breaking them up."

"Nicci is a close friend of mine, and I don't believe a word of it," Renee said.

"I didn't think you would."

Jenna jumped when a door slammed and then frowned when she heard a woman humming and a second door close.

"Did you hear that?" Jenna whispered. "I wonder why Sophia is stirring the pot."

Jenna peered into her empty mug. "Do I want tea or wine?" She sighed. "Neither; I'm too lazy to get up."

While she continued to read, she heard a creak on the stairs and Katy's ears perked up.

I should have gone to my room after they went upstairs.

"There you are." Renee came into the room. "I saw the light on and hoped you were still up." She raised the almost full bottle of wine she had brought with her.

"Would you care to share a glass of wine with me?"

"Sure. I'll get two glasses."

Jenna carried the diary with her and dropped it off in the kitchen.

When Jenna returned with two wine glasses, Renee was staring at the cold fireplace.

"I suppose it's too late to build a fire," Renee said as Jenna held out the two glasses.

Renee emptied the bottle as she filled both glasses before Jenna could say anything.

"It is; when it's cold, we start the fire in the middle of the afternoon and let it die out during happy hour."

Jenna handed Renee the glass that was filled to the brim and sat in her yellow chair.

Renee sat on the sofa and raised her glass. "Cheers."

"Cheers," Jenna echoed and took a small sip.

Renee took a large gulp of her wine then sighed. "Did you hear what Sophia said?"

"No, I was focused on the book I was reading and didn't realize you were back until I heard a door close upstairs." Jenna took another small sip.

"Orion told me I should fire Sophia, and now I'm wondering if he was afraid she might tell me something he didn't want me to know. Nicci is my best friend; she's too professional to date the boss, but if she had been, she would have told me." Renee shook her head. "I really am torn."

Jenna nodded as she set her glass on the table next to her. *This wine would never get past the Paisley Business Association's wine connoisseurs.*

Jenna's mouth quivered. *I've turned into a wine snob.*

"What would you do?" Renee asked.

"Sleep on it, for sure," Jenna said.

"You were always so sensible." Renee sighed.

Why does that sound like I was boring?

Renee stared at Nettie's portrait.

Maybe because I was.

A gust of wind rustled the wind chimes on the front porch. The chimes sounded like a woman giggling.

Jenna smiled. *Thank you, Nettie.*

"We may get some rain tonight," Jenna said. "You'll hear it on the roof. You'll love it; our guests tell me it's nature's white noise. One guest recorded it, but she said it wasn't the same when she listened to it at home."

"It would be nice to have a good night's sleep." Renee droned on about Orion and his past escapades in his youth.

"Of course, that was years ago." Renee stared at her still half-full glass. "I think the day has caught up with me. I'll see you in the morning."

Renee sat her wine glass on the end table and left for her bedroom.

After Jenna heard Renee's door close, she carried the two wine glasses and the empty bottle into the kitchen. After she poured out the wine, she rinsed the glasses and the sink and placed the wine bottle into the bin for bottles.

Katy was waiting for Jenna in the hallway. Jenna threw on her jacket, and they went outside. After a quick break, Katy nosed the back door, and they went in.

Jenna picked up the diary from the kitchen then paused when she heard voices coming from the second floor.

Sophia growled, "I've already told you, Renee. There was never anything between me and Orion. If you're going to play that jealousy card, why don't you talk to your so-called good friend, Nicci?"

"Sophia, you can pack up your things and leave. I'll authorize one month's of severance."

Sophia snorted. "You can't fire me. I work for Fred, not you."

Renee's voice was shrill. "You mean Fred Haas, the Chief Technology Officer at Orion's company?"

"Oh, you know another Fred?"

"Since when?" Renee's tone dripped with vitriol.

Jenna heard footsteps, and Sophia's voice faded. "A month ago; check with him yourself, if you don't believe me."

"I don't expect you to be here in the morning." Renee shouted.

A door slammed upstairs.

After Jenna quietly closed the bedroom door, Katy stretched out on her rug.

"Wasn't that something?" Jenna put the diary in a drawer and then dressed for bed.

As Jenna slipped under her covers, the rain slammed against her window.

"Good night, rain."

Jenna turned off her light.

"Good night, Katy."

Katy settled down on the soft rug at the foot of the bed while Jenna slipped under the covers and listened to Katy's soft snoring and the rain.

CHAPTER SIX

Jenna woke to the sound of rain and Katy whimpering in her sleep. She opened her eyes and glanced at her phone. *Still dark. Five thirty.* Katy whimpered again.

Jenna rolled out of bed and stroked Katy's back. Katy sighed and settled down.

After Jenna was dressed in the dark, Katy stood at the bedroom door.

"It's raining, pretty girl. You want to take a quick break then I'll make coffee while you eat breakfast?"

After Jenna opened the back door, she and held it open while Katy took her quick break then dashed back inside. Jenna grabbed the towel she kept by the back door and gave Katy a good rubdown. After Katy was not as soaked as she was when she came inside, Jenna hung up the towel, and they went into the kitchen.

Jenna sat at the counter. While she drank her coffee and read Darlene's instructions for the morning breakfast, Katy ate hers.

"I would have figured this out eventually, Katy, but it's handy just to read it and avoid thinking so early in the morning."

While Jenna refilled her cup, her phone buzzed a text from Morgan. "Are you awake? Call me."

Jenna immediately called Morgan. "What's wrong?"

Morgan sobbed as she spoke, but her words were completely unintelligible.

Jenna furrowed her brow at Morgan's rising panic. "Slow down, Morgan. Deep breaths."

"Okay." Morgan exhaled. "They took Shane in for questioning; the detectives obviously think he murdered Bobbie. I should call a lawyer for him. Do you know any lawyers?"

"No, but I'll call Ethan; he'll know."

After Jenna hung up, she stared at her phone then exhaled and sent a text to Ethan. "Sorry so early. Shane needs a lawyer. Call me."

Her phone rang immediately.

"What's going on?" Ethan asked.

"Morgan said the detectives think Shane murdered Bobbie and took him in for questioning. That's all I know."

"I'll call the sheriff to find out where Shane is." Ethan hung up.

Jenna called Morgan. "Ethan will help. Are you okay?"

"Not really. I don't want to be alone; can I come there? Shane finished his sketches. We can look at them."

"Sounds good, and I'm sure he'll join us by this afternoon."

"I'll be there in time to help with breakfast." Morgan hung up.

Jenna put the Danishes in the oven to take off the chill then filled a pitcher with orange juice. After she added juice glasses, cups, silverware and napkins to the utility tray, she removed the Danishes and put them on a ceramic platter that was ringed with tiny pink blossoms.

She pushed the cart into the dining room as the coffee maker beeped twice to indicate it was ready. After she arranged the morning's breakfast on the sideboard, she checked the time on her phone. *Five minutes until seven.*

Her phone rang.

Ethan said, "Shane's at the sheriff's office; his lawyer will be there in fifteen minutes. Jenna, they haven't arrested him. After I drop Ryan off at school, I'll come to the inn. Tell your guests to use the side door to exit for today and leave the front and back doors locked."

Jenna frowned, but Ethan hung up before she could complain. *I need to tell him the doors are always locked.*

When she unlocked the dining room door to the hallway, she heard footsteps on the stairs.

I wonder what our drama is going to be today.

Jenna returned to the kitchen to give them a chance to drink some coffee before she greeted them.

At least, that's my excuse. She gave Katy a treat.

When she didn't hear anything from the dining room, she peeked in. Sophia sat by herself at a table with a glass of orange juice, a cup of coffee, and a small plate with a Danish on it.

Jenna went into the dining room. "Good morning, Sophia. How did you sleep?"

"I don't know if it was the room or the bed, but I haven't slept this well in ages."

Jenna poured herself a cup and joined Sophia at her table.

"Morgan decorated all the rooms; I find it relaxing to sit in mine. In fact, I've discovered I can't work for long in my room because I'll fall asleep."

Sophia chuckled. "The Peach Blossom Retreat is an amazing inn. I love everything about it. How long does the walk to the peach orchard take for most people? I was thinking about that for my next break."

Jenna smiled. "From personal observation, I'd say anywhere between one and three hours or more. The walk from the inn to the orchard takes twenty minutes if you walk briskly and don't slow down to watch the rabbits, squirrels, or hawks. Most people take the peach orchard tour or visit the gift shop, so that adds another one to two hours. Everyone tells me coming back is slower, but it might not be if you aren't worn out by all the activities at the orchard."

"That sounds wonderful. What about the walk to the barn?"

"It's about fifteen minutes, but again, you have to ignore the wildlife and not stop to pick blackberries."

"I love blackberries. Are we allowed to pick them?"

"Of course. They are wild blackberries, so they're a little tart, but I love the adventure of finding food in the wild."

"I'll try to schedule a stroll to look for blackberries."

Jenna rose. "Enjoy your day."

Sophia smiled. "At least it's starting out relatively calm."

Jenna went into the kitchen with Katy and read the instructions for the evening's happy hour. *Doesn't sound too hard.*

She raised her eyebrows when she heard voices from the dining room.

I've heard the rumble of noise from the dining room, but I've never paid attention to how clear the voices are when there are only two people talking.

"What's on the agenda for today? I thought you'd beat me down to the dining room this morning after you cut the evening so short," Sophia said.

"We left the restaurant early because I was tired. You make everything about you sometimes," Renee grumbled.

Jenna settled in her seat at the counter after she refilled her cup. *Of course, it's quiet in the kitchen, which is rare, and they aren't trying to be quiet.*

"You're a fine one to talk, and don't tell me I'm fired again. It's boring."

"I'd fire you in a minute if you didn't have an ironclad contract," Renee hissed.

"So, you did check. I wasn't sure you were smart enough to take a hint."

Jenna rose and partially opened the door to the dining room. "Come on, Katy. It's time for my breakfast."

Jenna smiled as she strolled into the dining room. "How did you sleep?"

When she glanced at Sophia, Sophia side-glanced at Renee then put her forefinger in front of her mouth. Jenna nodded. *We're in a conspiracy.*

"You were right about last night's rain; it was exactly like an expensive white noise machine found in high end hotels. I understand why your guest recorded it; I was tempted too," Renee said as Jenna picked up a fork and a napkin before she put a Danish on a plate and poured a small glass of juice.

When Jenna joined them at the table, Sophia pulled out her phone. "No rain today, but I suppose the ground will be too wet for a walk."

"Were you thinking about taking the path to the peach orchard? Most of the path is pea gravel," Jenna said.

"I was thinking about walking to the barn," Sophia said.

"The path is mowed grass and probably won't dry out until tomorrow afternoon, assuming it doesn't rain. We plan to improve it, so it will be more like the path to the orchard." Jenna took the last bite of her Danish and refilled her coffee.

She held up the pot. "Anyone else?"

Sophia shook her head. "I like my coffee with more oomph and a little frothier."

Renee glared at her. "Just a splash more, Jenna. Your coffee tastes freshly ground."

"Thank you," Jenna said. "We try to serve what we think our guests will like. Is the coffee you like a darker roast, Sophia?"

Sophia glanced at Renee and jutted out her jaw. "I guess so, but it's served with frothy almond milk."

"That sounds interesting; we don't have any way to froth milk, so that wouldn't be an option for us." Jenna smiled. "I'm always interested in new ideas. Maybe we could offer almond milk so guests could add their own. I'll send a survey to our recent guests to get their opinion."

Sophia raised her eyebrows. "Have you ever offered hazelnut or French vanilla coffee as an alternative?"

"No, but you just gave me another question for my survey. Thanks," Jenna said.

Sophia smirked at Renee. "I have a technical call with our support team. Did you want to sit in?"

Renee glanced at her phone. "I have a conflict; my conference call starts in fifteen minutes, but thanks for including me."

Jenna sipped her coffee. *The air is thick with contempt.*

Jenna forced herself to smile until they left then she shuddered. She stacked the dishes on the utility cart and rolled it into the kitchen.

"Why would anyone want to lie about a tech call or a conference call? Were they trying to impress each other?" Jenna whispered.

Katy sneezed.

"I think I'm allergic to liars too."

Jenna heard a car come up the driveway. "Doesn't that sound like Shane's car?"

When Morgan came into the kitchen, she said, "I'm sorry I'm late. Shane's car is newer and much fancier than mine. I should have realized I'd need a little time trying to figure out what all the buttons, levers, and knobs were supposed to do. It took me ten minutes to start the dang thing. I need coffee."

Jenna cocked her head. "Shane's car? Is something wrong with yours?"

Morgan took a big sip of coffee. "Ahh. I really needed coffee. Don't tell Shane I couldn't figure out how to start his car. Mine is at my apartment. We actually didn't plan on Shane going somewhere without me."

Jenna smiled. "When were you going to tell me you were staying with Shane?"

"Maybe tomorrow."

"Okay, I can wait. I'm a very patient person." Jenna fluttered her eyelids.

"My foot." Morgan laughed and rose to pour more coffee. When she held up the pot and raised her eyebrows, Jenna said, "None for me; thanks."

While Morgan refilled her cup, she said, "I designed business cards for the Peach Blossom Barn and made some samples. I'll show you."

Morgan set her cup on the kitchen table and left. When she returned from their office, she had a small stack of business cards in her hand and set them on the table.

Jenna picked up one and examined it while Morgan sat and sipped her coffee.

"Very sharp. I like the logo colors of peach and green with the peach blossom and the intertwined PBB initials. The font you chose for your name and title has a crisp, professional look."

"I found a template I liked then played with it, but it didn't take long because I knew what I wanted. If you don't see any changes, I'd like to order a box of professionally printed copies. Do you want me to design business cards for you?"

"Maybe later. Can I keep a few of your samples?"

"Of course. What's your news?"

"I had coffee and a show earlier."

While Morgan nibbled on a Danish and sipped her coffee, Jenna told her about the argument followed by more sniping between Renee and Sophia.

"If their original purpose was to interview Bobbie, why are they staying?" Morgan asked.

"Renee told me she wanted to stay so she could focus on a second project she had going on, but I'm not sure when she's had time to work on anything. So, what's this about staying with Shane?"

"You'll accuse me of being a conniving sneak," Morgan grumbled.

"I'd never do that; were you?"

Morgan chuckled. "No, but only because I didn't think of it."

Jenna smiled. "Still waiting."

"Three weeks after I started working with you, I stopped on the way home at the gas station. After I filled up the tank, the engine wouldn't start. I was looking under the hood when this creepy guy got way too close to me and told me I needed a man to take care of me. I slammed the hood shut and told him my fiancé was on the way. Shane pulled in, and I rushed to him and hugged him."

"He didn't know what was going on, but he knew it was something and hugged you back. Am I right?"

"Almost. He hugged me and whispered, 'Did you rob the store?'"

Jenna laughed. "He did not."

Morgan smiled. "He actually asked if I needed a jump for my car, but I like the other story better. My car was in the shop for three weeks while they waited for a part, and then four more weeks after the supplier sent the wrong part. He was my ride to work and home, and we had dinner together every evening, so it just made sense for me to stay at his place."

"Is this one of those exciting only one bed stories?" Jenna asked.

"I'm not saying." Morgan snickered. "Actually, Shane's apartment has two bedrooms."

Jenna smiled. "I'm happy for you, but why is it such a big secret?"

"I was in an unhealthy relationship for a long time; everything I did or said was criticized. My self-confidence is still more fragile than I'd like to admit. After I escaped, I was certain the isolation of my job at the hotel before I came here offered me a chance to recover. I was desperate for privacy because I hadn't had any in such a long time. Until I met Shane, I didn't realize I had to feel safe before I could heal. So, that's kind of where we are now."

"Safe and healing?"

"Working on it." Morgan exhaled and stared out the side window. "On Sunday, Shane was absolutely livid when he came home from the grocery store. He told me Bobbie picked a fight with him in the produce department over the décor for the barn. He said he thought she was kidding at first because she was insisting he change something she had hated the day before. Shane said she became really loud and the entire situation deteriorated because he told her he'd turn in his resignation on Monday. Shane left his cart and was walking out of the store when Bobbie screamed, 'Over my dead body.'"

"Oh, no. That is so unfortunate." Jenna peered at Morgan. "There's more, isn't there?"

She nodded. "He told me he kind of mumbled, 'Whatever it takes.' He said no one heard him, but you know how it is. Shane would have been completely exhausted from dealing with her."

"He's afraid someone heard what he said, isn't he?" Jenna rubbed her forehead.

"Shane's convinced no one heard his words, but I'm certain anyone could have picked up his tone."

"And spun a story to go with it, which I sure must have triggered the investigation against him. What else?" Jenna asked.

"Nothing," Morgan growled as she slammed Shane's keys on the table.

Jenna picked up the keys, and her eyes widened. "He went to the barn to talk to Bobbie on Monday morning."

Tears welled up in Morgan's eyes. "He was convinced he could patch things up with her, and they would come to an agreement. He gave me the sketches to bring to you and told me we'd talk later."

Jenna set the keys back down on the table. She put her hand on Morgan's. "He didn't hurt her."

"I know." Morgan sobbed. "But I'm scared for him."

Jenna handed her a tissue. "Straighten up, girl. We've already agreed Shane wouldn't have hurt Bobbie, so we need to find out who did."

Morgan blew her nose. "Why would anyone want to hurt Bobbie?"

"That is a great place to start. I have some ideas."

Morgan rose and started pacing. "Like what?"

Jenna paused. "Ethan's truck is coming up the driveway. Do you want him in on this?"

"I do, but it's up to you."

"It's your say, not mine."

"Okay, then, maybe."

Jenna giggled. "We have a wishy-washy maybe, so we might tell him what we know."

Morgan grinned. "I agree. I'll let him in then follow your lead."

Jenna sighed. "I should let him in, or he'll accuse me of being anti-social."

"Look at you being all sensitive and charming."

When Jenna glared at her, Morgana giggled. "I'll warm a few Danishes. You want to split one with me to be social?"

"Might as well," Jenna muttered.

When she opened the door, Ethan stepped out of his truck. He raised his eyebrows when he saw her and quickly strode to the door.

"Is everything okay?" he asked. "I didn't expect you to be waiting for me."

"I heard your truck. Come in; we have coffee and Morgan is warming pastries."

As he strode into the kitchen, Ethan said, "The lawyer is on her way to the sheriff's office. She said Shane should be here before lunch. I wanted to see if you or Morgan knew what Shane had in mind for today, so there would be something the crew could get started on."

"I have a copy of the final draft Shane finished last night and planned to have Jenna review today. We could go over that," Morgan said.

Morgan poured a cup a coffee for Ethan then pulled out the Danishes from the oven. "I'll bring my laptop in here."

After Morgan returned, she put her laptop on the counter and pulled up a copy of Shane's sketch on her screen.

While the three of them huddled around the screen, Ethan was so close to Jenna that their shoulders were touching. Jenna felt the warmth from his shoulder spread through her chest and down to her toes. She sighed. *It's so comforting.*

Ethan asked, "Peach Blossom Barn and Peach Pit? Are those their names?"

When Jenna inhaled to speak, she was almost overcome by the now-familiar, tantalizing aroma of the no-frills man soap mixed with the distinctive scent of the outdoors that was Ethan.

She cleared her throat and nodded. "The Peach Blossom Barn is the name for the barn; Peach Pit has to be changed later to something more elegant, but that's its name for now."

Morgan added, "The Peach Blossom Barn is a final, though; I've already built its website."

"I like them; they fit. Did you know about these large rooms in the reception center, Jenna?" Ethan asked.

Morgan jumped in. "Those are changing rooms for the bridal party when we host weddings. It was Jenna's idea."

Ethan raised his eyebrows at Jenna. When she felt her face growing warm, she rubbed her temple and turned her face. *Why am I embarrassed about thinking about the wedding party?*

Morgan pointed. "This is the storage for the table linens and cleaning supplies."

"The reception center looks comfortable. Where's the office?" Ethan asked.

"We decided against an office because Morgan and I are comfortable with our shared office, but what's this room where the office used to be?" Jenna asked.

"Shane thought our clients might like a work room. He suggested guest internet access, a computer desk with a laptop and an office chair, a work table, a copier, and a few office supplies for the clients to use."

Jenna furrowed her brow. "So if the organizers had any last-minute changes or additions for place cards, they'd have the space and tools at their fingertips?"

"Yes, that's a good example. I asked for a small refrigerator to keep our drinks when we're working at the barn," Morgan said. "He said if we changed our mind about an office at the Peach Pit, the work room is large enough to add a small conference table and three more chairs."

"That shows me how oversized the original office was," Jenna said.

Ethan pointed to the storage area for extra tables and chairs. "Nice wide exterior door and a ramp going out the back. After that's built, we'll add a concrete walkway to roll the tables to the barn and back. What do you think, Jenna? Is there anything you'd like to change, or do you need more time to study it?"

"No, we've discussed and studied enough. Let's get moving."

Ethan said, "Thanks, I'll be at the Peach Blossom Barn or the Peach Pit if you need me."

After Ethan left, Morgan said, "I'm excited about the work moving ahead, but I wish Shane was here."

Jenna's phone rang.

"It's Renee," Jenna sighed.

"Do you want me to give you some privacy?"

Jenna shook her head as she answered.

"Do you have a minute?" Renee asked.

"Sure; what can I do for you?"

"A friend of mine is in town, and he'd like to meet you. Would you join us for lunch? You'll enjoy his company; he's the most thoughtful, charming man I know. Now don't tell me you have to stay at the inn for guests, because you'll be having lunch with me, and Sophia went to Atlanta for the day." Renee tittered.

"What time, and where?"

"I have reservations for three at noon at the little tea shop on the square. I talk like a local, don't I?"

Jenna frowned. *Renee's cheerful voice sounds forced.*

"You certainly do; I'll see you at noon."

After she hung up, Morgan asked, "Are you having lunch with Renee?"

"She said Sophia went to Atlanta for the day, and she has a friend who wants to meet me. She didn't explain how those two things are related, but the invitation to lunch feels contrived to me. I couldn't come up with an excuse fast enough so I could gracefully decline. I need some canned responses of regret prepared for these early calls."

"Contrived like a matchmaking or hidden agenda thing?"

Jenna shrugged. "I won't know whether she has an ulterior motive, or it's actually important, unless I go, will I?"

"Want me to tag along? You can borrow my car story. You could say you can't make it because your car broke down, but I offered to give you a ride, or come with you. I don't know why I'm trying to spin your story; you're better at it than I am."

Jenna peered at Morgan. "If Ethan had said that, I'd have tossed him out; when you tell me I'm good at adding imaginative details, I take it as a compliment."

Morgan smirked as she sat in front of her computer. "I'm proud of your new insights, but you'll still toss him out if he crosses you, won't you?"

Jenna shrugged. "So, I'm going to wait a while before I call Renee. I'm expecting Foster Kincaid soon. He's bringing me a notebook he thinks might have belonged to Bobbie, and he wants to visit with Nettie."

Morgan glanced at Jenna. "Foster Kincaid was the caretaker for Nettie's portrait for a long time, wasn't he?"

"He was; I don't think he would have given me her painting except he knew she belonged in the Wyndham house."

"I'm glad she's here. When I'm overstressed, I sit in the living room for a while; it's very calming."

Jenna's phone buzzed a text from Foster Kincaid.

"I forgot to tell you I'm on the way."

Katy yipped.

Jenna smiled. "We have company."

"I need to complete my list of what we need in the barn and in the pit so I can place an order today. I'd be embarrassed if Shane's sideboards arrive before the tables, chairs, and tablecloths."

Jenna waited in the foyer with Katy and watched while Foster Kincaid strolled to the house. He stopped midway and gazed at the front yard and the old inn, and then smiled as he continued to the front porch.

Jenna opened the front door with her electronic key and returned his smile.

He stepped onto the porch. "You've made a few changes but kept the inn's personality. Well done."

"Come on in. I'll give you a quick tour."

"I'd like that."

After he was inside, Foster scanned the foyer. "I feel like I stepped back in time. Where do I drop my calling card?"

He glanced at the registration desk. "You've kept the old wooden registration desk and have a guest sign-in book." He chuckled. "I'm surprised you don't have a pen and inkwell."

"We seriously considered it, but Mr. Morgan pointed out our guests wouldn't know how to use it and would just make a mess, so we have a feather quill and empty inkwell as a decoration. Our reservation system is online, but we wanted to preserve the feel of signing into an old inn."

"You have certainly done that." Foster gazed at the staircase. "I can imagine Nettie Wyndham running down the stairs to greet guests."

"So can I." Jenna smiled. "We have five guestrooms upstairs and four downstairs. The rooms are basically similar in layout; the furnishings and linens are different for each of the nine rooms, though. We didn't want our rooms to have a hotel feel. I'll show you one of our guestrooms."

CHAPTER SEVEN

Jenna unlocked the door of the guestroom next to hers.

Foster smiled as he peered into the room. "It looks very plush in an understated way. How did you do that?"

"Morgan Farley is a design genius."

Foster nodded as his eyes twinkled. "There's no television. How do you get away with that?"

"Our guests know there is no television here when they register, but we have excellent Wi-Fi available for them, so they take advantage of it for their streaming services."

On the way to the dining room, Foster handed Bobbie's notebook to Jenna.

"I appreciate you taking Bobbie's notebook. I didn't know if it was something Mr. Moore would want or not, but I knew you'd be a better judge of that."

When they stepped into the dining room, Foster's eyes widened. "How did you get that monstrosity of a table out of here?"

"I stayed out of the way while Mr. Moore and his men did the work."

Foster chuckled. "Smart."

Jenna continued, "We're renovating the barn to be an event center and moved the table to the barn. It's perfect as a sideboard. We're reusing and renovating everything we can to preserve the Wyndham estate heritage."

She pointed to the doors. "That door closest to us goes to the kitchen and the door in the back of the dining room goes to the office Morgan and I share."

"What about the cottage? How's that coming along?"

"It's close. I have my fingers crossed; hopefully, I can move in early next week."

"Are you taking Nettie with you?"

"I don't think so; she belongs in the house."

As they continued to the living room, Jenna said, "You're welcome to stay as long as you like. If you need me, I'll be in the office; just tap on the door, or I'll hear you if you're in the dining room and call out."

Foster chuckled. "I remembered your sensitive hearing. I'm glad it comes in handy for you."

While Foster strolled to the blue overstuffed chair that sat next to Nettie's yellow chair, Jenna returned to the office.

Morgan was hunched over her computer screen with a scowl on her face.

"Everything okay?" Jenna asked.

Morgan leaned back in her chair and exhaled. "I'm bummed. This is not in my budget."

Jenna peered at the screen. "A custom, hand-hewn wooden sign? It's beautiful and would be perfect for the barn."

Morgan scrolled to the price.

"Ouch," Jenna said, "Maybe we can set a goal and order it when we meet our goal."

"I like that; I'll think about what would be an appropriate goal. Meanwhile, let me show you the three styles of tablecloths and the four sideboard runners. Don't ask me how many tablecloths are in a set, but they are discontinued styles, so we got a great price."

After Morgan pulled up the tablecloths on her screen, then scrolled to the reviews, Jenna gaped. "These are perfect for us, and the reviews are excellent."

"I bought all they had," Morgan said.

"What about the covers for the chairs?"

"We're not getting them after all. Shane and I priced the slip covers and the chairs, and we can get sturdier, more comfortable chairs at a price that is less per chair than the cheaper chairs with slip covers."

Jenna nodded. "Plus, we're saving the extra cost of washing and drying the covers and the labor to put them on the chairs. I've been a little stressed about the slip covers anyway, because I can't tie a pretty bow. My square knots are impressive, though."

Morgan raised her eyebrows. "I'll keep that in mind. I'm keeping a journal of our decisions and rationale as we go along in case we want to review our choices. For example, if we discover slipcovers are frequently provided by our competition."

Morgan's phone buzzed a text. When she picked up her phone, she squealed.

Katy woke up and howled.

"Shane has been released and wants me to pick him up at the sheriff's office."

"Well, go, but don't speed. That would be embarrassing if you got a ticket," Jenna said.

"What about your lunch with Renee and your new boyfriend?" Morgan asked as she grabbed the keys and picked up her purse.

"I'll tough it out, and don't start any more rumors about me and another new boyfriend. I still haven't decided what color of flowers I want at my wedding."

Morgan giggled as she headed toward the door. "That's right. I've been waiting for an answer."

"Don't forget your phone and your jacket."

Morgan wheeled around and snatched her phone off her desk. "I wasn't going to. You're extra bossy today."

After Morgan left, Jenna said, "Let's go for a walk. I'll let Foster know we'll be outside."

When Jenna opened the door to the dining room, Foster was entering from the hall.

"I have to get to work. Thanks for letting me visit Nettie. She's still as sassy as ever."

"Let me grab my jacket. Katy and I were going for a walk, so we'll walk with you to your car."

On the way, Jenna said, "You're welcome to visit Nettie any time."

"Thank you, but we're good for now. I was worried about her, but she's settled. She's been worried about me, but I'm better now after talking to her. I might visit her once in a while for old times' sake; we have history and sometimes it's pleasant to reminisce with an old friend. Good friends are hard to find." Foster put out his hand, and they shook.

A tear slipped down Jenna's face; she choked back the tears as Foster turned toward his car. *His wife died.*

"I'm so sorry for your loss, Foster."

"It's been rough, but it helped to talk with Nettie. Thank you for understanding."

Jenna watched as he drove away, and then she couldn't hold the intensity of his grief back any longer, and his loss combined with her own slammed her to her knees. She hung her head and sobbed. Katy whined, and Jenna put her arms around her. "He's just so sad, Katy. I'm sad too."

She dried her tears. "Nettie helped him. I'm glad he came to see her."

Jenna exhaled and rose. "Let's walk to the road and back."

When they returned to the inn, Jenna went into the living room and sat in the yellow chair. "Thank you for helping Foster, Nettie."

A shadow of a tear slipped down Nettie's cheek.

"It never goes away completely, does it? The grief."

No.

"I won't be a chump and let my grief put me behind the eight ball." Jenna's smile was weak, but when the chimes on the front porch jingled and clanged, she giggled, and the chimes sounded like bells from a steeple.

"Thank you, Nettie. Foster told me good friends are hard to find, and he was right."

Jenna and Katy went into the kitchen. Jenna refreshed Katy's bowl of water and poured herself a cup of long-cold coffee. After she took a big gulp, she dumped the rest of it down the drain and rinsed her cup.

She smiled when her phone rang.

Morgan said, "I sprung my main man from the pokey. That's what Nettie would say, right? We're going to our apartment first so Shane can take a shower. We'll grab burgers and fries on our way to the inn. Don't tell Darlene what we plan to eat in her kitchen. Shane wants to see the tablecloths and the new chairs I found and talk to Ethan to see if he has any questions. Are you sure you'll be okay going to lunch without me?"

"I'm positive."

"See you after lunch. Want me to text you at one o'clock?"

Jenna furrowed her brow as she hesitated. "No, that's okay."

"I'll take that as an affirmative. Later."

Jenna hurried to her room and hopped into the shower. After she dried off, she stared at the closet.

"What do I wear to a lunch at a tea shop, Katy?"

Jenna closed her eyes and pulled out a black long-sleeved T-shirt. She added a black and gray plaid flannel shirt and a pair of clean jeans. After she slipped her carry pistol into its inside waistband holster, she twirled. "Am I too fancy?"

Katy yipped then grinned.

Jenna examined herself in a mirror then brushed her hair one last time. "I'll leave it down."

After she put on her boots, she picked up her jacket and purse.

"Will you be okay by yourself for a while? Morgan and Shane will be here soon. Do you want to wait for them in the kitchen?"

Katy trotted to the bedroom door and nosed it.

"Kitchen, it is."

Jenna rubbed Katy's ears and stroked her back. "Be a good girl. I'll be back later."

Katy flopped down on the kitchen floor and closed her eyes. Jenna left.

On her way to town, Jenna gazed at the puddles on the side of the road. *I have to check the backyard for puddles.*

Jenna parked on the street across from the tea shop. She exhaled after she turned off her car's engine. *I'd say I'm not in the mood for this today, but I'd never be in the mood.*

"Let's do this." Jenna opened her car door and climbed out.

As she approached the door of the tea shop, she frowned. *I should have worn something less informal.*

When Jenna went inside, Renee glanced up from a table near the back. Her face transformed from bored to a cobra smile. Next to her was a beefy man who faced the door and studied the menu in front of him on the table.

Jenna continued to scan the room to avoid making eye contact with Renee. *Evidently, oranges and browns are the colors to wear this time of year. My gray and black isn't too bad.*

After her slow survey reached Renee's table, Renee waved, and Jenna smiled as she returned the wave.

The man rose as Jenna approached their table.

"Jenna, this is Fred. Fred, Jenna."

Jenna abruptly sneezed into her elbow. "Excuse me; sometimes my allergies flare up this time of year. It's wonderful to meet you. Renee had nice things to say about you."

"I have random allergy attacks myself." Fred chuckled as he extended his hand.

I gave him the opportunity to not shake hands. Interesting. Jenna held her breath. His handshake was firm and all business.

After Jenna sat next to Renee, Fred sat in his chair.

"It's a pleasure to meet you. Thank you for taking the time to have lunch with us. Renee tells me you're the owner of an inn and an event center. I expected you to be much older." His smile was so contagious that Jenna reflexively returned his smile.

"I've had guests compliment me on looking after the inn so my parents could take a vacation."

He nodded. "I understand; that's exactly what the older generation would assume. What do you tell them?"

"Thank you."

Fred chuckled.

Maybe I'm not as bad at small talk as I thought.

The server brought Jenna a menu. "What can I get you to drink?"

Jenna cleared her throat. "Hot tea, please."

"Good choice. I'll bring the tea box."

After the server returned with the small tea pot with hot water and the tea box, Jenna selected a tea.

The server pulled her order book from her back pocket. "Our soup of the day is carrot cashew ginger soup, and our sandwich of the day is ham and brie. Ready to order?"

Renee said, "Chicken salad sandwich for me."

"I'll have the soup of the day," Jenna said.

"The Cuban sandwich sounds good to me," Fred said.

"I'll have your order out shortly."

After the server left, Fred said, "Renee said the two of you attended the same college. Are you from Paisley?"

"My family is from Paisley and I inherited the property. I'm an accountant, so managing the family business was a good fit for me. What about you, Fred?"

"I'm a geek from way back and manage the technology staff at the Orion West Industries."

While they waited for their food, Renee told Fred about her contact with Bobbie.

Fred turned to Jenna. "Did you know Mrs. Moore well?"

"Not really; her husband was the general contractor for renovations for the inn, which is how I met her."

Fred nodded. "I'll bet an old inn would need a great deal of work. Did you have to close during renovations?"

Jenna turned her head, covered her mouth with her napkin, and lightly coughed before she sipped her tea then responded. "Not really; Mr. Moore was careful to affect our guests as little as possible."

Before Fred could ask his next question, their food was served.

Jenna smiled, nodded, and focused on her soup while Renee talked about her projects.

Fred asked thoughtful questions and smiled at Renee's answers. When Renee said something that

Jenna considered only mildly funny, Fred's laugh was so engaging, the couple at the next table chuckled. While Renee continued her story, Fred smiled at Jenna, and she automatically returned his engaging smile.

Jenna listened, smiled, cleared her throat, and nodded. *This small talk stuff is exhausting.*

The server approached their table. "Dessert? Our special today is cheesecake with fresh strawberries."

Jenna shook her head. "I have to pass."

"Lightweight," Renee sneered. "I'll have the cheesecake, but hold the strawberries because I'm allergic."

Fred frowned then exhaled. "Cheesecake with fresh strawberries sounds great."

While they waited for their dessert, Fred said, "Sophia was right about the Peach Blossom Barn. She told me I should take a day off and check it out."

Renee interrupted. "I told Sophia to tell you about it; I'm pleased to hear she followed through so promptly."

Fred side-glanced at Renee then shrugged. "Jenna, is it possible we could tour the barn this weekend? We'd like to have an off-site strategy session for our senior staff, and we've had trouble finding anything that would host a small-scale, one-day event."

Jenna pulled out Morgan's business card. "Morgan Farley is the operations manager of the Peach Blossom Barn. You can coordinate with her. The barn won't be ready for an event this weekend, but you could discuss a tour of the facility with her if you don't mind that the barn isn't furnished or ready for an event."

"A tour of the facility is exactly what I was looking for. I'll let Orion know and make reservations at the hotel for this weekend."

Renee smiled. "That's a wonderful idea; I'll make reservations for all of us for dinner on Friday night. You'll join us, won't you, Jenna? Of course, you're welcome to bring someone, if you like."

Jenna smiled. "That's very kind of you, but it's difficult for me to get away from the inn on a weekend night."

"You'll have time to rearrange your schedule; I'll let you know what time," Renee said.

Fred glanced at Renee with a slight frown. "We don't want to put any pressure on you, Jenna, but if you can make it, I'd enjoy seeing you again, and I know Orion would like to meet you."

Jenna sipped her tea. *Maybe Fred's okay after all.*

After they finished eating, Renee and Fred had a half-hearted scuffle over who would pick up the check.

Renee smiled as she rose. "You win; thank you." Renee left before the server appeared.

After Fred gave the server his credit card and returned with his card, Jenna rose and put on her jacket. "Thank you so much for lunch."

While Fred left, Jenna stopped the server. "I'd like two slices of the cheesecake to go, please."

"Yes, ma'am."

After she was in her car, she texted Morgan. "Leaving. Gave Fred Haas your business card. He'll contact you for a tour of the facility this weekend. He knows it won't be ready for an event."

When she reached the inn, she hurried inside and put the cheesecake in the refrigerator. *No Katy.*

She continued to the office, and Katy met her at the door.

While she stroked Katy's back, Morgan looked up from her computer. "I got your text; I'm excited about our first potential event. How was lunch?"

"My lunch was great. Have you ever had carrot cashew ginger soup? It was delicious and soothing on my scratchy throat. I couldn't participate in the small talk at all because of my allergies."

"You have allergies?" Morgan peered at Jenna.

"Not anymore."

"Ah ha, so you aren't a fan of Renee's friend."

"Fred was actually nice; he even had the redeeming quality of telling Renee to back off when she insisted I have dinner with them on Friday evening; he definitely has a contagious smile and a winning personality."

Morgan cocked her head. "Too much to be true?"

"Maybe so, but maybe I'm just irritable."

"From your allergies."

"Of course, but more from being around Renee. After I had an uncomfortable feeling that I had to be careful of what I said, my sudden scratchy throat was all I could come up with on such short notice. I don't remember her as being so shallow, but she could have been. I really didn't know her all that well. Fred Haas was easy to talk with, though. He told me it was not a problem that the barn won't be set up for an event, but you can ask more questions when he calls you. If his expectations of what he'll see are greater than I thought, feel free to schedule his visit later in the month. That's your call. How's your day?"

"Much better. I ordered what we'd need for our first event and expect to have everything here before the end of next week. I can't wait to get the tables so we can run through different scenarios. Shane said if we come up with how we'd set up the tables depending on the number of guests, he'll draw templates for us."

"He's a real find, isn't he?"

Morgan sighed. "He certainly is. I couldn't ask for a better man than him."

"I love that for you." Jenna smiled. "Wendy's vacuuming upstairs. I'll run up to tell her hello."

"I'm still tweaking the event reservation system, so it will be as automated as possible, and I'm close. Will you have time tomorrow to sit through a training session? I'll write up a cheat sheet this afternoon."

"I'd love it."

After Jenna went upstairs, she found Wendy in Sophia's room. Jenna raised her eyebrows at the two laptops and three computer screens on the small table next to the window. She peered closer at the window. *Is that a camera?*

Wendy turned off the vacuum cleaner. "Hey, Boss Lady. I'm almost through in here. These ladies could give lessons to some of our guests on how to be organized. I've never seen anyone with three computer screens, though, and that's one fancy camera on the window ledge, isn't it? I guess I'm used to our vacationers who come to relax, not guests who bring their work with them."

Jenna smiled. "Don't tell Morgan about the computer screens. She'll decide she could use three too."

Wendy chuckled. "She does get into that computer work, doesn't she? I'm not surprised, though, because she definitely has the talent for it."

Wendy turned on the vacuum cleaner as Jenna headed for the stairs. When Jenna joined Morgan in the office, she said, "I'd like to see how things are going with the construction at the barn. You don't think Shane would be offended, do you?"

"Not at all; he'll be flattered you are interested."

"Good. Are you going with me, Katy?"

Katy opened one eye, but when Jenna reached for her coat, Katy hopped up and trotted to the door that went to the kitchen.

"You weren't going to move unless it was serious, were you?" Jenna chuckled. "Let's go. Call me if you need me, Morgan."

Morgan absently nodded as she focused on her computer screen.

While Katy explored the brush, Jenna examined the trail. *Ethan has widened it and leveled it too. I wonder if he's planning to put down pea gravel on it like the trail to the orchard.*

When Jenna reached the barn, her eyes widened at the number of work trucks and the construction noise from the barn and from the Peach Pit.

A man called out, "Hey, Miss Jenna. Shane's in the Peach Pit, and Ethan's in the barn."

"Thanks." She waved and headed to the Peach Pit.

When she opened the door, Shane greeted her. "Take a quick peek, then let's go outside. It's noisy and dusty in here."

After they were on the porch, Shane said, "Ethan's crew are framing in the rooms first. When the frames are up, it won't take them long to finish the rooms. Last on the list is painting. Let's go around back. We've cut out the back door to the storage area. It's rough, but you'll get an idea of what we have in mind."

When they reached the back, Jenna furrowed her brow. "Are you putting in a roll-up door or double doors?"

"Ethan and I went back and forth with the pros and cons. While a roll-up door would be cheaper, we decided on the double doors. Ethan wanted double doors because of the aesthetics both inside and outside the building, and the potential noise of a motor bothered me because if we installed a roll-up, it would have to have an automatic opener."

As they strolled to the front, Jenna said, "Things are finally on a roll, aren't they?"

"They are; we were close, but I think pulling you and Morgan into the project smoothed the friction between Ethan and me."

Jenna listened to the sounds of nail guns and saws coming from the barn.

Speaking of friction. "Do you think it would be okay if I peeked into the barn?"

"Why not? It's your barn." Shane side-glanced at her then strode into the Peach Pit.

While Jenna stared at the barn, Katy nudged her leg and whined.

"Shane's right; it's my barn, but would I be interfering?"

When Katy whined again, Ethan came out of the barn and smiled when he saw them.

Jenna gazed at his eyes as they crinkled with his smile. *His eyes are so expressive.*

She returned his smile with a chuckle. *Not even his mustache can hide his lopsided grin.*

"I'm glad you're here, Jenna. Would you like to see what we've accomplished in the barn so far?"

When Ethan opened the door, Jenna gasped. "Who approved taking out part of the back wall?"

"What do you mean, who approved? Shane's a structural engineer."

"What are you talking about? Shane's an architect, and what does that have to do with anything? You've ripped out the wall." Jenna's voice became shrill.

Two men stopped working and turned to stare at Jenna.

"Why don't we take this outside? You're drawing attention to yourself, or is that what you in mind?" Ethan growled.

Jenna turned and stormed to the trail to return to the inn, and Katy trotted alongside her.

"Wait a minute," Ethan called out. "I can explain if you'd calm down and bother to listen."

"You want me to calm down?" Jenna shouted and put her head down to walk even faster.

Ethan caught up with her. He reached out for her then drew back his hand. "Jenna, can we start over?"

Jenna stopped, crossed her arms, and glared at him. She narrowed her eyes as she examined his face and then put her hand on his arm. A flood of warmth encircled her.

When she dropped her hand, Ethan asked, "What?"

Jenna tilted her head. "I think I can rephrase my question. What was wrong with the wall?"

"I didn't know Shane was a structural engineer either, until he told me we needed to replace the wall because it wasn't originally designed to be load-bearing. I argued with him until he explained where our changes would stress it and cause it to collapse. After he got that through my thick head, we shored it up so we could safely replace it."

"So I can yell at Shane for not telling me he's a structural engineer?" Jenna's mouth quivered.

Ethan beamed. "Be my guest."

Jenna gazed at him. *There's that cute smile again.*

"Can I show you what he showed me?" Ethan asked.

"Yes."

As they strolled back together, Ethan asked, "Did you know Bobbie told me to never underestimate how fierce you are? I should have realized what a shock it would have been to see half the wall gone. I should have explained what we were doing before we went inside."

"Is that an apology?" Jenna asked.

Ethan groaned.

Jenna smirked. "I'll take that as a yes, and I accept your sincere expression of regret."

Ethan rolled his eyes. "We should get you a hard hat. A construction supervisor wears a white one."

"Mine should be pink."

"You'll have one in the morning."

When they reached the barn, Ethan said, "We'll stay close to the door since you don't have your hard hat yet."

After they went inside, Jenna listened carefully as Ethan explained what Shane saw. When he finished, Jenna said, "That was very clear; now I understand why the wall is gone. Will you have to take out the rest of that section?"

"We might, but now that we have it open, Shane can get a better idea of what else has to be done to make sure everyone is safe."

"I don't need to get into the middle of any construction, but this is really interesting. How did you know where to shore it up before you took out the wall?"

"That's my area of expertise. Shane's the what, and I'm the how."

Jenna giggled. "I must be the why."

When Ethan laughed, the workmen froze and stared at him.

"Let's get out of here," Ethan said. "These guys need to work."

After they were outside, Jenna said, "Thanks for explaining what was going on. How much of a delay to the schedule do you expect?"

"No more than a day. We already had all the materials, so that didn't slow us down. We'll have to reorder the lumber we're using, so we'll have what we need later, though. Are you going back to the inn now?"

Jenna nodded. "Come on, Katy."

"Are we still having dinner together this evening?" Ethan asked.

"So far." Jenna smiled as she and Katy hurried to the inn.

Chapter Eight

When Jenna and Katy went into the office, Morgan looked up. "I'm glad you're here. We shouldn't have talked about filling up all the rooms because I have two more reservation requests for this weekend, and both of them want to arrive on Thursday afternoon. What do I do about the second one?"

"I'll send Ethan a text to see if it's possible to get a certificate of occupancy or whatever it's called by Thursday for the cottage. If not, then I think we should invest in a rollaway bed. It might be handy to have anyway, and I wouldn't mind testing it before we ask a guest to sleep on it." Jenna sent the text.

Morgan rubbed her forehead. "Should I approve both of the registrations or wait until we hear from Ethan? After I read the reviews for rollaway beds, do I order one? Do we want one on hand even if you don't need it for this weekend?"

Jenna exhaled. "Your turn to take a cleansing breath."

Morgan breathed in and then exhaled.

Jenna smiled. "I don't see any reason to wait to know where I'll be sleeping because we'll come up with something, so approve the registrations. A rollaway bed might come in handy in the future; check the reviews and let me know what you find. If they don't sound comfortable enough, we'll skip the extra bed because our next problem would be where to store it. If you get antsy, research the typical charge other B&Bs quote for an extra person."

"Good thinking, which is why you're Boss Lady."

Jenna's phone rang; Morgan peered at the phone and chuckled. When Jenna answered, Ethan asked, "What did you do? Give away your room for the weekend?"

"You're a very suspicious man. It was just an idle question, and yes, Morgan gave away my room, so I've been tossed out into the snow."

Morgan covered her mouth to stifle her giggles.

Ethan laughed. "Morgan's right there, isn't she? Can you run faster than she can?"

"No, but if I told her I found a glitch in our reservation system, I could get a head start. So, what about the cottage?"

"I'll see what I can do." Ethan hung up.

"What did he say?" Morgan asked.

"He'll try, which is all we can ask, except I'll bet he comes through. He doesn't like loose ends."

"You mean he doesn't want to disappoint you. If he pulls this off, we owe him a big parade," Morgan said.

"If I can sleep in my cottage on Thursday night, I'll make a big pan of lasagna next Thursday, and you and

Shane are invited to dinner. Maybe we'll even invite Ethan. We'll have a housewarming party."

"You can cook?" Morgan stared at her.

"I'm actually not bad except I never got the hang of cooking for one, and I've gotten out of practice the last few years, but my lasagna recipe is a classic. I just have to call Mom and ask her to send it to me."

"Do we still get lasagna if you can't move into the cottage until next week?"

"Of course, but we'll have to see how busy we are."

"Thursday is your day off, so it doesn't matter how busy we are because you are free to make lasagna."

"You're a fine one to talk; your days off are Monday and Tuesday, yet here you are. You're going to get burned out. Your days off this week are Wednesday and Friday."

"I can't take off Friday; that's when all our guests arrive."

"I covered Fridays by myself for a long time; I can do it again. Maybe you should clock out immediately, so your days off this week are Tuesday and Wednesday."

Morgan slammed her laptop shut. "You play dirty, you know that?"

Jenna shrugged.

Morgan stopped at the door and cocked her head. "Wait a minute; how am I supposed to clock out? I've never even seen a physical time-stamp machine; have you?"

"Doesn't matter; you got the point. See you on Friday because my day off is Thursday."

"Well, you better not be here on Thursday, then." Morgan sniffed.

"It's a little different; I live here. Maybe I'll go hang out at the barn and ask questions. Ethan said he'd get me a pink hard hat."

"Really? Can he get me a pale blue one?" Morgan asked.

Jenna cleared her throat, and Morgan slammed the door as she left.

Twenty minutes later, Morgan returned. "We have to talk, Boss Lady. Do you want to take a walk or sit at the table?"

Katy stared at Morgan then trotted to the door that led to the kitchen.

"Katy votes for a walk. Is it still chilly?"

"No, it's comfortable unless there's an occasional gust of wind; you'll want your jacket."

As they strolled along the trail to the orchard, Morgan asked, "How many friends do you have in town?"

"You mean besides you and Shane, and of course, Katy? Foster Kincaid is a friend."

Morgan nodded. "You two bonded immediately when you saw Nettie's portrait at his office, didn't you? Who else?"

"Maybe the sergeant at arms? He's a nice man."

"He doesn't count. Who else?"

"Mr. Moore and the sheriff."

"They don't count either, but you still have one more friend than I do. If the purpose of a day off is to keep from burning out, what will you do?"

Jenna furrowed her brow in thought. "I'll do my laundry and take Katy for a walk."

"After that half hour is over, what would you do for the rest of the day?"

"It would be more than that; maybe even an hour." Jenna snorted. "I could check the progress on the barn and maybe analyze the expenses over the past quarter to see if there was anything we could change to save money or be more efficient."

"That's technically not taking a day off."

Jenna sighed. "I'm the owner of a business; I have to stay focused."

Morgan nodded. "You're right, and I'm a professional in a new position with the responsibility for the operations of a business. I want to drink from the fire hose and learn everything."

Jenna glanced up. "We're almost at the orchard. Let's turn back."

After a few moments of silence as they walked, Jenna asked, "I heard what you said, but what are you telling me?"

"My friends are at the inn. I'm new at my job; there's so much to learn, and I love learning, so I'm energized and nowhere close to burn out. Why can't we take our days off when we have something we have to do or feel like it, not when the calendar says we should? Give me another month to feel more proficient in my job, then we'll talk again about days off for both of us."

As they neared the inn, Jenna broke the silence. "I reserve the right to tell you to take a day off because you're getting close to exhausting yourself and need it."

Morgan nodded. "Okay; same for you?"

"As long as it's because I'm draining my reserves; cranky doesn't count."

Morgan's dark eyes twinkled. "If you're peevish and Ethan's not around, I'll assume you are suffering from burn out."

Jenna laughed.

When they got to the back door, Morgan said, "You're still the Boss Lady. Nobody else would have listened to me."

"Thanks. When I was in the corporate world, successful people did their jobs and kept their mouths shut. I guess I still remember how unsuccessful I was."

Morgan smiled. "That's our secret to success; we're completely unsuccessful."

Jenna chuckled. "We need to come up with a tagline for the Peach Blossom Retreat and the Peach Blossom Barn, but I don't think that's it."

"Okay, let's scratch that one off the list. I have work to do, Boss Lady, and my reputation as an overachiever to maintain."

"I have reading to catch up on. If you need me, I'll be in my room." Jenna headed down the hall with Katy padding along behind her.

"That's refreshing, but suspicious to hear. Let me know if you need me."

When Jenna and Katy were in her bedroom, she kicked off her boots and exchanged her jeans for sweatpants and her black T-shirt for an oversized one.

"Now, I can read." Jenna pulled out Bobbie's diary and took notes as she read.

After three hours, she rose and stretched then looked over her notes. "So far, I've found ten groups, and each group was supporting a young girl and an elderly man in their group. Bobbie numbered the groups, so it was relatively easy to follow the conversations. I'll take a shower then go to the office so I can get all this on the computer. I want to analyze the information I have so far to find patterns."

Jenna flipped through the rest of the diary. "Looks like I'm about two-thirds of the way through."

After she showered and changed into a fresh T-shirt and jeans, Jenna gathered her notes, the diary, and the notebook Foster had brought her and put them into a small tote bag.

"We'll put all this in the safe in the office."

Before she left her room, her phone rang.

When she answered, Adrienne said, "We just got an offer from Clarence Moore's lawyer. Mr. Moore wants you to buy Bobbie's business from him."

"Her business? What does that include besides the events for the barn?"

"That's basically it. The offer is reasonable. Are you interested? Do you want to think about it?"

"Can I get back to you tomorrow?"

"That's what I told his lawyer." Adrienne chuckled as she hung up.

"Let's put the tote in the safe then take a walk. When we get back, it will be time for your supper and for me to set up happy hour for our guests."

After they were outside, Jenna asked, "Which way, Katy?"

Katy bounded toward the orchard then stopped and glanced over her shoulder at Jenna.

"I could use a brisk walk to stretch my legs for a change." While Jenna power walked down the path, Katy trotted ahead.

When they reached the orchard, Jenna stopped and gazed at the trees and their reddish-orange leaves. After she pulled out her phone and snapped a couple of pictures, she said, "Morgan mentioned my blog. If one of these photos turns out, wouldn't it be the perfect blog for this month?" Katy yipped and raced up the path then zoomed back to walk alongside Jenna.

When they returned to the inn, Jenna peered down the driveway at the empty visitor parking lot.

"I'm sure they'll be here soon enough."

While Katy ate, Jenna preheated the oven and read the directions a second time. "This is easy."

She put ice into their new water dispenser, filled it halfway with water, and put it on the utility cart. When the oven had reached temperature, Jenna put the candied bacon and dates on a tray and slipped them into the oven while she whipped the goat cheese to fluff it up. She put the sausage rolls into the oven to warm while she poured chips into a festive bowl. After Jenna folded the bacon into the goat cheese and decorated the top with dates, she set aside some of the appetizer for Ethan and herself.

Katy followed Jenna as she rolled the utility cart into the dining room and set up the appetizers on the sideboard.

Jenna sighed as she heard a car come up the driveway. "I was hoping they'd go somewhere with Fred and skip happy hour here. I need to clean up my attitude, don't I, Katy?"

Katy yipped then nosed the door to the kitchen.

Jenna giggled as she opened the door to the kitchen. "At least you understand."

Jenna waited in the foyer until Renee and Sophia were close to the porch.

Before she opened the front door, Renee hissed, "You ask too many questions."

"I just asked why Nicci was coming here. I didn't know you two were that close."

When Jenna opened the door, Renee's scowl quickly shifted to a smile. "Well, we are. You learn something new every day, don't you?"

"I'm going to run upstairs for a quick shower." Sophia handed a bottle of wine to Renee. "Save me some appetizer and a glass of wine."

Renee handed the bottle to Jenna. "I need to clean up a bit myself. Just open this so it can breathe. I'll be down in twenty minutes. No telling when Miss Priss will join us."

Jenna carried the bottle to the dining room and set it on the sideboard next to the corkscrew then went into the kitchen and texted Morgan.

Morgan immediately called her. "I can't believe Renee ordered you to open her wine bottle. Have you already poured it down the sink?"

Jenna chuckled. "I knew I'd feel better if I told you what she said. What are you doing tonight?"

"Something that involves sweatpants, popcorn, and a movie session. We take turns picking the movie, and it's my turn tonight. Shane will drink a beer, fill up on popcorn, and fall asleep. I read when it's his turn. Watch out for Sophia. On our way home this evening, Shane told me this evening she asked him last night if he was married. When he told her no, he said she made a throaty growling sound. When I told him she was trying to be sexy, he said he was afraid she was going to be sick."

Jenna giggled. "Shane's so cool. Do you want me to say something to her?"

"No, she'd mock Shane or something, I'm sure. For the record, I don't like her at all, but I'm on your side, so I like Renee even less."

"That makes me feel better; thanks."

Jenna hung up and returned to the dining room. *Sophia better stay clear of Morgan.*

Renee stood at the sideboard as she struggled to open the bottle of wine. She glanced up at Jenna, and her glare quickly turned to a smile. "You forgot to open the wine so it could breathe."

I recognize your cobra smile for what it is, Renee.

Jenna turned to the water dispenser and filled a glass halfway.

"Anything new on what happened to Bobbie? I heard they were investigating foul play." Renee exhaled when she finally popped the cork. She carried the bottle and the platter of appetizers to her table.

"People like intrigue, don't they? The doctors say she had a stroke while she was changing a light bulb. How was your day?"

Renee filled her wine glass then launched into a long discussion of the exciting cases she was working on and how skillful she was in searching out the facts. "I have a nose for the truth. All I need is a thread, and I can weave an entire blanket. Did I tell you I'm up for an award?"

Renee refilled her glass as Sophia came into the dining room. "Very prestigious. Which reminds me, Sophia, did you finish that article on ten unusual crimes? I have to submit it first thing in the morning."

Sophia snorted. "I sent it to you last night."

"I'll read it later." Renee shifted in her chair away from Sophia and popped the rest of a sausage roll into her mouth.

"We have dinner reservations in thirty minutes, Renee," Sophia said. "Fred Haas will meet us there."

"Five minutes." Renee picked up her glass then put it down. "Why did Fred hire you?"

"I told you when he offered me the position. I can't help it if you refuse to listen to what I say. He admired my photography skills; I've been testing new digitized products."

Renee snorted. "A likely story. Let's go. I'm driving."

"No, I am."

"Give me the keys, Sophia."

"You can choose the music."

Renee stormed out of the dining room. Sophia groaned then followed her.

Jenna held her breath until the side door closed, then locked the dining room door to the hall. She hummed as she loaded up the utility cart and rolled everything into the kitchen. Jenna dumped the opened bottle of wine into the sink and tossed the uneaten food from the sideboard into the trash bin.

Katy eyed the sausage rolls and whined as Jenna slid them into the bin.

"Seems wasteful to me, too, but Darlene said unless we eat the leftovers the same night, that's what we do. When you think about it, Darlene's right, because we don't want a refrigerator filled with leftovers that we have to sort through and toss later."

Jenna returned to the dining room to change the linens and vacuum the floor. After she replaced the tablecloths and finished cleaning, she replenished the supplies.

When she heard Ethan's truck coming up the driveway, Jenna exhaled, and Katy yipped.

"Right on time, isn't he? Do you supposed he drove around, so he wouldn't show up early?" Jenna chuckled as she and Katy hurried to the back door.

After she put on her jacket, Jenna and Katy went outside. When Jenna shivered, Katy grinned.

"I'm not excited to see Ethan; it's just chillier than I expected."

Katy raced into the woods then returned when Ethan parked.

Ethan climbed out of his truck and smiled as Katy dashed to him. "Hey, Katy. How are you doing?" He bent down and scratched her ears then stroked her back.

When he rose, his face quickly slid to neutral as he strolled to Jenna with a large white paper sack in his hand. "I should have asked if you had any food allergies or preferences. I hope you don't mind an old standard of cheeseburgers and fries."

"Sounds good to me; do you want coffee or sweet tea to drink? We have one of Darlene's dips too."

"Sweet tea sounds good."

"We can eat in the kitchen unless you'd rather eat in the dining room."

"Eating in the kitchen is more my style."

Katy dashed to the back door, and Jenna and Ethan followed her.

After Jenna unlocked the door, Ethan held it for her then followed her inside.

While Ethan pulled out the food and set it on the table, Jenna poured their iced tea. "Did your brother pick up Ryan?"

Katy whined.

Ethan smiled and reached down to pet Katy. "Yes, and Katy and I miss that energetic dynamo, don't we, girl?"

Katy grinned.

Jenna put the dip, plates, and napkins on the table, and they unwrapped their food in an awkward silence.

Jenna took a bite of her cheeseburger, and the juice ran down her chin. She felt her face warm as she grabbed her napkin and wiped her chin. She side-glanced at Ethan who averted his eyes and dipped a fry into the goat cheese dip.

After he took a bite, he said, "This is interesting."

Jenna's face grew warmer. *He hates it; I shouldn't have put it on the table.*

Ethan turned his burger upside down. After he removed the bottom bun, he smeared a generous portion of the dip on his burger.

Jenna widened her eyes as he put his burger back together and took a bite.

"This is great. I've never had a goat cheese bacon burger before," he said. "It's my new favorite."

Jenna tilted her head then flipped her burger over and added goat cheese. After she took a bite, she said, "This is good; what made you think of it?"

After Ethan took another bite, he said, "Bacon."

Jenna giggled. "Bacon goes with everything."

Ethan smiled. "Ryan and I really like hearing you laugh. Ryan said it's like hearing fairies sing. Pretty poetic for a twelve-year-old boy, don't you think?"

"It really is. Katy and I really enjoyed his company. She's looking forward to seeing him this weekend."

"I think Ryan has already packed for the weekend. How was your day?"

"The polite answer is fine, but why don't I tell you one interesting thing about my day, and then you can tell me one interesting thing about yours."

Ethan had just taken a big bite. His eyes crinkled as he nodded.

"Morgan created business cards for the Peach Blossom Barn. I had lunch with Renee and Fred Haas, the Chief Technology Officer for the Orion West Industries. Fred is interested in the Peach Blossom Barn for a one-day executive strategy meeting. I gave him one of Morgan's business cards."

"That is interesting. Does Shane know?"

"I told Morgan, so the answer is yes."

Ethan chuckled. "You're right about that. Shane talks about structural stress points and Morgan nonstop."

When Ethan picked up a handful of fries, Jenna said, "Enjoy your fries, then it's your turn."

"You're not giving me a pass?" His eyes twinkled when Jenna rolled her eyes.

After he ate the fries, he said, "My interesting news is that the county inspector will be at your cottage tomorrow right after lunch, so you can move in on Thursday."

Jenna squealed, and Katy yipped.

"That's not interesting; it's super exciting!" Jenna narrowed her eyes. "When were you going to tell me?"

"In the morning." Ethan stared at his plate. "I couldn't think of the best way to tell you without sounding too proud of myself."

"What are you talking about? Why wouldn't you be proud of yourself? I'm proud of you."

Ethan's cheeks developed spots of bright red, and he shoved the rest of his burger into his mouth.

Jenna swallowed hard. *Did I go too far? That sounded condescending, didn't it?*

Her shoulders slumped. She exhaled then rose and wrapped her burger. As she put it into the refrigerator, Jenna asked, "Ready for dessert?"

"If you are." Ethan's tone was polite and formal.

Jenna glanced over her shoulder at him, and his face had returned to neutral.

"I have cheesecake; it's from the restaurant in town. Fred Haas said it was the best he ever had, so I thought we could try it. I'm pretty full, but I always have a corner saved for dessert."

Ethan furrowed his brow.

Why is he overthinking dessert?

"That Fred Haas sounds like a nice guy."

"He was very charming. I enjoyed lunch despite the dour Miss Renee with her snippy remarks."

"He was charming?" Ethan shrugged, and his voice had a tinge of sadness. "I'll have some if you do."

Why can't I interpret what he is saying?

"Would you like to split a slice?"

"Sure."

Jenna pulled out the sack. "They packed the fresh strawberries separately. I didn't expect that."

She cut a piece of cheesecake in half and put each half on a small plate. Before she spooned fresh strawberries over the slender slices, she examined the cheesecake carefully.

"Is something wrong?" Ethan asked.

Yes, I want to weigh the slices.

"No, except I'm not sure the two halves are equal."

Ethan narrowed his eyes. "They look the same to me."

Why is he being polite? She put the two plates and two forks on the table then put away the sack.

When she sat at the table, she examined the plates. *I think I gave myself the bigger piece, and I might have more strawberries. I should switch plates real quick.*

She glanced at Ethan, who hadn't picked up his fork. *He's waiting for me. I'm a klutz.*

Jenna picked up her fork and took a bite. "This is good."

Ethan took a large bite of his cheesecake. "It is good. I don't think I've ever had fresh strawberries with cheesecake, have you?"

Jenna shook her head as she took another bite.

After they finished their cheesecake, Jenna picked up the plates and took them to the sink.

"I enjoyed supper." Ethan rose. "I'm sure you have a busy day tomorrow; I know I do."

Ethan headed to the back door, and Jenna and Katy followed him. When they reached the door, Jenna put on her jacket and accidentally brushed Ethan's arm with her elbow.

The wall is back. Why?

After they were outside, Ethan waited with Jenna at the back door while Katy explored the backyard.

When Katy returned, Jenna impulsively put her hand on Ethan's upper arm. Jenna was startled when the wall dropped, and her hand became warm.

She gazed up at him. "Thank you for the cheeseburger; I enjoyed your company."

Ethan smiled and leaned down and gave her a brief kiss that made her lips tingle. "See you tomorrow."

Jenna was stunned as Ethan swaggered to his truck.

When he turned and waved, she returned his wave then went inside with Katy.

"Wowser, Katy. What do you think?"

Katy yipped.

Jenna touched her lips. "His mustache didn't bother me at all; it was nice."

Jenna went into the living room and sat in the yellow chair. She smiled as she gazed at Nettie's portrait. "I didn't say anything about his mustache."

I know. The wind chimes sounded, and Jenna giggled. "I knew you did."

Jenna leaned back in the yellow chair as she cocked her head. "What about the wall? Why is it there in the first place, and why does it go away?"

Because of you.

"It's there because of me, and it goes away because of me? That doesn't make sense."

No, it doesn't.

Jenna rose. "At least we agree."

The chimes jingled again as Jenna left the living room with a smile.

Jenna went into the office and removed Bobbie's diary of secrets and her notes from the safe. She set them down on the kitchen table then opened the diary where she had left the pamphlet as a bookmark.

While she slowly went through the diary, she continue to take meticulous notes.

She was close to the end of the diary when she heard voices from the hallway. Jenna rolled her eyes. *I'll call it a night as soon as they go upstairs. I'm not in the mood for more of Renee's drama.*

Jenna took her notes and the diary to the office and locked them in the safe.

"Are you ready for bed, Katy? Let's take one more walk."

After they were outside, Jenna shivered. *I'll have to pull out a warmer coat to keep by the back door. It's gone from chilly to downright cold when the wind blows.*

When Katy returned from her patrol, they went inside.

Jenna tiptoed down the hallway. Katy clicked alongside her.

After they were in the bedroom, Jenna whispered, "Success."

Jenna changed into her pajamas then climbed into bed. "I'm not sure I can go to sleep right away, Katy. I need something to read."

Jenna peered over the side of her bed at Katy, who was sleeping. Katy snuffled in her sleep then resumed her light snore.

Jenna saw the furniture pamphlet on the floor close to Katy. "The pamphlet must have fallen out when I was putting everything in the tote bag. I could read that, but I'd have to climb out of bed and touch the floor with my bare feet. What should I do?"

Katy twitched in her sleep and softly barked a quiet "boof".

Jenna leaned back, turned off the light next to her bed, and closed her eyes.

CHAPTER NINE

Katy whimpered and nudged Jenna's arm. Jenna opened her eyes and stretched then picked up her phone. *Six thirty.*

"Oh no. Look at the time; I've never slept this late before. I must have forgotten to check my alarm. Thanks, Katy." Jenna changed to her sweatpants and T-shirt from the day before and hurried with Katy to the back door.

After Katy went outside, Jenna rushed to the kitchen and exhaled with relief at the sight of Darlene and Morgan. "I overslept."

"No kidding, Boss Lady, but we figured you needed it. We were just debating about how we could get Katy out of your room without disturbing you," Darlene said.

"She woke me up."

"Katy's a good girl. I'll let Katy back inside, and we'll feed her while you take your shower and get dressed," Morgan said.

"Don't have to tell me twice." Jenna rushed to her room.

While she waited for the water to be hot enough to jump into the shower, Jenna checked the weather. "Today's weather calls for a long-sleeved T-shirt with a flannel shirt for a second layer," she mumbled.

After her shower, Jenna quickly dressed then hurried to the kitchen.

"Your hair's still wet, Boss Lady." Darlene pointed at Jenna's hair with her wooden spoon while she set a cup of coffee on the counter.

Jenna picked up her coffee and held the hot cup with both hands. "The kitchen is warm; it will dry in here."

"Morgan's working on her ads this morning, so you'll need to cover breakfast this morning. She already set everything up. Go dry your hair, and I'll have a one-egg and cheese omelet waiting for you. You've got five minutes."

Jenna downed her coffee and rushed to her room as Morgan and Katy came in the back door.

Jenna waved the hair dryer around her head a few times then after a half-hearted swipe at her hair with her brush, she dashed to the kitchen.

"How's that?"

Darlene pointed to the plate with a one-egg and cheese omelet. "There's your omelet and a fresh cup of coffee. Your hair is a little wild, but good enough. Katy went with Morgan to the office after I gave her a treat."

Jenna hurried to unlock the dining room door then returned to the kitchen to enjoy her omelet. After she took her first bite, Jenna furrowed her brow then took a second. "My omelet is delicious; how did you make it spicy?"

Darlene chuckled. "Cook's secret."

Jenna took another bite. "Pepper jack. Am I right?"

Darlene shrugged, but a slight smile slid across her face.

"I knew it; I'm right." Jenna heard the clink of a coffee cup from the dining room. "I have guests."

When Jenna carried her coffee into the dining room, Sophia sat alone at the table with her coffee and a pastry on a small plate.

"Good morning, Sophia. How did you sleep?"

"Very well. I woke up early because I thought I'd get a few things done, but I'd brought a tech brief on new cameras, so I put up my feet and read it. It was very relaxing to do what I wanted to do."

Jenna stared at Sophia. "A tech brief relaxes you?"

Sophia sniffed. "Not just any tech brief; it was on cameras."

Jenna tried to control her face, but she giggled. "My mistake."

Sophia laughed. "Good; you got it."

Sophia bit her lip then went to the sideboard and refilled her coffee. "Jenna, Renee said you told her you had security cameras for the property, including the visitors' parking lot, and the cameras were monitored by a security company."

Jenna stared at her cup sipped her coffee.

Sophia joined Jenna at the table and gazed at her. "Is that true?"

Jenna met her gaze. "It's true that I told her that, but since you're such a camera aficionado, you probably already know there aren't any. Renee said something that got on my nerves, and I don't even remember what it was, but I made up the security cameras on the spot."

"That's what I thought; she gets on my nerves too, so I didn't correct her. What about the records of room key use?"

Jenna sighed. "It wasn't you, it was the timing. You asked your security question right after Renee irritated me, so I gave you a partially phony security story. We don't get alerts on our phones. That would drive me crazy. I guess I was on a roll; I'm really sorry."

"Don't apologize; I understand completely, but I'm deeply disappointed because I was impressed by your dedication to security to the point of enduring the alerts of endless ins and outs."

"Then I apologize for being unimpressive." Jenna smiled.

Sophia laughed. "Apology accepted. Time to get to work. Thanks for talking to me. My life lately has been listening to lies and exaggerations. Have you ever heard of Angel Girl?"

"I don't think so. Is that a new singer?"

"I have no idea; maybe so. Renee swore me to secrecy, but she does that all the time, then told me she would take over knitting. She's always spouting off about something, but she's mentioned it several times. I've been researching knitting to see if it has a double meaning with no luck. I guess I need to dig deeper. It's been my job to keep track of Renee and distract her as much as I could."

"I could never take that on."

Sophia chuckled. "I understand. Thank you, Jenna. It has been so pleasant to talk to someone without having to weigh each word."

Sophia picked up her dishes and put them in the bus bin. "Watch out for Renee, Jenna. She seems like a total flake, but she is very technical and very calculating. She's actually quite dangerous."

Sophia stopped at the table and said quietly, "I have a camera with photos I want Nicci to review. Would you give it to Nicci for me?"

"Of course."

"I'll be right back."

Sophia returned with her camera. "I really appreciate it."

When Sophia handed the camera to Jenna, Jenna was instantly slammed by a sense of Sophia lying lifeless on the barn floor with a pink scarf tied around her neck.

Jenna steeled herself and carefully set the camera on the table.

Jenna swallowed hard. "Do me a favor, Sophia. Stay away from the barn."

Sophia peered at Jenna's face. "Okay, I will. Thanks."

Sophia reached into the top of her shirt, pulled out her room key, and smiled. "I love my tight skirts, but they don't have pockets."

"Makes sense to me." Jenna returned her smile then after Sophia left, she wrapped the camera in a large napkin and went into the office from the dining room.

As she carefully set the wrapped camera in the bottom drawer of her desk, she said, "Morgan, I need you with me if Renee makes it for breakfast."

Morgan examined Jenna's face. "Are you in danger?"

"Not me, but I'm a little tired and might not be on my toes. I need back up."

"You got it, Boss Lady."

"You won't be crazy about this, but Sophia might be in danger. We need to watch her back."

"You're kidding me."

Jenna shook her head.

Morgan crossed her arms. "I'd feel better if you said I could stalk her instead of watching her back."

Jenna chuckled. "Okay, then stalk her. We don't want her to go to the barn."

"Now that is the perfect assignment for me, because Shane spends all his time at the barn and the Peach Pit."

After they went into the kitchen, Darlene said, "I see there isn't any of the goat cheese dip left. Was it too much trouble?"

"You don't allow leftovers, so we ate all of it." Jenna smiled. "Your instructions were easy to follow. The goat cheese was fluffy, and the bacon didn't lose its crispness at all."

"It was an experiment; I'm glad it worked out."

"We can do it more often with your instructions because they were very clear."

"I think I hear someone in the dining room," Morgan said.

After they were in the empty dining room, Morgan said, "Tell me about the goat cheese dip in case Darlene asks me for details."

Renee strolled in and headed for the coffee.

Jenna said, "It was absolutely delicious, Morgan; we can ask Darlene for a repeat next week."

Renee poured a cup of coffee and put two Danishes on a plate then carried her breakfast to a table. Jenna filled a small cup with ice water and joined her while Morgan rearranged the Danishes.

"Would you like to split a Danish?" Morgan asked. "I need to get back to my ads in a few minutes, but I can't pass up one more bite of Darlene's pastries."

"Sounds good to me." Jenna sipped her water. "How did you sleep, Renee?"

While Morgan cut a Danish in half, Renee said, "I've been terribly anxious since Bobbie's death, which I thought would seriously affect my ability to focus; on top of that, the looming deadlines are piling up. I finished up my latest article, ten unusual crimes I have investigated and solved, in thirty minutes last night, and promptly fell asleep. The Peach Blossom Retreat is magical, but you probably already knew that. My normal style is to have a polished article ready at least a week, if not more, in advance, but I still submitted it on time with a much snappier title, so everything is okay."

"I think it's wonderful that you can remain so centered." Morgan set the two small plates on the table and sat down.

"Thank you. It means a lot coming from you because I can see that's an area where you excel." Renee smiled at Morgan.

Morgan stared at her Danish. "Time for me to get back to work." She shoved her half of the Danish into her mouth then took her plate with her into the kitchen.

Jenna watched her leave. *So much for back up, but I don't blame her. I wonder if Renee realizes how condescending she sounded?*

"What time do you expect your friend Nicci?" Jenna asked

"She's a bit of a flighty free spirit. I've always said you'd know what time Nicci was going to arrive when she walked in the door."

"We'll be here when she shows up; her room is ready."

"Which room will she have?"

"I don't really know; Morgan assigns the rooms. Nicci will be upstairs with you and Sophia."

"Can we ask Morgan which room? I'm worried we might be crowded with all of us upstairs."

Jenna raised an eyebrow at Renee. "It really doesn't matter which room she has, because we'll have a full house on Friday. Four of the rooms upstairs are registered for your group, and there will be a couple in the fifth room. You know how large our guestrooms are. No one will be crowded."

Renee's face turned red; after she scrunched her eyes, a big tear ran down her face. "I'm sorry. I'm really claustrophobic around crowds of people."

Jenna stared at her phony tear then with one sweeping motion of her arm, encompassed all the tables in the room. "Look around. There will be plenty of room in the dining room for everyone. It won't be crowded at all because our tables are large enough for each group. How can we fix this? Do you want to cancel your reservations and stay at the newer hotel near town?"

Morgan strolled into the dining room from the office. When Jenna held up her hand for Morgan to stop, Morgan leaned against the wall like an impartial spectator.

Renee glared at Jenna, who maintained her casual, open stance. Renee swallowed hard. "I overthink sometimes. I'm sure you're right; this is nice.."

Jenna smiled. "Yes, it is."

Renee exhaled then left the dining room.

Jenna locked the door from the dining room to the hall, and then she and Morgan went into the office.

"There's just something about her that rubs me the wrong way," Jenna said.

"I don't have your sensitivity, but I could tell you were close to kicking her out. I came into the dining room to tell you the rollaway bed I ordered for you is on back order. Shouldn't we have a contingency plan?"

"Yes; if the cottage fails inspection tomorrow, we'll scramble and come up with something else."

Morgan chuckled. "The scramble plan; why didn't I think of that? What is your plan for today? After we have the room ready for happy hour, I'd like to go over my drafts for ads."

"I want to blog today. Maybe I should do that first and publish it so it will be done. Then you can teach me about ads and marketing."

While Jenna and Morgan worked in the office, Jenna heard Renee and Sophia arguing as they hurried to their car.

Morgan hopped up and peered out the window. "Sophia's driving. I'll be right back." Morgan sprinted to the door to the kitchen and dashed out.

Jenna hurried to the window as Morgan raced down the driveway with Katy running alongside her. Morgan and Katy reappeared as Morgan jogged and Katy trotted up the driveway back to the inn.

When Morgan came into the office from the kitchen, she left the door open as she carried a large glass of sweet tea. She kicked off her shoes and plopped down in her office chair.

Katy came in the door Morgan had left open. Her tongue was hanging to the side, but Katy's big grin told the tale of how much fun she had running with Morgan.

Katy leaned against Morgan, and Morgan stroked her back. "I know you could have left me behind, but you stayed right there with me, didn't you, sweet girl?" Morgan hugged Katy then rubbed her ears.

"Jenna, Sophia turned toward town."

"On their way out the door, they were arguing, as usual, and Sophia said something about being late for their meeting. Renee said Fred needed to come down a peg or two. She was still talking when they reached the car, but I couldn't make out what she was saying."

"What does that mean, come down a peg?" Morgan asked.

"She was saying he wasn't as important as he thought he was."

Morgan snorted. "Why wouldn't a Chief Technology Officer of a major company be important? Renee Sabot is a respected investigative journalist, but the Renee who is here isn't a respected anything."

Jenna sighed. "I could easily embrace an imposter theory, but the Renee Sabot who is a guest of the inn looks, talks, and acts like the Renee Sabot I knew in college, except she's much more abrasive. That obviously must work for her, or she wouldn't have honed it so well."

"I wish I could go snoop on them in town. I'd be completely incognito. You know, like casually blend in as I walk into the restaurant or wherever they are and have a nice cup of coffee. Maybe chat with the server."

"Business professional isn't incognito in Paisley. You dress, talk, and even walk like a business professional. You'd have to be more casual, like jeans, boots, and a flannel shirt to blend in."

"Jeans, boots, and a flannel shirt? That's you, Jenna. I'll blend in because I go shopping almost every day, and this is what I wear. How often do you go shopping? Write your blog while I go into Paisley and find out what's going on."

"That's not a bad idea. I can do that. While you write my blog, I'll be back later."

Jenna giggled at the shocked look on Morgan's face. "You don't have to write my blog. I'll get it done this afternoon."

Morgan put her hands on her hips. "There aren't many places to have a meeting in Paisley. It won't take me long to find them."

"Give me a minute to think." Jenna strolled to the window and gazed at the sky. *I don't want Morgan to go against Renee because Renee is truly a cobra, but what if she's just a puppet, and Bobbie found the ultimate monster?"*

She turned to Morgan. "Maybe it's Renee's job to distract us. Think about it; who have we ever met that is as obnoxious as Renee?"

Morgan relaxed her arms. "So what do we do?"

"There has to be somebody behind Renee. I need more time to think, but I'm certain we have to watch Sophia, not Renee, because Sophia is in danger."

There's more for me to find, and Bobbie's my key.

"In that case, I have an excuse to go into town and stalk Sophia." Morgan asked. "I've dropped by the gift shop occasionally to discuss colors and trends with the owner and promised I'd show her the tablecloths we're ordering. I can cruise around and see where Sophia parked their car."

"Renee is dangerous because she's so volatile. As long as you avoid her, that's actually a good idea."

After Morgan left, Jenna went into the living room. "Is there more for me to find?"

She sat in the yellow chair and exhaled as she gazed at Nettie's portrait. "I'm going through the diary and taking notes. I'm certain I'm right. There's more than just Renee, isn't there?"

Follow the key.

"Okay, but I'm totally lost."

The tones of the chimes were deep and mournful.

"Are the chimes for Sophia? Is there anything I can do?"

Jenna sat quietly in the chair for an hour, but there was no answer to her question.

She rose and strolled into the kitchen. Darlene had her back to her, so she didn't hear Jenna. Katy followed Jenna into the office.

Jenna unlocked the safe and sat at her desk with the diary and her notes. After she finished taking notes from the last page in the diary, she said, "Now it's time to find the key."

Jenna opened the spiral-bound notebook Foster had given her and flipped through it. On the first page Bobbie wrote, "I am Pink Lady, and I have a friend, Arti, which is short for Artemis. Arti is in all ten groups, but using different character names. Arti isn't very active, but her alternate characters are. I think I found them all. It is odd Artie has favorite numbers. I have alternate characters for each group too, but I'm less predictable. A wise person could use one of my alternate characters to see what's going on. There are hundreds of groups. I thought I'd start with ten to keep it easy for me to track."

"This is odd. Bobbie drew a circle around Beansy and said Otis elevators have a lovely front and an ugly rear door. What does that mean?"

Katy sat up and cocked her head while Jenna searched online for Otis elevators.

After spending thirty minutes reading about the history of elevators and the different styles of elevators, Jenna returned to the notebook. "Maybe that was just a random thought. So, back to Beansy; she's in Group One."

Katy had stretched out on her side while Jenna was searching; she closed her eyes.

Jenna followed Bobbie's instructions in the notebook that detailed how to log into the group as Beansy, so Beansy couldn't be traced to her computer. She was greeted by another member.

"It's been a while. Where have you been?"

Jenna as Beansy replied, "Too busy. You know how it goes."

"Do I ever."

The conversations immediately resumed to a discussion about Angel Girl and the problems she was having.

While Jenna read and occasionally jumped in with a comment, she furrowed her brow when the discussion turned to rallying around Angel Girl and the different ways the group could help her.

When Angel Girl signed in, Jenna leaned forward to focus on her screen in anticipation.

"How is your mum?" a member asked.

"She's much weaker. She told me she found a doctor who might help her."

Jenna watched as the group probed for more information, but Angel Girl's replies were vague.

She's setting the hook.

"Did you lock your bedroom door last night like we said?" a member asked.

Angel Girl replied, "No, I was afraid he would hurt Mum when he came home."

After everyone expressed their outrage and fear for Angel Girl, she continued, "He didn't come home last night because he was in jail, but he's getting out today."

Jenna watched the drama unfold as the members continued to advise Angel Girl what she should do until Angel Girl suddenly posted, "I have to get off now. He's home."

When Angel Girl logged out, the outrage continued until someone suggested starting up a secret fund for Angel Girl and her mum, and Knit One volunteered to spearhead the collection. Knit One promised to have details soon.

When members started dropping off, Jenna did too.

She exhaled. "That was classic. I see why Bobbie circled Beansy."

Jenna moved on to Group Two. When she logged in as Old VA Cook, the group was in an argument about a cake recipe that a member had posted two days earlier.

Jenna raised her eyebrows. "Katy, evidently the controversy is that the recipe used a cake mix. It doesn't look like they have their Angel Girl yet, but they were on Bobbie's list, so we'll check back tomorrow."

After Jenna went through all ten groups, she said, "I'm getting a feel for all the Angel Girls and Knit Ones. This must be what Bobbie was working on. We'll finish it for her, won't we, Katy?"

"Boss Lady, you gonna make me eat lunch alone?" Darlene shouted from the kitchen.

Katy trotted to the door and was poised to dash into the kitchen the second Jenna opened the door. Jenna put all the notes, the diary, and the notebook into the safe and locked it.

When she opened the door, Katy scrambled to Darlene then sat politely. Darlene poured a small bowlful of chopped roasted chicken into Katy's bowl. Katy gazed at Darlene's face; when Darlene nodded, Katy dug in.

"I made chicken salad for the main appetizer tonight; do you want a sandwich or a fork?"

"I'll take a fork." Jenna spoke clearly and loudly enough for Darlene to hear her.

While Darlene dished up chicken salad onto two small plates and added fresh peach slices on the side, Jenna poured two glasses of sweet tea.

Jenna took a bite of chicken salad then followed it up with a bite of a peach slice. "This is really refreshing."

Darlene ladled soup into two mugs then put saltines on a plate. Darlene set a mug in front of Jenna. "Since the cold weather is sneaking in, I decided the chicken salad needed a warm side dish."

Jenna tasted the hot soup. "It's got a little spice to it; that's nice."

Darlene beamed. "Should we go with saltines or crusty rolls?"

"The saltines are perfect with the chicken salad and the mushroom soup; the crusty rolls would be good, but they might be too filling for an appetizer. Is this the appetizer for today and tomorrow?"

"No, I checked the registration book, and we'll be getting close to a full house at happy hour tomorrow. We'll have something else."

Jenna smiled. "I am thrilled you released me from having to approve the menus. It's more fun being surprised."

"When do we expect our guest who is arriving today?" Darlene asked.

"I don't know, but I'm assuming she will be here before happy hour."

While they were eating, Morgan returned from town.

"Sit down, and you can have lunch with Boss Lady."

Morgan smiled. "I'm starved."

While Darlene made a chicken salad sandwich, Morgan brewed a cup of tea. "It's not really all that cold, but there's a wicked blast of wind that chilled me to the bone just walking from my car to the back door. Are you ready for a progress report, Boss Lady?"

"Sure am."

"I had coffee with Sophia and Fred Haas. Renee had a hair appointment, and it was wonderful to skip all her negativity."

"I'm almost jealous I didn't go with you."

"Fred Haas asked about you. He said to tell you he was sorry you weren't there. He really is a charming, kind-hearted man, but very sharp. Fred and Sophia had a heated technical discussion that I didn't understand, but it was obvious from their banter that they had a good working relationship. Can you believe no one has snapped him up yet? I can see where he might seem to be almost too good to be true, but he's a keeper for some lucky girl."

"I'm glad you could talk to him and Sophia without Renee's interference. She really does like to keep the spotlight on herself," Jenna said.

"My friends and I were pretty self-centered in college, but we didn't realize we were. Most of us outgrew it, but a few didn't; I guess Renee's in that second group."

"That would explain why I never noticed it in college."

"What's this cheesecake doing in my refrigerator?" Darlene grumbled as she held up the white sack with her thumb and two fingers.

"I bought it at the restaurant at lunch yesterday because it came with fresh strawberries. Do you want to split it, Morgan?"

"Sounds good to me."

Darlene waved a knife. "I'll slice it so you two don't get into a squabble over whose piece is larger."

"We wouldn't do that, would we, Boss Lady?"

Jenna shrugged. "I don't know, Morgan; fresh strawberries sounded good to me."

"Don't get your hopes up too high; I'll divide them in half too," Darlene said.

After she sliced the cheesecake and placed the two slices on dessert plates, Darlene weighed the plates. "Perfect."

She spooned strawberries over each slice and measured again. She removed half a strawberry from one plate and popped it into her mouth. "Mmm. Sweet."

Darlene put two forks and the plates on the counter. "There you are. Take your pick."

Morgan picked up the plate that was closer to Jenna, and Jenna giggled.

"I never had a sister, but this must be what it would have been like," Jenna said.

"I have two brothers," Morgan said. "This is nothing. A brother would have taken a huge bite out of one then run off with the other."

Jenna took a bite of her cheesecake. "It's not as good as yours, Darlene, but the fresh strawberries are a hit."

"Maybe I'll do individual cheesecakes for dessert this weekend," Darlene said.

"Sounds good to me," Morgan said.

Jenna tilted her head. "We have a car coming up the driveway. Maybe it's Nicci."

Morgan hurried to the office to peek out the window. "She's taller than you, but not by much, but she's got at least thirty pounds on you. She's wearing an olive green jacket and a pale green blouse. I love her style."

Jenna joined her.

When Nicci gazed at the inn and smiled, Morgan said, "She has a pleasant smile. Maybe she's here to smack down Renee."

CHAPTER TEN

When Jenna opened the door, she was startled by Nicci's clear green eyes. *Nicci does outweigh me, but she's so polished that I feel like I've got ragged edges.*

"I'm Nicci; you must be Jenna. It's nice to meet you." Nicci set down her suitcase and held out her hand.

They shook hands. *Secrets.* Jenna examined at Nicci's face; Nicci averted her eyes.

"You too; come inside."

Morgan stood behind Jenna. "Hi, I'm Morgan. I'll get you checked in so you can get settled."

Nicci sighed. "That sounds nice. It was a long drive."

After Nicci registered, Morgan gave her the tour of the downstairs and her usual spiel that now included the history of the Wyndham family and the estate.

"Your room is upstairs."

Nicci picked up her suitcase she had left at the registration desk and followed Morgan up the stairs.

Jenna's phone buzzed a text from Ethan. "Inspector signed the occupancy certificate."

Jenna stormed out the back door with Katy at her heels. When a frigid blast of wind hit her, Jenna returned to grab her coat then joined Katy outside again.

"I need a good long walk, Katy. Ethan fixed it so I can't check the cottage because I don't have a key. I should have a key. Let's go to the peach orchard."

Jenna lengthened her stride as Katy ran in front of her. When she reached the edge of the orchard, Jenna stopped to catch her breath and read her text again.

"That man who always calls and never texts just sent me the most important news of the week in a text," Jenna grumbled.

She replied, "Thanks."

Jenna snorted. "There. I thanked him."

As they headed back at a much slower pace, Jenna stopped and looked at her phone.

"Ethan put in extra effort so I could move into my cottage tomorrow. My reply sounds snippy."

Jenna sent a follow up text. "I appreciate your extra effort."

When Jenna reached the back door she pulled out her phone. "Does that sound too impersonal? It does to me; I might as well have added yours truly, J. Ross."

After she hung up her coat, she read the texts. "It's not me; it's him. He followed up last night's surprising moment of tenderness with a business text, and now, nothing. Well, Mr. Ethan Bentley, licensed general contractor, best regards from Jenna Carlson Ross, proprietor."

Jenna stopped in the empty kitchen. She refilled Katy's water bowl then read the instructions for happy hour while Katy took a long drink.

When she went into the office, Morgan said, "I'm the winner of the day. Nicci told me she loved her room because the walls were pale yellow, and the flowers on the fabric of her soft chair were yellow wood sorrel. Can you believe she knew the name of those tiny flowers? She told me yellow was her favorite color. She said she never wore yellow to work because someone told her at the beginning of her career that yellow made her look timid."

Jenna giggled. "I can't imagine anyone calling Nicci timid."

"She asked if she could tour the barn today. I checked with Shane, and he said it was a good idea. He went with Ethan to the peach orchard to discuss an addition to the orchard's country store. The farmer wants to put in a small café with drinks and maybe an ice cream bar. When Nicci comes downstairs, we'll take a walk to the barn. Do you want to go with us?"

"I'd like that," Jenna said.

"Do we leave a note on the registration desk in case Renee and Sophia return?" Morgan asked.

Jenna opened her mouth then pressed her lips together and shook her head. "I almost said yes, but we are not available twenty-four hours a day for guests except for emergencies. We open the dining room at seven in the morning during the week for a light breakfast and at six in the evening for happy hour and to provide a clean, safe, comfortable inn. We're a retreat, not a resort, and we do not have an activities director on the premises. Our numbers are posted at the registration desk for emergencies, so there's our note."

Morgan's eyes twinkled. "Say that again real slow, so I can type it up and slip it under Renee's door."

Jenna giggled. "Print two extra copies so we can tape one on each of our doors, so we can't leave the office without the reminder."

Morgan stopped at the door to the kitchen. "If we're conducting tours of the barn for potential customers, we have to rename the Peach Pit, tout de suite."

Jenna was deep in thought as they walked toward the kitchen door to the hall.

Before they left the kitchen, Jenna's mouth quivered. "You're right, so let's call it the Peachy Suite. Suite is spelled s-u-i-t-e, which is pronounced like Peachy Sweet, s-w-e-e-t. What do you think?"

Morgan gaped at Jenna. "I love it, but how do you come up with stuff like this? I'll be right back."

Jenna and Katy followed Morgan to the office.

Morgan sat at her computer. She tapped on the keys and frowned at the screen. "Okay, this is just a first draft."

Morgan sent a document to the printer.

Jenna examined it. "Our peach blossom logo with Peachy Suite. Oh, this is so cute."

"I think so, for now. We might add some garland with peaches. I'm in love with Peachy Suite. You accountants are remarkably multi-talented."

Jenna laughed. "At least you didn't say I was remarkably talented for an accountant."

"Dang. Missed opportunity." Morgan laughed. "I'll text Shane."

After she sent the text the two of them stared at Morgan's phone.

"If he doesn't answer this in three seconds..." Morgan was interrupted by the buzz of a text.

Shane texted, "Perfect AND hilarious!"

"He got it!" Morgan danced a jig; Jenna and Katy joined her.

When she was out of breath from dancing, Jenna said, "I forgot to tell you I can move into the cottage tomorrow. The inspector signed the certificate of occupancy."

"That is great news. Is our scramble plan to move you into the cottage tomorrow?"

"Must be because I haven't packed one thing yet. I hear Nicci on the stairs."

Nicci reached the bottom of the stairs and glanced at the surroundings, including the hallways behind her. Her face was pale.

When she saw Jenna, Morgan, and Katy, her smile was weak. "The wind is cold, but I'd like to walk to the barn if it isn't too far because I've been driving all day."

"We all have warm coats, and Katy loves to run. It's actually not very far. We can walk there and back and then monopolize happy hour while we complain about how cold it was," Jenna said.

"Deal." Nicci chuckled.

"So, are you here to help Renee or Fred?" Jenna asked.

"Good question. I'm actually here at Orion's request."

"Well, I, for one, hope we're looking at three different events," Morgan said. "My boss might let me have a day off if I can swing three contracts at once."

Jenna laughed. "Nicci, you're in the company of two workaholics. The only battle we've ever had was over days off. Morgan refuses to take even one, and I don't have any use for a day off, so we're at an impasse."

Nicci laughed. "Sounds like me and a great guy who used to work with me. Sergio left Orion Tech Industries for a promotion at a start-up and is doing very well. It's difficult to lose talented people, but it was time for him to move on; he had outgrown us. Orion and Sergio were the original developers of the system. In fact, they were the only two on the team for the first eight months. They were the typical garage development team living off pizza and popcorn."

"It's hard to stay inside the tidy corporate box when your wings want to breathe," Morgan said.

When Jenna and Nicci stopped and stared at her, Morgan said, "Sorry, I've been working on ad copy most of the day."

"I'm in the presence of genius; you two are remarkable. I heard besides the barn there's also an auxiliary building on the property," Nicci said.

Jenna nodded. "That's right; about half of it is storage for our tables and chairs. We've converted the half that faces the barn to two large dressing rooms we expect to be invaluable for weddings, a cozy waiting room for the mamas or whoever, a workroom with a computer, printer, copy machine and office supplies for last-minute emergencies, and two wheelchair accessible restrooms."

What's the building called? Reception Center?" Nicci asked.

Morgan smiled and showed her the flyer. "It's just a first draft. The art needs work."

Nicci stopped. "Peachy Suite. This is great."

"It was Jenna's idea," Morgan said.

"That I got from Morgan when she said we needed a name tout de suite," Jenna added.

"What a great team," Nicci said.

As they strolled to the barn, Nicci was tense and remained on alert.

Jenna caught her mood and listened for footsteps or rustles in the leaves. Her senses were heightened for anything out of the ordinary.

When they neared the barn, Nicci said, "I'd heard Bobbie Moore was the project manager for the Peach Blossom Barn. Did she retire?"

Jenna and Morgan exchanged glances.

"She had a fatal fall earlier this week, so we stepped in to carry on her dream," Jenna said.

Nicci turned her head as a tear slipped down her cheek. She mumbled under her breath, "The Pink Lady is gone."

Nicci cleared her throat. "What a tragedy, but I'm sure her family appreciates the project being finished. It looks like you are ready for business, but that's from my uneducated eye."

"The buildings are close, but we're waiting for tables and chairs."

"If someone wanted to hold an event, couldn't they rent tables and chairs?"

"It depends on the size of the group; for a small- to medium-sized groups, renting might be an option, but it would be important to factor in delivery and labor."

Nicci's eyes were sad. "I liked it better when I was ignorant. Could I reserve the barn, knowing that the date could change?"

"You certainly could. Let me know when you want to discuss options." Morgan handed Nicci one of her new business cards. "We can work something out."

"Could we get together tomorrow after breakfast? That gives me time to sort out our must haves versus nice to haves. What about Wi-Fi?"

"We have a strong signal, even out here."

Nicci chuckled. "Our crowd would sit on the floor and eat sawdust if the internet signal supported their needs."

"If we aren't talking fancy, let's get together in the morning and see what we can pull together for your group in the morning," Morgan said. "I have a project work sheet I'll give you when we get back. We'll talk where it's warm."

Jenna hurried ahead to peer into the barn and exhaled in relief. "All clear."

When Morgan and Nicci joined her, Jenna said, "This is barebones. Morgan can talk to you about everything else."

"Which we'll do at the inn." Morgan's teeth chattered.

"Can we take a peek at the Peachy Suite?" Nicci asked.

"There's not much to see, but the workers store their equipment inside the building, so it's locked when they aren't on the job site. We can come back tomorrow after lunch with a key," Morgan said. "We could come in the morning, but it's going to be colder than it is now."

Nicci shivered. "That sounds smart. I'm ready to go back."

Nicci set a fast pace, but it was an easy pace for Morgan, and Jenna matched Nicci's stride. Katy dashed ahead.

When they reached the inn, Morgan opened the back door.

"Where's Katy?" Nicci asked. "Are we leaving her outside?"

"Our chef would have let Katy in before she left for the day. I'll bet Katy's in the living room soaking up the heat from the fireplace," Jenna said.

Nicci smiled. "Warming up in front of a fire? I'm going to join my new best friend, Katy." She hurried to the living room.

The camera.

"I'll bring you a project planning sheet," Morgan said.

"I almost forgot. Sophia gave me a camera to give to Nicci. I'll be right back."

Jenna opened the desk drawer where she had put Sophia's camera, still wrapped in the sturdy napkin. She carried the still-wrapped camera into the living room and exhaled in relief at Nicci who sat on the floor in front of the fire.

"Sophia asked me to give you this camera. She said it had photos she wanted you to review."

"Why is it wrapped in a cloth napkin?"

"I put it in my desk drawer and didn't want to scratch it."

Nicci furrowed her brow, and Jenna hurried back to the office. Morgan had printed two copies of the planning sheet and put one on Jenna's desk.

Jenna said, "I don't have much to move since I lost everything in the fire except what I brought here for the weekend, but the move would be easier if I had boxes. I expected the furniture we ordered to have been delivered by now."

"I'll follow up on that for you while you're in town," Morgan said.

"Thank you. Is there anything else we need?" Jenna pulled out a notepad to create a shopping list.

"Not that I know of, but I'll text you if I think of anything."

"I'll be back before happy hour. Katy will be sad, but I'm not taking her."

"She has a new friend and me to hang out with, and she won't starve because she's smart and reminds us when it's time for her to eat. How's your shopping list going?"

"It's finished."

Morgan strode to Jenna's desk and peered at her list then pointed. "I suggest you wait to replenish this section of kitchen supplies until you see how much space your cupboards have."

"That's a good idea. I'll pick up boxes and packing tape, and then shop for a few more outfits. I should have bought more clothes right after the fire, but the laundry is so handy to my room that I developed a routine of washing small loads of laundry every other day."

When Morgan headed toward the door, Jenna said, "Text me when Sophia returns."

"Will do."

After she put on her coat, she shifted her holster a little farther forward for access when her coat was open. *That's better.*

As Jenna drove into town, she smiled. *Why do I feel like I'm playing hooky?*

Her first stop was at the gas station. While she stood at the pump and refueled. A man she didn't recognize who was a few years older than her pulled into the pump behind her. He wore a beat-up ball cap, jeans, and a brown hunting jacket. The man had a scraggly, four-day beard.

He's not from around here. She chuckled to herself. *I'm such a local.*

After she returned the gas nozzle to its cradle, she turned to open her car door.

"Excuse me," the man said.

Jenna glanced at him and tilted her head.

"You left your fuel door open."

Jenna smiled as she closed it. "Thanks."

"Is there a restaurant in town you'd recommend?" he asked.

"It depends on what kind of food interests you, but I hear all the restaurants in town are excellent. They're in the middle of town fairly close together. I hate saying this, but you can't miss them."

The man chuckled. "I know what you mean. It's so tempting to say you'd be surprised by what I can miss."

Jenna laughed. "I'll have to borrow that."

"Be my guest. It was nice talking to you," he said.

Jenna nodded and climbed into her car. Before she pulled away from the pump, she glimpsed a man who went into the station. *Was the Ethan? No, he would have at least waved.*

When she went into the clothing store, the owner had emptied a box of folded T-shirts and was arranging them on a shelf.

"Hi, Jenna. Are you looking for anything special?"

"I need some long-sleeved shirts and jeans."

"Button-down or T-shirts?"

"Button-down unless I don't find anything I like, then T-shirt."

The owner pointed to the shirts hanging on a circular rack. "You're in luck. I just got a shipment in. You'll find several there I'm sure you'll like. It's funny; I thought of you when I opened the box."

After Jenna picked out five shirts, she read the content tag then took three of them to the dressing room.

After she tried them on, she carried the three to the register.

"Well, that was easy," the owner said. "Jeans your size are over there."

Jenna found two pairs of jeans in her size that were the style she always bought. After she took them to the register, the owner said, "Under things and socks next?

We just got in some new boot socks. I know how partial you are to your boots. They are on the back wall."

After Jenna picked out underwear and socks, she said, "I'm ready to check out."

While the owner folded the shirts, she said, "I was sorry you lost your cottage in that fire, but I heard you're rebuilding. I'll bet you're ready to move into your new home. You've been staying in a room at the inn all this time, haven't you?"

"I have, but I worry every weekend that we won't have enough rooms for all our guests who want to register."

The owner nodded. "That would make me a nervous wreck."

Jenna furrowed her brow. "It may have been bothering me more than I would admit to myself."

"I can imagine. There are enough worries as a business owner without the added stress of not having your own space, and worse, taking up a room your customers could use. If I had something like that here, I'd be sleeping in the back room."

"My plan was to sleep in my office."

The owner smiled. "Some would say it's the pride of ownership, but I think it's just hard-headed orneriness."

Jenna returned her smile. "Which is all part of a normal day."

The owner laughed. "Welcome to the club."

After she climbed into her car, Jenna checked her list. "Boots and a hat. I want another warm jacket that's a little longer. When the wind blows, it's brutal."

While Jenna was trying on boots, Fred came into the store. "I thought I saw your car, Jenna, and decided I'd pop in. How are you?"

"Doing well. What about you?"

"Not bad at all. I'm enjoying the pace of a small town, and I don't miss the city traffic. I need to pick up a few things for the family while I'm here. Is the orchard country store a good place for gifts?"

Jenna smiled. "We have quite a few guests who spend at least three weekends a year with us, so they can visit the orchard and shop at their country store."

"I'll head that way then. See you later."

Jenna found a coat that fit her and fit her criteria of being long enough to cover her backside when the wind blew. She selected a pair of warm gloves and rolled her small cart to the cashier.

"These boots are so cute," the cashier said. "Did you notice they were on sale? Fifteen percent off."

"Oh wait. I need a hat."

"Ball cap or winter?"

"Both. Do you have anything in creamy peach?"

The owner laughed. "I have peach orchard caps, so the answer is yes."

Jenna grabbed a pale blue denim ball cap with a peach blossom on it, and a navy blue wool knit cap with the same logo.

After she loaded her packages into her car, Jenna headed toward the inn.

When she went in the back door with her packages in-hand and the flattened boxes under her arm, Katy met her at the door. Jenna dropped her packages and hugged Katy. "I missed you, Katy girl."

After Jenna picked up all her things, Katy followed her to the bedroom. Jenna removed the tags from her new clothes and added them to her laundry basket with its small load of clothes.

"After I start my load of laundry, I'll put on my new coat and my wool cap so we can see if I'm dressed warm enough for this weather."

When Jenna and Katy went outside, Jenna put on her new gloves and pulled up the hood to stop the icy wind from blowing across the back of her neck.

"My fancy new coat is warm. Which way do you want to go, Katy? I hear a tractor coming from the orchard. Want to see what's going on? Maybe they need a sidewalk superintendent to meddle in their business." Jenna giggled.

Katy grinned then raced toward the orchard. Jenna strolled down the trail. When the noise of the engine stopped, a mockingbird trilled through its songs.

When Jenna neared the curve in the trail, Ethan was standing in the middle of the road with Katy standing next to him.

"Isn't it too cold for you to be out?" he asked.

Jenna glared at him. *It doesn't take any special talent to feel that the wall is back.*

Jenna turned her back to him and stormed back to the inn with Katy at her side.

Before she reached the inn, the engine noise behind her started up again.

When they went inside, Jenna said, "Thanks for the walk, Katy. It was an excellent test for my new coat and a solid confirmation of Ethan's wall and his volatility."

After Jenna tossed her clothes into the dryer, she went to her office and opened the safe. *Morgan said she'd stalk Sophia. Wasn't there something about stalking in Bobbie's diary?*

Jenna sat at her desk with the diary, the notebook, and all the notes. She skimmed the diary. "Here it is, Katy. It's one of Bobbie's notes next to Daffodil. It says, 'Why is the daffodil following the goddess of wild animals and the hunt? What is the connection? Next step: find Arti and Daffodil in the same group or groups.'"

Jenna opened the notebook and after an in depth review, she exhaled. "Daffodil and Arti are in three groups." Jenna reviewed the groups again. "And neither one is in any other group."

Jenna signed into Group Three as Beansy. She searched for Arti. *Last session was this morning.*

Jenna began reading Arti's posts from the most recent to older posts and saw a pattern. After Arti posted, Daffodil added to the thread. *Makes sense. Daffodil can track Arti's posts by searching for her own.*

Okay, I have a theory. Jenna typed faster and hopped from group to group as she scanned the posts and noted names. *So far, so good. I don't know why, but I'm seeing what. There's my old friend Skillet. She's relatively active in all ten groups. She posts when she signs on and again when she signs off. Good way to track your time, Skillet.*

This is odd. A member named Jazzy comments on the beginning of every one of Daffodil's posts after Daffodil signs off. How does she do that? "So, is Jazzy stalking Daffodil?"

"What?" Morgan asked.

"A soap opera." Jenna closed out the groups. After she put the notes, diary, and notebook into the safe, she locked it.

"Sure, soap opera. Look at my planning sheet. I feel like I forgot something or maybe I'm going into too much depth. Should I just tear it up?" Morgan handed the planning sheet. "You hate it, don't you?"

"Oh, stop. You sound like what has been going on in my head all day."

Jenna raised her eyebrows as she read. "This is great, Morgan. It has good flow, but you've created a template for the client to be creative rather than just list the cold data."

Morgan swiped away a tear. "You've been so good for me."

"It's what friends do. Did you see Sophia or Renee when you went into town?" Morgan asked.

"No."

"I'm going to the barn," Morgan said.

"No, I will. Text me if they show up."

"They'll be here soon; it's almost happy hour. I'll get busy."

Morgan muttered as she opened the door to the kitchen. "We need a golf cart."

Jenna followed her into the kitchen then rushed to the living room. *Nicci must have gone up to her room.*

Jenna put on her heavy coat and her wool cap. "I'm going to the barn, Katy. Are you going?"

Katy trotted to the door then raced to the trail that went to the barn and disappeared. Jenna ran after her. When she was halfway, she had to stop and get her breath.

Katy yelped.

Is she hurt or was that a happy yip? I'm too scared to think.

Jenna ran as fast as she could to the barn. When she reached it, she groaned at the figure standing in front of the barn. *I should have known. Katy is a traitor. It's Ethan.*

Jenna raced to get past him, but he sidestepped, and she slammed into a wall.

CHAPTER ELEVEN

Ethan caught her before she fell, and Jenna squirmed. "Let go." She leaned to the side to gaze into the barn and exhaled with relief even though her knees threatened to collapse from running.

"The barn is empty," she whispered.

"Yes, it is." Ethan continued to hold her. "We have to talk."

Jenna's teeth chattered as she gazed up at him. "Can we talk where it's warm?"

"Good idea. Let's take my truck."

"I can't go anywhere; it's almost happy hour. I can't abandon Morgan."

"We're taking my truck to the inn."

Ethan kept his arm around Jenna's waist as he helped her to his truck. Jenna tensed her muscles to keep from leaning against him.

As they neared his truck, Jenna pushed away from him. "Thank you for the help, but I'm okay now."

They rode to the inn in silence.

After he parked near the back door, Ethan left the engine running. "So, what's going on with you?"

"Me? What are you talking about? Nothing's going on; I'm doing great."

"No, you're not. You just tried to knock me down."

"I did not; you stepped in my way with no warning. Why did you do that?"

Jenna's phone buzzed a text from Morgan. "Sophia is here."

"Oh, good." Jenna sighed with relief then replied, "Thanks."

Ethan tapped his thumb on the steering wheel then exhaled. "What were you even doing at the barn?"

Jenna glared at him. "It's my barn."

Ethan narrowed his eyes. "You were there for a reason."

"Thank you for the ride; we appreciate it."

Jenna climbed out of the truck and opened the back door for Katy, who hopped out.

Ethan followed Jenna inside. "Where can we talk without interruption?"

"My office."

When they went into the kitchen, Morgan said, "I can't tell you how relieved I was to see her. Nicci's in the dining room too. So far, no Renee." Morgan stared at the two of them.

"We'll be in the office if you need me," Jenna said.

When they went into the office, Ethan scanned the room. "You've rearranged your office. It looks bigger."

"We can sit at the table." Jenna examined his face. *It is a nice mustache.*

After Jenna sat, Ethan sat next to her. She shifted her chair so she could watch his face.

Jenna tried to glare, but she gazed at him instead. "Why did you text me about the county inspection?"

Ethan smiled. "I knew you'd be happy about it. Are you moving this evening or tomorrow? Do you need any help?"

Jenna bit her lip. "You've always called me when I text you."

"I know, but I wanted you to know right away, and Shane and I were in a meeting with our new client. Shane is positive we got the job."

"Oh." Jenna furrowed her brow.

Ethan narrowed his eyes. "Is something wrong?"

"I didn't realize you were busy; that's good news." Jenna cleared her throat. "I'm going to move tomorrow. I don't have much to move, but I bought two boxes today so I can pack this evening."

"Shane and I will be here at eight in the morning, so we can carry your boxes."

Jenna stared at him. "My clothes aren't that heavy."

Ethan shrugged. "Boxes can be bulky. Can I ask about the barn?"

Jenna's eyes twinkled. "You want the short, dramatic answer or the long, boring one?"

Ethan stroked his chin. "The long one, please."

Jenna exhaled. "At breakfast this morning Sophia was warning me about Renee and asked me to give a camera to Nicci. I can't explain it, but when I touched the camera, I suddenly envisioned her on the barn floor close to where I found Bobbie. There was a pink scarf tied around her neck, and I knew she was gone. I've been worried about her all day. Morgan and I tried to keep track of her, but we couldn't."

"That's not boring."

"But it is long. I went into town to do some shopping..."

Ethan interrupted. "Oh, so that's what you were doing in town."

Jenna furrowed her brow. "What else would I be doing?"

"I don't know. Meeting an old friend?"

Jenna peered at him. "Why didn't you say hi at the gas station?"

Ethan stared at his hands. "Is that where you went shopping?"

"No. Where was I?"

"Shopping," Ethan said.

"Right, and I went shopping at the boutique and the farm store. So, when I returned to the inn, Sophia still wasn't here, and you know the rest."

"Have you ever had a loose connection like this before? That doesn't sound right."

Jenna stared at him then pursed her lips to keep from smiling. *I can't imagine how angry I would have been if he'd said that to me this morning. Now, it's kind of funny.*

"I've never had something not be true, but I'd love it if this one is a warning, not a fact."

"Is that possible?"

Jenna sighed. "I don't know."

Morgan came into the office from the kitchen. "Shane's here, and we were talking. Why don't the four of us go out to dinner? It's not a weekend, so we won't have any problems getting reservations. I told Shane what you said about not being on call twenty-four seven for the guests, and he was impressed. When I told him he could decide where we eat, he declined, so I told him I would select a place unless you have a suggestion, Jenna. What do you think?"

Jenna glanced at Ethan, but he was staring at the floor. She chuckled. "Don't pick anywhere fancy because I don't want to do laundry again. All I have on my agenda is to pack, and that will take me all of ten minutes. After that, we all know I'm free."

"If you are, I am," Ethan said.

"Good. We can leave after we have the dining room ready for tomorrow morning and the kitchen spotless for Darlene," Morgan said.

"I'll go pack," Jenna said.

"I'll give you fifteen seconds to get to your room then start a timer," Ethan said.

Jenna jumped up. "Don't you dare."

She dashed to her room and put her boxes together then packed all her clothes in one box. She glanced at her phone. *Not bad. Three minutes.* She hurried to the laundry room with the second box and emptied the clothes from the dryer into the box. When she returned to her room, she selected the clothes she would wear in the morning and folded all the clean clothes and put them into the box.

She glanced around the room. *All that's left is the bathroom, and that will be one swipe and everything goes into the second box.*

She hurried to the kitchen where Ethan and Shane were sitting at the counter. Ethan stopped the timer on his phone.

"How many minutes?" She asked.

"Seven and a half," Ethan said.

"Nice try. It was five minutes."

"Five and a half." Ethan said.

"You looking for a fight, mister?" Jenna growled.

"Oh no, ma'am. I've had my quota for the day." Ethan smiled as he held up his hands.

When the two of them laughed, Shane shook his head and went into the dining room.

A few minutes later, Shane returned. "Jenna, Renee told Morgan she wants to speak to you privately. I'll stay here and keep Ethan company."

When Jenna opened the door to the dining room, she glanced at Katy. "Are you going with me?"

Katy closed her eyes.

Good choice, Katy.

Only Renee and Morgan were in the dining room when Jenna closed the door behind her.

"I really need to speak to you privately, Jenna. I have a delicate problem and could use some homespun advice," Renee said.

Jenna cocked her head as she examined Renee's face. *Why does everything she says sound like an insult?*

Morgan stared at Renee then cleared her throat. "I'll load up the dishes and take them to the kitchen."

"Would you like to meet in the living room so Morgan can clean the dining room?" Jenna asked.

Renee grumbled, "Anybody could just walk by and hear what we're saying."

"Not really. The wood floor would give them away, and even if they took off their shoes and tried to tiptoe, the old boards would creak."

"I think we should go into your office," Renee growled.

Jenna nodded. "That would be a logical choice, but after Morgan and Shane clean the kitchen, which won't take long, Morgan will have to close out the day's receipts and check for reservations."

"Doesn't she do that in her office?" Renee asked.

"We share an office."

Renee gaped at her. "You're kidding me."

"Do you want to talk now or in the morning?"

"Now," Renee shouted.

"It's up to you, but you may want to keep your voice down."

Renee grumbled under her breath.

When they were in the living room, Renee sat in the middle of the sofa.

I'll play. Jenna stepped toward the sofa then glanced at either side of Renee and sighed as she sat on the yellow chair in the corner.

Renee smiled her cobra smile.

That's right, Renee. You won.

Jenna glanced up at Nettie's portrait. Nettie mocked Renee's smile, and Jenna coughed three times into her elbow to keep from laughing.

That was great, Nettie.

Jenna smiled at Renee as they sat in silence.

When Renee didn't speak, Jenna raised her eyebrows then leaned back in the yellow chair and held her gaze on Renee, who stared down at the rug.

Renee glanced at Jenna and cleared her throat. "This is completely confidential and can't go beyond this room."

Jenna nodded.

Renee exhaled. "I am having problems with your Wi-Fi. When Sophia is here, your network is so slow, I can't log into my database of articles. When she's not here, the network is still slow, but it's at least tolerable. I was walking past her room and happened to take a peek at her computer, and I was shocked. She was playing one of those games that takes up all the bandwidth. Could you speak to her about that? You could tell her she's slowing down both you and Morgan."

"That's really odd that you are being affected, and we aren't. I'll check the connectivity to the upstairs. We may have a hardware issue. If I can't find anything, I'll call our internet provider and ask them to check it. Our system is new, but maybe there's a software update we're missing. Thank you for letting me know."

Jenna rose. "If there isn't anything else, I'll check right now."

Renee glowered at her. "She shouldn't be playing games when she is behind on my projects."

"I'll let you know in the morning what I find. I may check several times tonight in case it's sporadic."

"That's not good enough. You have to kick her out," Renee shouted.

Jenna raised her eyebrows. "Why is that?"

"She's not doing my work. How dense can you be?" Renee screamed.

Renee ran up the stairs and slammed her door.

The chimes jingled as Jenna left the living room. Jenna smiled. *Thanks, Nettie.*

Jenna strolled into the kitchen.

"You're practically strutting. If it was so all-fired confidential, why was she screaming? She wants Sophia kicked out, doesn't she?" Morgan asked.

Jenna nodded.

"What if she's trying to protect Sophia?" Ethan asked.

Even Katy stared at him.

"If it was anyone but Renee, that could be a possibility," Jenna said.

Shane frowned. "Ethan has a point. Ask Sophia if there's been a change in Renee's attitude toward her since they've arrived here. You could catch her first thing in the morning."

Jenna and Morgan exchanged a look.

"I need an excuse," Jenna said.

"Give me your silver pen, Shane," Morgan said. "It's monogrammed, right?"

"Yes." He gave the pen to Morgan.

Morgan examined the pen. "The monogram is S. A. L."

"Perfect. Sophia's last name is Baker, and she signed in as S. M. Baker. I'll be right back."

Jenna hummed under her breath as she quietly slipped up the stairs. *I've caught that from Morgan.*

When she lightly tapped on Sophia's door, Sophia opened the door and motioned for Jenna to come inside. After she closed the door, Sophia asked, "What's up?"

"We found a silver pen in the dining room. Is this yours?" Jenna held out the pen, but Sophia didn't accept it.

"No, it's beautiful, but it's not mine. Why are you really here?"

"Has Renee's behavior changed since came to the inn?"

"She's always been self-centered and spiteful, so no change."

"Thanks; that's what I thought, but I needed verification."

"Why did you tell me to stay away from the barn?"

Jenna willed herself not to shudder. "Bobbie Moore was attacked in the barn. I'm very superstitious, so stay away from the barn."

Sophia peered at Jenna. "I thought it was something like that."

Jenna left as quietly as she had arrived.

When she returned to the kitchen, she returned the pen to Shane. "Thanks; it was nice to have an excuse to talk to her. Sophia told me Renee has always been as mean as she has been here."

Ethan shook his head. "I thought you'd be gone longer. Did you just ask her if that was her pen and has Renee always been obnoxious?"

Jenna shrugged. "Yes."

Morgan giggled. "She took Shane's pen so she could be subtle."

Ethan smiled. "Right, the Jenna version of subtle. My mistake; I should have realized that. Can we all be off duty tonight and have normal conversations?"

"I'm not sure that's what we want, Ethan. That means only you and I will be doing all the talking tonight," Shane said.

While the two men laughed, Morgan rolled her eyes.

"Jenna, our reservations are in twenty minutes. Let's go."

"Katy, we're going out for a while; do you want to wait in the kitchen or our bedroom?"

Katy trotted to the front of the stove and stretched before she circled an imaginary spot then laid down.

"Okay; I'll be back later."

When Jenna picked up her keys, Ethan cleared his throat. "You could ride with me, Jenna."

"There's no reason..."

Morgan elbowed Jenna. "That's a great idea. There's no reason to take four cars when we're all going to the same place."

"Honey, your car's not here," Shane said.

"I know, but if it was, I'd still ride with you."

"Works for me; let's go."

As Shane and Morgan headed to the back door, Ethan asked. "Jenna?"

Jenna gazed at him. "I'm ready."

After they were outside, Jenna slipped her arm through Ethan's and exhaled. *No wall. That last one might have been mine, not his.*

When he side-glanced at her and smiled, she said, "Just in case."

As Ethan started the engine, he asked, "Are you going to throw everything I ever say to you back into my face?"

Jenna's mouth quivered. "Sure; you got a problem with that, bud?"

Ethan laughed.

"Were you the same as you are now when you were a kid?" Ethan asked.

"If you want to know if I was super smart and loved dogs, the answer is yes."

"What about your sensitivity to objects and people?"

"Yes, but I thought everybody was sensitive like me until I heard the family whisper, 'Jenna is a troubled child.' My grandmother saw it, though, and tried to explain it to my mother. Grandma explained it to me when I was three, and it made sense to me. Of course, most of the family still thinks I have issues, except Mom and Dad."

"Was your talent inherited from you grandmother?"

"No, she told me she could see how strongly I reacted to things, so she watched me closely and realized what was going on. The aunts told Mom to take me to a therapist because I was too dramatic. Grandma banned them from our house." Jenna chuckled. "Grandma didn't even live at our house, but she was fierce when she wanted to be, and nobody crossed her. Dad told me I'd be okay because Grandma had my back."

"Is she still alive?" Ethan asked.

"No, she passed when I was in high school." Jenna sighed. "I still miss her. Mom tells me she'll always be grateful to her mother-in-law because she would have listened to the meddling relatives, and I'd be an over-medicated, angry woman."

"What did your husband think?"

Jenna smiled at the memory. "Tom called it my royal energy."

"Your princess power," Ethan said.

Jenna gaped at Ethan. "Why did you say that?"

Ethan shrugged. "It just makes sense."

How did he know that's what Tom called it?

Jenna swallowed. "What about you? Who had your back?"

"I never thought about him like that before, but I overheard Mom complain to Dad that Uncle Jack would have covered for me if I'd robbed Fort Knox."

"What did your dad say?"

"He said if I was smart enough to get into Fort Knox, he'd help his brother."

Jenna giggled. "You had a strong support system."

"I really did, but I didn't always appreciate it until I went into the army." Ethan slowed down. "There's Shane; Morgan must be inside."

After Ethan parked, Jenna shivered as she climbed out of the truck. *I am so tired of being cold.*

Ethan put his arm around her shoulders, and she leaned into his warmth. *No wall is nice.*

"Come on, let's get out of this wind," he said.

They rushed together to join Shane. Shane opened the door when they reached him, and the three of them scooted inside.

Jenna inhaled the inviting aroma of fresh roasted garlic, sweet tangy tomatoes simmering in a pot with basil, rosemary, and thyme.

Ethan leaned down and whispered, "Do you think we've been transported smack into the middle of Italy?"

Jenna smiled and nodded.

As they were being led to a table in the back away from the door, Jenna heard Renee's voice over all the voices in the crowded restaurant. She glanced at the room on their right and raised her eyebrows. Nicci, Renee, Sophia, Fred, and another man were sitting at a table. Nicci raised an eyebrow when she glanced at Jenna, and she waved with her hand under the table.

Jenna kept her hand low and gave a quick wave in response.

When they went into the small room, Morgan was sitting at the round table with four chairs around it. "I told them we would like to be as far away from the cold air as possible, and they offered the small room."

"This is wonderful," Jenna said as she studied the menu the server had handed her.

The server returned with four glasses of water; after she recited the specials, the server took their drink orders.

Morgan continued, "I thought so too. When I checked in, the host told me large groups always ask for a private room for their parties, but this room is too small. I told her Shane and Ethan could easily expand the room for them and gave her Shane's card."

Shane's eyes twinkled. "I thought everybody was supposed to be off duty."

Morgan snorted. "I wasn't on duty for the Peach Blossom Retreat; I was sharing a review of your company, which is reaching out to the community and is completely different. What's everybody going to order?"

Shane said, "I noticed her engagement ring; I'll bet you did too. Did you also give her a business card for the Peach Blossom Barn?"

Morgan shrugged. "My card might have gotten stuck to yours."

Their server brought glasses of wine for Jenna and Morgan and coffee for Ethan and Shane.

"Are we ready to order?"

"We're sharing, right?" Morgan asked. "You pick, Jenna."

"Carbonara," Jenna said.

The server nodded. "I'll tell the chef you are sharing so he can serve it on two plates. He hates seeing a messy plate."

After the server took Ethan's and Shane's orders, she spun around and left the room.

"Did you see who was in that side room?" Morgan took a sip of her wine. "I wouldn't have noticed if I hadn't heard that familiar, irritating voice."

"Her voice definitely carries. Let's change the subject. I can't ask about work, so help me out, Morgan. Small talk is not my strong suit." Jenna bit her lip. "Wait, I've got it. How's the wine?"

"It would definitely tickle the taste buds of the Paisley Business Association wine connoisseurs."

Jenna took a sip. "Wow, it really is good."

"So, an old friend of mine called me because she heard I had become an event coordinator. She's been an event coordinator for ten years and was asking me for advice. She must have forgotten I interned with her company for a year when I was in college."

"What did you tell her?" Jenna asked.

"I told her my key was to adjust when things didn't go as planned, but then she launched into a lecture that everything must follow the plan."

Shane snorted. "How's that working out for her? She wouldn't last two seconds around here."

"Funny you should say that. She finally told me she was available to manage my events for me because the convention center where she has been working for the last two years cut back their staff."

"That's too bad," Jenna said. "Did you tell her your skinflint of a boss wouldn't give you the budget for any more staff?"

Morgan nodded. "Kind of. I told her there was no budget for any additional staff for at least five years because we were a startup."

"Did that slow her down?" Ethan asked.

"She told me ninety-eight percent of startups fail in the first year, so she wasn't interested after all. She hung up on me like I had called her."

"Ninety-eight percent? Is that true?" Shane asked.

Morgan shrugged. "I've seen that number quoted, but it's such a broad brush because there are so many types of industries from service to manufacturing, so I'm skeptical of how relevant it is to any specific industry."

Ethan added, "The Peach Blossom Barn is not a true start-up, although it feels like one, because it is essentially another service of the Peach Blossom Retreat."

"I didn't think of it like that. I'm glad we had the time to discuss that phone call because it would have gnawed at me, and I wouldn't have brought it up in one of our quick meetings," Morgan said.

When their food arrived, their conversation stopped except for an occasional comment about how delicious the food was.

After all of them had eaten their fill, their server reappeared and handed out dessert menus. "What are we having for dessert?"

Jenna and Morgan shook their heads.

Shane glanced at Ethan. "I don't think any of us have room for dessert. We'll take the check now."

"It's already covered. Come back and see us real soon."

Morgan narrowed her eyes as she rose. "That was you, wasn't it, Boss Lady?"

Jenna grinned. "I knew we'd talk about business. It was a team bonding event."

"You might have been a little sneaky, but it was a great idea to get the four of us together away from the Peach Blossom Retreat," Ethan said.

Jenna sniffed. "I'm not sneaky, I'm strategic, and it actually was not my idea. This was a Morgan scheme."

Shane laughed.

"I'll see you in the morning, Boss Lady," Morgan said.

"Do you want to wait inside while I warm up the truck?" Ethan asked.

Jenna gazed at his face. *He's being nice.*

Even over the busy dining area, Renee's voice carried to where they stood near the door. "I think it would be a perfect place for a wedding."

Jenna shuddered. "No, I'll brave it."

Ethan smiled as he opened the door. "Renee's voice really carries, doesn't it?"

The wind took away Jenna's breath as she dashed to the truck, but Ethan strode alongside her. He opened the door and held it until she climbed in then closed the door.

After he climbed into the truck, Jenna said, "That wind is fierce; I'm not sure I could have closed the door."

The wind buffeted the truck as Ethan drove toward the inn.

"Thank you for offering me a ride. My car would be all over the road in this wind."

"I thought about that too; I'm glad you went with me. We had an interesting discussion, didn't we? It was nice to talk with Shane outside of work, and I enjoyed getting to know you and Morgan better. I didn't realize how close you two are."

"I'm a little surprised myself because I'm definitely not an extrovert."

Ethan smiled. "Morgan makes up for it, doesn't she?"

Jenna giggled. "We do keep each other balanced."

"Ryan called me right before I left. He wants me to tell Katy he'll be here on Friday afternoon."

"I don't know why, but I thought he'd be here Saturday, not Friday."

"Plans change." Ethan chuckled. "He wants to take her to a dog park on Saturday."

"She'll love it."

Ethan nodded as he parked. "I'll hold the door."

As they hurried to the inn's back door, Ethan shielded Jenna from the sharp wind gusts. "I'll watch Katy if you want to go inside."

"I've stood outside with her on a lot of frosty nights." Jenna side-glanced at Ethan's sad face. "But I'll take you up on it."

Ethan smiled. "Good."

Jenna released Katy from the kitchen, and then Ethan took Katy for a walk. Jenna hovered by the back door. When Ethan and Katy returned, she opened the door and Katy dashed inside.

"Did you want to come in for a bit?" Jenna asked.

"You probably have a few things to do, so I'll see you in the morning." Ethan leaned down to kiss her, and Jenna stood on her tiptoes. After a lingering kiss, Ethan said, "Good night, Jenna."

She smiled. "Good night."

After she closed the door, Jenna said, "I'm going to make some tea and take it into the living room, Katy."

Katy followed Jenna into the kitchen then into the living room.

Jenna sat in the yellow chair and talked about her evening. The chimes blew in the wind, and the yellow chair was warm and comforting.

"When we arrived home, Ethan took Katy for a walk then we shared a sweet kiss. I'm not ready for a man in my life, but it was a pleasant kiss."

Jenna gazed at Nettie's portrait. Nettie smiled. *Sure.*

"No, really. It was just a friendly goodnight kiss, but I'm not interested in a complication right now."

Nettie's eyelids fluttered.

"Cut it out," Jenna growled.

As she and Katy headed toward her bedroom, the chimes jingled.

After Jenna changed into her pajamas, she yawned, and Katy yawned. Jenna turned off her light and tensed when she heard Renee in the hall.

"Jenna must already be in her room; I wanted to tell her what a great night I had. Maybe she's just reading. I'll go knock on her door; she'll want to hear this."

"She might be asleep, Renee. You can talk to her in the morning," Sophia said.

"I can just see if she's awake. The first thing she will say to me in the morning is why didn't you tell me this last night? My evening was absolutely fascinating."

"Leave her alone, Renee. If she was awake, she would be in the living room, and she isn't. Do you see any light coming from her door? I don't. Let her sleep."

Renee grumbled all the way up the stairs and to her room.

Thank you, Sophia. Jenna rolled over and the quiet darkness settled around her.

Chapter Twelve

Jenna woke at five thirty and threw on her robe. Katy nosed the bedroom door as Jenna opened it. They hurried to the back door.

"I'm staying inside, Katy. I'll go out with you later this morning."

When Katy returned, Jenna fed her breakfast.

After Jenna showered and changed, she finished packing her things in the open box then sealed it. "Darlene's probably here. You can spend some time with her if you like or go with me to the office after I grab a cup of coffee."

When they went into the kitchen, Darlene smiled at Katy. "Good morning, beautiful girl. Are you ready for your second breakfast?"

Katy grinned, and her tail went into overdrive.

"Darlene, the vet said we shouldn't overfeed Katy; it's not good for her health."

"I just have a tiny sliver of chicken for her. Lean protein is good for her." Darlene held the tidbit, and Katy sat.

After Darlene sneaked a second snack of chicken to Katy, she poured a cup of coffee. "Here you are. Take it to your office; Morgan's not here yet."

While Jenna reviewed her notes from the previous day, Morgan came into the office. "Nicci stopped me in the hallway. She was looking for you but asked if they could use the barn or the dining room for an important all-hands meeting of Orion Technical Industries. Orion called a meeting of his senior staff, and they needed a space where they could meet for about three hours. She said they will cover the cost of furnishing the barn and any other extra charges if that would make a difference."

"How many people?"

"She said a maximum of six."

"It's too early to call the local big box store, but we need the retail price of a round table that seats eight, and eight folding chairs. Look it up online for a price and add in shipping. I'm assuming retail would have higher prices than what we're paying for the tables and chairs we've ordered. Find a caterer who can cater coffee and snacks on short notice and get a quote from them. Add our fee to the caterer's and give Nicci a quote for the use of the barn for a day plus the furniture and the caterer with our fee."

"Shouldn't I charge them a half day?"

"No, we don't want to get into that. Our minimum is one day."

"Okay, Boss Lady." Morgan sent a text. "I let Nicci know you approved it, and I would get her a quote within the hour unless I had trouble finding a caterer on short notice."

Before Morgan sat at her desk to make calls, her phone buzzed with a text. "Nicci said we're awesome."

"We knew that." Jenna grinned.

While Morgan was on hold with a caterer, Jenna said, "Would it help if I found tables?"

Morgan nodded as she explained to the caterer what they needed and the short lead time.

After she hung up, Morgan said, "We've got a caterer. What do you have, Boss Lady?"

"Our local super center's website says they have the tables and chairs. I ordered them for curbside pickup at eight thirty; we should rent a work truck. Do you want to do that?"

"I'd love to. I'll check the price and availability of a rental truck or panel van. The hardware store opens at eight, so I'll go early and scope it out to see if they have any available. That gives me the option to look somewhere else if they don't. If they have one available and their paperwork doesn't take too long, that should work. I'll be the first delivery guy in heels."

"I'll snap a photo at the barn when you get there. Let's pull together a grand total and send a quote to Nicci by email that can be signed electronically. Don't put it in the quote, but tell her their meeting can begin at eleven. Does that give our caterer enough time?"

Morgan nodded as she pulled up a quote template then typed.

She sighed. "Okay, that's done. I'll follow up with a text."

"It's almost seven. I'll take care of the breakfast."

When they hurried into the kitchen, Morgan left.

Darlene said, "You were busy, so everything is set out. You just need to unlock the door at seven. Where's Morgan going in such a rush?"

"Thank you, Darlene; I really appreciate it. We have our first customer for the Peach Blossom Barn. Orion Tech Industries is assembling all their senior executives here, so Nicci asked if they could have a meeting at the barn, and it looks like Morgan and I have pulled it together, except now we're hustling to get everything ready."

"Congratulations; I'm not surprised. You and Morgan are the unstoppable team."

"Thank you," Jenna said.

Darlene ducked her head to hide her red cheeks. "Anybody could have seen it; I was just the first to tell you."

When Jenna unlocked the dining room door a few minutes after seven, Nicci was waiting in the hall.

"Thank you for scrambling for us, Jenna. I told Orion you could do it. He called one of Renee's old friends to occupy her for the day. Can you pretend her friend is a day guest? She still hasn't confirmed, but we're hoping she can be here by eight."

"Deception? Me? It might be a stretch, but I'll do my best." Jenna giggled.

Nicci chuckled as she poured herself a cup of coffee and wrapped silverware in a napkin then used the tongs to put two mini-quiches and a strawberry Danish on her plate.

She put her plate on a table. "It's been my experience that too many times the hotel continental breakfast was who-knows-how-old commercial mini-pastries and yogurt sitting in a pan of water with melting ice."

"Ugh. I remember those days when I was corporate."

"Your Darlene is a treasure. Everything I've eaten here has been freshly baked and prepared with wholesome ingredients."

"We have to keep up with our Italian neighbors."

Nicci smiled. "My food last night was delicious. I have not eaten a meal that authentic since my last trip to Rome when Sergio and I found a small restaurant off the beaten track. We need to hang out in small towns more often."

After Nicci left, Jenna stayed in the dining room since Sophia and Renee would be down any minute. At seven-thirty, she frowned. "Maybe they went to pick up Renee's friend."

Her phone buzzed a text from Sophia. "barn"

Jenna grabbed her coat and keys and shouted, "Darlene, call Ethan and tell him Sophia is at the barn."

"Right away."

When Jenna opened the driver's door, Katy leaped over her and into the passenger seat. Jeanna climbed in and spun gravel as she accelerated down the driveway.

"Hang on, Katy."

Jenna swerved into the left lane when she made her nearly uncontrolled turn onto the road, but she accelerated to straighten up and eased back to her lane. She slowed when she neared the turn to the driveway to the barn. After she turned, she sped up the driveway then slammed to a stop.

When she jumped out, she left her door open, and Katy leaped out behind her. Katy growled then snarled as she raced ahead of Jenna to the barn.

Jenna sprinted into the barn. Katy growled as she stood guard next to Sophia who lay awkwardly on her back with a black hood over her head. Jenna raced to Sophia and pulled off the hood.

Sophia's lifeless blue eyes stared at the rafters. Jenna kneeled next to her and screamed as she pulled out her pocket knife and cut the pink silk scarf wrapped around Sophia's neck.

As darkness closed in around her, and her head began spinning, Jenna bent down to rest her head on her thighs and sobbed.

When she heard Ethan's truck, she slowed her breathing and then she exhaled. *I have to know.*

She picked up the silk scarf and clutched it to her chest.

A sharp pain in the back. Pink scarf! Send barn to Jenna.

Jenna gently rolled Sophia toward her and tasted iron in the back of her throat. She fought the rising bile, then she saw the knife in Sophia's back and swallowed hard.

Ethan shouted, "Jenna!"

Jenna whispered, "Barn. She told her phone to send me a text. I was too slow."

After Ethan called nine-one-one and reported what they had found, he gently lifted Jenna up from the floor and held her.

"She texted me barn."

"It's okay; I gotcha."

"I picked up the pink scarf and held it close to my heart. It told me. Sophia felt a sharp pain in her back. There's a knife buried to the hilt in her back. Then she saw the pink scarf, so she told her phone to text barn to me. And then she was gone. I got here as fast as I could." Jenna broke down. "But it wasn't fast enough."

"Jenna, she bled out from the knife wound. There is a lot of blood under her."

"I took off the black hood, and her eyes were staring past me. I saw the pink scarf and cut it."

"That was good."

Jenna sobbed. "I didn't know about the knife until I held the scarf next to me."

"Let's go sit in my truck and wait for the sheriff."

"I think I left my phone in my car."

"I'll get it for you."

After Jenna and Katy were in his truck, Ethan handed Jenna her phone.

Jenna's hands shook as she held her phone and sent a text to Morgan. "Abort. Complete change of plans. Cancel tables and chairs and van rental. Cancel caterer and send her full payment for her trouble. Tell Nicci they can have their meeting in the dining room. Will talk later. I will let Darlene know."

Morgan replied, "Okay, Boss."

Jenna sent a text to Darlene. "Meeting in the dining room today from ten until mid-afternoon. Can you do snacks and lunch for six people?"

Darlene replied, "Sure can."

Jenna dropped her phone into her lap and covered face with her hands as the tears flowed. "I tried to warn her. What made her come here?"

Jenna swiped at her face to clear away the tears. "Her phone. I need to see her phone. I know where it is."

When Jenna jumped out of Ethan's truck, he shouted, "Jenna, wait."

Jenna ignored him and raced to Sophia.

She didn't have her purse. Her tight skirt has no pockets.

Jenna pulled her gloves out of her coat pocket and pulled out Sophia's phone from the top of her shirt.

"What are you doing?" Ethan asked.

"I have a theory. Do you have a pencil with an eraser?"

"You mean the one I always have behind my ear?"

"Yes, I want it." Jenna used the pencil to tap so she could check Sophia's messages and found a text Sophia had received not long before she sent the text to Jenna. *From Morgan?*

She read the text. "Jenna needs you at the barn ASAP."

Jenna closed Sophia's messages and returned her phone to its spot where Sophia carried it.

"Here's your pencil, thanks." Jenna's teeth chattered as she spoke. "I'm have to go back to the truck. I'm cold to the bone."

Ethan gaped at her. "Are you saying that's my fault?"

"Don't crab at me."

Jenna continued to shiver after she was in the truck. She texted Morgan. "Do you see a text from you to Sophia about forty-five minutes ago?"

Morgan replied, "No. No texts from me to her all day."

When the sheriff pulled in next to Ethan's truck, he approached Jenna.

"Jenna, come sit in my cruiser so both of us can be warm. I've got the heat cranked up. Ethan, would you show me what you found?"

After Jenna was in the cruiser, she sighed. "The heat feels good."

Katy followed Ethan and the sheriff as they walked to Sophia. Jenna watched them. Ethan spoke, and the sheriff nodded. The sheriff kneeled close to Sophia's body and peered at her back. He frowned at the hood and shook his head at the pink silk scarf.

The two of them returned. Ethan opened the back door of his truck, and Katy jumped in. While Ethan climbed into his truck, the sheriff joined Jenna in his cruiser.

After she told him about the text and finding Sophia, he asked, "What was it about the barn that made you dash here right away when you got the text?"

"I've been nervous about the barn since I found Bobbie. Sophia and I chatted a few times, so she knew how I felt about the barn."

"Jenna, I know there's more," the sheriff said.

Jenna bit her lip then exhaled. "Sophia wanted me to give a camera to Nicci. When she handed me the camera, I had a vision of her lying lifeless on the barn floor with a pink scarf tied around her neck. I immediately put the camera on a dining table and warned her not to go to the barn."

"What was her reaction?"

"She knew I was serious."

"What do you know about the relationship between Morgan and Sophia?"

"Sophia was a guest, so both Morgan and I were friendly toward her."

"Did Morgan know how you felt about the barn?"

"Yes."

"But you and Morgan moved forward to have an event there today."

"It was my idea because I was certain the energy of a group of people being here would give me a fresh perspective on the barn."

"Why do I always feel like I'm talking to the tip of an iceberg when I talk to you?"

"Is that how you feel?"

The sheriff exhaled. "Not really. Was that too dramatic?"

"For you, yes. For me, it would be something I would say."

"Why is your car here? Didn't you come here with Ethan?"

"No, when I got the barn text, I told Darlene to text Ethan and tell him I went to the barn before I left the inn."

"So Ethan knows how you feel about the barn."

Jenna nodded.

"Who else?"

"Shane. I think that's all."

"Are you okay with driving yourself to the inn?"

Jenna nodded.

"If I think of any more questions, I'll drop by. The barn and the surrounding area will be off limits for anyone for a while."

The sheriff walked with Jenna to Ethan's truck. After she opened the truck's back door, Katy jumped out.

When Jenna headed down the driveway, Katy leaned over the backseat with her head on Jenna's shoulder. Jenna glanced in the rearview mirror; Ethan was following her.

He joined her as she and Katy strolled to the back door. "Do you feel safe moving to the cottage?"

"Of course."

"Let's go inside. Is Morgan here?"

"She's on her way back from shopping."

Ethan sent two texts. "Shane will be here soon too."

"Who did you send the second text to?"

"Nothing gets past you, does it?"

Jenna smiled. "Nope, except I didn't know you always had a pencil behind your ear."

"When they get here, let's get you moved. Are you all packed?"

"All packed. I guess I'm ready to move." Jenna sniffled. "I can't get Sophia out of my mind. Seeing her was like seeing Bobbie again."

Ethan hugged her. "I understand, and I'm so sorry."

Jenna leaned against him. "Thank you."

She exhaled. "We should probably take my boxes from my room to the kitchen, so Wendy can clean my room for its next actual guest."

When they went into her room, Ethan glanced around. "Wendy's already been here."

Jenna frowned. "No, she hasn't. This room still needs to be cleaned."

"It looks okay to me."

"It isn't. I guess Wendy's job is safe with you around." Jenna's smile was weak.

"Maybe Wendy will give me some lessons." Ethan returned her smile. "You want these two boxes in the kitchen, right?"

While Ethan picked up the two boxes, Jenna said, "Let me take one more look to see if I've left anything."

When Jenna looked under the bed, she frowned. "How did that get there?" She pulled out the pamphlet that was Bobbie's marker. After she folded it, she stuck it into her back pocket.

Ethan stopped in the doorway. "What's that?"

"A random pamphlet. I'll look at it later to see if it's a throwaway, or if there is some reason I wanted to keep it."

When they reached the kitchen, Jenna opened the door for Ethan.

Darlene waved her wooden spoon. "Are those the boxes that go to your casita, Jenna?"

Jenna nodded.

"How have you been getting by all this time with practically nothing?"

"I've been doing laundry every other day or so."

Darlene shook her head and mumbled in Spanish.

Ethan elbowed Jenna and smirked.

He's right. I'll hear more about this later.

Morgan and Shane came in the back door together.

"We need a quick meeting in the office," Ethan said.

Jenna furrowed her brow. *Since when is he the boss of my office?*

When Morgan looped her arm through Jenna's as they headed to the office, Jenna exhaled. *Maybe we are a team.*

After they were in the office, Ethan told Morgan and Shane about finding Sophia.

Morgan moved her chair closer to Jenna. "You tried your best."

Jenna nodded. *No, I didn't.*

"Morgan, should we cancel the meeting at the barn?" Shane asked.

Morgan glanced at Jenna, who shook her head.

"No, it's been shifted to the dining room. Boss Lady caught me before I bought the tables, and I let Nicci know their meeting location changed. We'll pay the caterer, and Darlene will provide their snack and lunch."

Shane and Ethan gaped at Jenna.

"Are those the texts you sent while we waited for the sheriff?" Ethan asked.

Jenna nodded. "I knew we couldn't have set up at the barn, and the sheriff confirmed it."

Ethan shook his head and mumbled, "Amazing."

"Give me a minute. I'll be right back," Morgan said.

"Under the circumstances, is it right for us to assume they'll still hold their meeting?" Shane asked.

"The choice is theirs, not ours," Ethan said.

Jenna nodded. "That's true, but I wanted to have an alternative to offer them."

"But what if Darlene cooks all that food and they decide to cancel?" Shane asked.

Jenna and Ethan stared at him.

Shane's face reddened. "I just realized what I said. The food won't go to waste."

Morgan returned. "I told Darlene and Wendy about Sophia. Wendy hadn't gotten to Sophia's room yet, so she'll leave it alone for now. Nicci called me. The sheriff contacted Orion who decided to move forward with their meeting because everyone is already in town or on the road."

"It was genius to develop an alternative plan on the fly and immediately put it into action, Jenna," Shane said.

Jenna glanced at the floor. "Thank you, but I knew I could hand off everything to Morgan."

"So, what do we do now?" Morgan asked.

Jenna exhaled. "We need to set up the dining room for a meeting."

"But first, let's move Jenna into her cottage," Ethan said.

Shane grinned, and Morgan beamed.

"Darlene wants to go too," Morgan said.

As Jenna rose from her seat, she frowned. "There are only two boxes."

"Yes, and I'm embarrassed for you." Morgan giggled. "I'll carry one."

"I'll get the other one," Shane said.

Before they left the inn, Darlene shouted, "Wendy, we're leaving."

Wendy dashed down the stairs to go along.

Jenna stared at the gathering. *It takes this many people to move two boxes?*

After they were outside, Ethan put his arm around Jenna while Katy waited to see which direction they were going.

When she side-glanced at him, he said, "It's cold."

She shivered. "You got that right."

As they strolled toward the cottage with the parade of people behind them, Jenna noticed a truck parked in the spot where the construction workers always parked. "What's Terrell doing here? I thought the cottage was ready. Is there a problem?"

"If there was one, you'd fix it," Ethan said.

Jenna tensed and bit her lip. *How do I take that?*

Ethan whispered, "That was a compliment."

"Oh."

When they were close to the cottage, Terrell grinned as he waved from the cottage porch near the door.

Ethan reached into his pocket and pulled out a silky pale green ribbon with a bright brass key tied to it. "This is your key to your cottage."

Jenna stuck the key into the lock and glanced at her grinning friends.

After she unlocked the door and stepped inside, she froze. "Wow, this is beautiful."

"Move it, Boss Lady, so we can all see; it's cold out here," Darlene growled.

Jenna stepped inside, and everyone went in with her. Katy immediately began investigating the rooms.

Morgan said, "I'm in charge of your tour. If there's anything you don't like, Shane did it, but if you love it, it was my idea."

"If you absolutely hate it, it was my idea." Ethan's eyes twinkled.

Jenna giggled. "Good to know."

Terrell grinned. "Enjoy your new home, Jenna. I'll let Mr. Moore know how pleased you are."

After Terrell left, Darlene asked, "When do we get our tour?"

Morgan smiled as she swept her hand in a wide arc. "This is your great room. You have a sofa, a matching armchair, a coffee table that Shane and I found in a secondhand shop, and a gas fireplace to keep you toasty. Let me show you something special by the front window."

Jenna's eyes widened at the pale green soft chair with creamy pink camellias. "It's the sister of Nettie's yellow chair. I didn't know there was a second chair."

"None of us did except Mr. Moore. He told Foster about it, and Foster went on a quest to find it. He found it in the back of a junk shop in the next county. We had a professional clean it, and here it is," Morgan beamed.

Jenna sat in the chair and leaned back. When she sighed and rested her hands on the soft arms, the wind blew the tree tops. *Welcome home.*

Tears welled up in Jenna's eyes. "This is so sweet, and the key's ribbon is the same color as the chair."

Darlene swiped at her eyes with the back of her forearm. "Let's keep moving."

Morgan headed toward the bedrooms. "You have two bedrooms. I decorated them like the rooms at the inn."

Jenna followed Morgan to the larger of the two bedrooms.

"It's completely furnished and absolutely beautiful. How did you find time to do all this, Morgan?" Jenna asked.

Morgan grinned.

"This lovely cottage is you, Jenna." Wendy sniffled. "You'll hire me to clean the cottage once a week too, right?"

"Done," Morgan said.

"Don't I get a say?" Jenna asked.

"Of course you do. We'll talk." Morgan winked at Wendy who beamed.

Jenna rolled her eyes. *I was set up by those two.*

After Morgan showed off the second bedroom and the office that overlooked the woods at the back of the cottage, she opened the bathroom door. "Shane designed your bathroom to be like the ones at the inn."

"That was really smart, Shane; I love those bathrooms." Jenna peered inside the bathroom. "Morgan, new towels with our peach blossom logo?"

"Don't you love them?" Wendy asked.

Darlene went into the bathroom. "Boss Lady, you have to see this."

Darlene pointed at the pale green throw rug in front of the sink. "See the peach blossom in the corner?"

Wendy tugged on Jenna's sleeve. "There's more."

Morgan moved on. "This is your utility room, and here's the kitchen. You have plenty of room to cook and entertain. Peek out the back door."

"The porch is much larger than the front porch."

"We decided you needed somewhere you could entertain people," Shane said."

"Frequently entertain people," Morgan added. "Which is why you also have a dining table that seats six."

Jenna raised an eyebrow. "Does Mr. Moore know you people put all these extras in for yourselves?"

Morgan snorted. "He was the major instigator. If you have any issues, take them up with him."

Morgan strode to the front door and opened it. "And that, ladies and gentlemen, is the end of our tour."

Darlene and Wendy rushed out, and Shane followed them. When Jenna started toward the door, Morgan said, "Come to the dining room after you unpack."

"Do you need any help to unpack?" Ethan asked.

"No."

"See you later."

After Morgan and Ethan left, Jenna hugged Katy. "Don't you just love our cottage? It was worth the long wait, wasn't it? Did you see Morgan even found a throw rug for you like the one we lost in the fire? I'll bet Mr. Moore was behind that."

Her phone buzzed a text from Nicci. "Call when convenient."

Jenna called her.

"Thanks for calling so promptly. If it's possible, could you add a second person to my room? I have an overly protective friend who wants to stay close to me."

"I can add her; what's her name? We might be able to find a rollaway bed by tomorrow."

"The thing is, I don't want anyone to know he's here. Remember the man who left Orion Tech Industries for a startup? He left Orion Tech but still has access. Sergio found something, but he's sitting on it until we understand the source. Do the names Pink Lady or Daffodil mean anything to you?"

"Yes."

"Do you know who the Pink Lady is?"

"Pink Lady was Bobbie. You must be Daffodil."

Nicci smiled. "Have you ever heard of Beansy, Bean Counter?"

Jenna laughed. "I did not put that together. Bean-see."

"I didn't know until I met you. What have you put together so far?"

Jenna paced as she talked. "Daffodil is monitoring Arti, and Jazzy is marking Daffodil. The first sleezy character I saw was Angel Girl. After a group had donated a sizeable sum for Angel Girl, Knit One offered to make sure the money went to Angel Girl, and everyone was grateful because they were stressing over how to do it. Angel Girl and Knit One quickly disappeared from the group. All the groups had an Angel Girl with a different hard-luck story and with a different name. The Angel girls were in the middle of their story or suddenly disappeared after collecting a certain amount of money or account numbers. I'm not sure which. Every group also had a Knit One, which was actually easy to spot after I decoded something Bobbie said. She said it was odd Artie had favorite numbers, so I think Arti is Knit One, Viola Three, and all the others I found who offered to make sure the money or account information went to the current Angel Girl fund."

"Wow. Anything else?" Nicci chuckled.

"Bobbie mentioned Otis Elevators. I realized she was referencing OTI."

"Orion Technical Industries," Nicci whispered. "What did she say?"

"She said, 'Otis elevators have a lovely front and an ugly rear door.' My interpretation is that something at Orion Tech has a back door. It must be a conduit to divert funds, and the funds keep pouring in because Angel Girl is such a smooth talker. I felt the tug to open my wallet," Jenna said.

"So, what would you do?" Nicci asked.

"Even if we could find and close the back door, what if there is a contingency? I'd have one if I had that much money on the line. Say that you closed the back door; we'd have a celebration and move on. Angel Girl and Knit One can implement their contingency plan, which might not be as convenient, but will still be as lucrative."

"You know I'm picking your brain. I can see how one person could do all of this. What do you think?"

"This is definitely one of those scams that the fewer people involved the better. A person with good automation skills could have developed and managed the front end, but it doesn't seem like a set-it-and-forget-it system. It still would require a certain level of monitoring, and even if that was automated, there would be some situations that would require intervening and could be time-sensitive. I think the trickier piece is moving the money. I don't know if that could be automated without careful controls in place. That's your expertise, not mine."

"Maybe we could have a chat this evening while everyone goes out on the town unless you have plans," Nicci said.

"My only plans for tonight are to relax. I'll make you a second key and ask Wendy to slide it under your door." Jenna furrowed her brow. "Did you know Sophia very well?"

"Sophia and I have been working closely on this for a while. She could go where I couldn't because everyone saw her as just a kid with a camera."

Jenna smiled. "I think that is the way she saw herself too."

"You're right; she uploaded all her photos and videos to a cloud we shared. The only exception was the photos on her camera she gave you. There might be something there." Nicci hung up.

Jenna furrowed her brow. "How did Bobbie Moore know there was a back door at Orion Technical Industries?"

Jenna stared at her boxes. "I need to check her spiral notebook again, but first, let's help in the dining room, Katy. I can read and unpack later."

CHAPTER THIRTEEN

When Jenna and Katy hurried into the kitchen, Morgan was sitting at the kitchen table.

"Can I help with the dining room?" Jenna asked.

"All done. There actually wasn't much to do. Darlene is planning a light snack of sausage bites and mini-cinnamon rolls. What can I do for you?"

"Could you make a second room key for Nicci's guest room and ask Wendy to slip it under Nicci's door? I'll fill in the holes later."

"Sure can."

"Jenna!" Renee screamed out from the registration desk.

Katy slipped under the kitchen table at the sound of the screeching voice.

"Katy's got the right idea." Morgan covered her ears.

"Stay here with Morgan, Katy. I'll see what Renee wants."

"I'm right here, Renee. How can I help you?" Jenna asked.

"Did you hear about Sophia? She's dead! My closest friend is dead," Renee cried out.

Renee glanced wildly around her then whispered, "Fred has never liked Sophia. I warned her to keep her nose out of things she knows nothing about and not to cross him, but she wouldn't listen to me."

Is she saying Fred killed Sophia?

"What am I going to do without her?" Renee wailed as she flounced to the stairs then tromped up to her room.

"You might have to do your own work," Jenna muttered as she went into the kitchen.

"What was that all about?" Morgan asked.

"Renee was personally inconvenienced by Sophia's death."

Morgan shook her head. "So, I assume we'll meet our day visitors at the front door and show them the living room, the rest room, and the dining room. Should we tell them if they want to go to their car, they should use the side exit door? How would they get back in? Do we stay near the front door with our master keys to let them in?"

"Ugh. I'm really glad you thought of it. What do you think about issuing each one of them a guest day card?"

"What? We don't have any such thing."

"We could create them. Select a color for the cards that we haven't used, so the day key cards will be easily identifiable. Create room-less key cards that don't unlock a room but do unlock the side door until 8:00 PM. Issue them by number to each person and record their names, just like we do with our regular room keys, so we can track those that are not returned and charge them for their key."

"This is great. I'll send a quick text to Nicci to let her know before I create them."

Jenna heard a car then a knock at the front door.

She frowned as she hurried to the door. Renee dashed down the stairs. "Open the door, Jenna. It's Isabelle, my editor and my all-time best friend. I'll bet Orion called her because he knew how overwrought I am over Sophia."

When Jenna opened the door, she thought she was going to pass out from the decibels of the two women's screams. They clutched each other in a hug and hopped in a circle while they screamed.

"Can you give Isabelle a guest room for the weekend? Pretty please?" Renee pouted. "On Orion, of course."

"I'd love to, but we're fully booked."

Jenna turned toward the kitchen.

"You can take care of that," Renee said. "Come see my room, Isabelle. The maid cleans every day. Can you believe that?"

I'll ask Nicci if Orion plans to tip housekeeping.

When Jenna went into the kitchen, Morgan glanced at her.

"It has to be Renee. Ethan is with his crew working on the Peachy Suite."

"Renee wants her friend who just showed up to have a room, and of course, she assumes Orion would pay for it."

"We don't have any rooms available," Morgan said. "I can't see Renee sharing her room, can you?"

"Not really. I have to ask Nicci if Orion will pick up the housekeeping tip for all the rooms. If you can chat alone with Nicci before I can, would you tell her our guests always tip housekeeping, and we don't think Renee will."

"Are you sure?"

"That Renee won't tip? I'm positive. It will be a simple conversation to have with a glass of wine in hand. I hear cars coming up the driveway."

"Good. The day keys are in this envelope." Morgan pointed to the envelope on the table. "I'll be the tour guide and point out the guest entrance and exit then we'll move past the living room and rest room then into the dining room."

Jenna nodded. "After everyone is in the dining room, I'll welcome them and explain how their day key works. You can sit at a table and register them and give them a key. They'll have plenty of time to socialize and cruise the sideboard before their meeting starts."

"I hear car doors closing," Jenna said.

"How do I look?" Morgan asked.

"You look like a talented, unpredictable operations manager who gets things done because she knows what to do and does the opposite instead," Jenna said.

Morgan laughed. "That is how we work, isn't it?"

Before she left the kitchen, Morgan said, "Thank you, Jenna. I needed a good laugh."

Jenna stood near the dining room door and watched with horror as Renee tiptoed down the stairs with her friend standing on the top step with her arms crossed.

"Oh, come on, Isabelle. Orion would expect me to attend the meeting, and you're welcome to sit with me, so

I'll have someone to talk to while they talk about boring business stuff," Renee whispered.

"It was bad enough you talked me into crashing a B&B with no reservation when my days of couch surfing are behind me. I'm not crashing a business meeting," Isabelle said.

"You don't have to; you can just sit by yourself in my room and pout."

"Let's take the tour at the peach orchard or go shopping. I saw the cutest dress in their window that would look stunning on you."

"Really?" Renee preened. "Stunning?"

"Absolutely. We can go into town first so you can try on that dress. If you like it, it's my treat." Isabelle smiled and waved her wallet.

"Perfect. I'll just say hello to everybody then we can go."

Isabelle narrowed her eyes as Renee continued down the stairs.

Jenna quietly closed the dining room door.

Morgan opened the front door, and Nicci, Orion, and Fred came in first, followed by two women and two men.

After everyone was inside, Morgan began their tour. She explained the guest exit and entrance and how they could come and go during the day.

The group followed her to the living room. One woman sat on the sofa and patted the cushions. "I'll be right here if you need me. This room calls to me."

It does do that." Morgan smiled as she continued, "The restroom is here, and you'll be meeting in the dining room."

"I'm Jenna Ross, welcome to Peach Blossom Retreat."
She opened the dining room door. "This is your meeting
room for the day."

As Orion headed toward the dining room, Renee
caught up with him and slipped her arm through his.
He stopped and patted her hand, and she smiled and
fluttered her eyelashes.

"Sorry, Renee. I'll see you later. This is an executive
meeting," he whispered as he removed her arm from his.

Renee whined, "I know, but you need me to be there."

Orion shook his head. "Not this time. Let me know
when you're back in town, and we'll do lunch."

He turned his back on her and went into the dining
room. Renee jutted out her chin as she followed him, but
Jenna, Nicci, and Fred blocked her from going in. When
she tried to push past Jenna, Fred glowered at her. "Don't
embarrass yourself, Renee."

When Nicci and Fred went into the dining room,
Jenna closed the door.

Morgan entered the dining room through the kitchen
door and sat at her table.

When Jenna smiled and raised her hand, Fred
whistled, and the conversations hushed.

Everyone turned toward her. "We are so excited you
are here with us. We couldn't have found better partners
for our inaugural hosting event at the Peach Blossom
Retreat."

Jenna directed attention to the sideboard by
motioning with her open hand. "Please help yourself to
a morning snack, and coffee, hot tea, or water. We will
serve a lunch buffet at one o'clock, and I'm sure you will

be pleased. Our chef has gone all out to tickle your taste buds."

The two new women glanced at each other and smiled.

Jenna gestured towards Morgan's table, prompting a wave from Morgan. "Morgan will register you for a day key card you can use to return by the guest entrance."

Jenna continued, "We won't hover during your meeting. Nicci and Fred have our numbers to text us if you need anything. We are truly thrilled you are meeting at the Peach Blossom Retreat."

Everyone clapped, and Jenna felt her face warm.

Orion rose, and everyone became quiet. "Jenna, your spirit to overcome any obstacle and refusing to fail is an inspiration to all of us. We have hard choices to discuss today; I challenge everyone here to crush their obstacles and refuse to fail."

Everyone rose to their feet and cheered.

While the executives turned to the sideboard or strode to Morgan's table, Nicci rushed to Jenna's side and hugged her. "You are so inspiring. You've set exactly the right tone for our meeting. Thank you."

While Nicci joined the line at the sideboard, Fred strode to Jenna with a cup of coffee in one hand, and two pastries wrapped in a napkin in the other. "Your inn is a hidden jewel, Jenna. I told my wife earlier this week where we were meeting, and she checked your website early this morning. She has been looking for somewhere different for us to go for our anniversary this year. She'll make our reservations as soon as I clear my work calendar, which I was supposed to have done earlier this month."

Jenna smiled. "That's wonderful news. We'd enjoy meeting her."

"She's a dynamo, just like you. You two would definitely get along." Fred chuckled as he joined the line at Morgan's desk.

Jenna peered at the sideboard then went into the kitchen for another platter of Danishes.

When she returned, one of the men she didn't know snatched the single remaining Danish on the platter and held up the line behind him, so Jenna could make the exchange. He grinned when she set down the full platter and helped himself to another Danish.

Jenna smiled as she hurried to the kitchen. She poured a cup of coffee and sat at the counter to catch her breath. Katy leaned against her leg.

Jenna stroked Katy's back. "I didn't realize how much I dreaded speaking in front of a group. It was a small, friendly group, but they still terrified me. Isn't that silly?"

Morgan exhaled when she came into the kitchen. "Everybody's set. I'll never make fun of how much food Darlene prepares again. Those people are pastry vultures. Your opening talk was warm and welcoming while you told them what they could expect from us. It was very smooth; I should have recorded it."

"I'm glad you didn't. If I'd seen you recording, I would have passed out."

"No, you would have told me to cut it out." Morgan headed toward the office. "I have a lot of follow up to do for the barn. Our guests might need one more check to remove the empty platters, but they don't need to be refilled because all of them have a napkin with an emergency pastry on the table where they are sitting. This is obviously not their first meeting together." Morgan chuckled as she went into their office.

Jenna straightened the kitchen then peered into the dining room. The group was reviewing a document while Fred spoke. She slipped in, picked up the empty platters, and returned to the kitchen.

After she put the platters into the dishwasher, Jenna rubbed Katy's ear. "Let's join Morgan in the office."

Before she reached the door, her phone buzzed a text from Nicci.

"Sergio will be here in a few minutes. He has his key." Jenna replied, "I'll listen for him."

When she heard a truck in the driveway, she put on her coat and stepped out onto the front porch with Katy to greet Sergio and to show him where Nicci's room was.

Jenna watched while Katy chased a large grasshopper and then a small bird that flew up into a tree and taunted Katy.

When a man strode toward the inn, Jenna peered at him. *He looks familiar.*

The man with the scraggly beard and the beat-up ball cap smiled as he neared Jenna, and she returned his smile.

"Hello, Sergio," she said. "Nice to see you again."

"This is so funny; wait until I tell Nicci I met you long before she did." He held out his hand, and they shook.

Jenna exhaled as they released hands. *Strong and protective. No surprise there. Cop like Clint was a surprise though.*

Jenna chuckled. "I'll show you where the guest entrance is, and after you unlock the door with your key, I'll show you where your room is."

"What does your intuition tell you about me?"

Jenna side-glanced at him.

Sergio cocked his head. "I'm the friend of a friend. He mentioned you know things sometimes."

The sheriff.

She nodded. "Your friend must be the sheriff."

"Ouch. He was right. Does that give me creds?"

Jenna stopped at the door. "Unlock the door with your room key card so we know it works. The question is does it give me creds?"

"You earned your creds." Sergio unlocked the door.

"Stay, Katy," Jenna said. Katy sat on the grass while they went inside.

Jenna replied, "So did you."

"Do you have time to talk?" he asked.

"Sure. I'll show you where your room is then we can go for a walk."

Sergio dropped his backpack in Nicci's room, then they left the inn by the guest door.

"We're not likely to come across anyone on the path to the orchard," she said.

Katy dashed ahead to clear grasshoppers and small birds out of their way.

"If there was an online scam that was almost a duplicate of an old scam except it pulled in millions of dollars a year, what would it need?" Sergio asked.

"Automation."

"Okay, you know about the scam. If I told you the automation was managed at Orion Tech Industries, what would you say?"

"No surprise. There's the automation of the scam plus the automation of moving money. That's not being managed in a garage."

"You're right; how many people do you think it takes to manage all this?"

"I think two could do it, but there's always the possibility of a falling out. Only one would be better, but it would take someone highly skilled."

Sergio laughed. "The sheriff told me I should ask you to call me when you solved everything, but better yet, how about letting me step in here and take over?"

Jenna raised her hands shoulder-height. "It's all yours."

"Thanks, I think."

When they turned back, Jenna said, "Just let me know if there's something you want me to do or not do."

"If you hear or feel something I don't, let me know. Here's my business card. The cell number is mine."

When they reached the inn, Sergio headed to the guest entrance, and Jenna and Katy went in the back door and continued to the office through the kitchen.

"What's up?" Morgan asked.

"Nicci's friend is safely ensconced in her room. Nobody said anything, but I think after Renee leaves, things will change."

Morgan snorted. "I could have told you that."

Jenna nodded. "That's true."

Jenna sat in front of her computer, but before she opened her email, her phone rang. *Foster?*

"I'm at the café next to the shoe shop. Can you hear the commotion in the background?" he asked.

Jenna heard Renee's screeching voice wailing. "Renee. It sounds like she's standing right next to you."

"Seems like it to me too. She claims she was a dear friend of the woman who was murdered in the barn this morning. Of course, now everybody knows about the murder. She came in with another woman, and the two of them got into an argument about a meeting at the Peach Blossom Retreat. We all know the controversy about a promise of a room for the second woman by Renee, who is evidently a guest there. The second woman left, and I'll tell you most of the people in the café wished they had gone with her, because the caterwauling has continued. Do you suppose you could calm her down? Some people are talking about calling the police because she's making such a racket."

"Renee is very dramatic; I'll see what I can do. If I can't convince her to leave, somebody might have to call nine-one-one for an ambulance because it sounds like she's having a breakdown."

"I'll suggest that to the café owner. Can you head this way? I think he's reluctant to do anything because he's hoping she'll run out of steam, but so far, it doesn't seem likely to me."

"I'm not sure what I can do, but I'll be there as quick as I can."

After she hung up, she said, "I have to go into town. Renee was causing a commotion in the café. Foster asked me to come talk to her before someone calls the police. Hopefully, I won't be long."

"Call me if you need me," Morgan said.

As she drove to Paisley, Jenna grumbled, "Renee has to be in the spotlight for everything."

After Jenna parked at the café, she furrowed her brow. *I can't let down my guard. Sophia told me Renee was calculating and dangerous.*

When Jenna strolled into the café, Renee sat alone at a table while she screamed and pounded on the table. All the patrons turned to look at Jenna. She spied Foster sitting on a stool at the counter; he lifted his coffee cup to her and smiled. *Foster has my back.*

Jenna exhaled then strolled toward Renee who glanced at her. Her cobra smile was fleeting, but Jenna saw it. Renee continued her rant as she watched Jenna stroll to her table.

After Jenna sat with Renee, a young server rushed to her with a cup and a pot of coffee. The server poured the coffee then pointed to the menu. *Smart girl. I couldn't outshout Renee either.* Jenna shook her head, and the server moved on with her coffee pot.

Jenna sipped her coffee and watched Renee. When Renee finally took a breath, Jenna asked, "Mind if I join you?"

"What are you doing here?" Renee hissed. "Isabelle is hiding in the bathroom."

"Just a minute; I'll check on her."

Renee inhaled to resume her rant, and Jenna said, "Renee, I'm trying to help."

"Well, then hurry."

Jenna went to the women's restroom then returned to Renee's table. "She's not there."

"That sneak slipped out on me. The joke's on her; she can't get very far, I drove here. What are you doing here?"

"A friend of mine called me and said you were sick, so I came to see if I could help."

Renee snorted. "You don't know who you're messing with. I know stuff about him that could take him down, and he knows it. Orion thinks Fred is such a stellar Chief Technology Officer, and his pet Nicci is such a rock star. Nicci is nothing compared to me. I read Fred's notes that time I went to visit Orion."

She rolled her eyes. "Fred was sloppy, leaving his office unlocked like that, but his so-called administrative assistant told me to get out and called security. I knew Nicci was after Orion, so I wanted her to quit, but she was stubborn. He knows I work rings around her. I can do the work of two people, and I don't need him. He doesn't have the versatility I have. Nobody does. You really need to keep your nose out of my business. I'm going to find Isabelle and give her a piece of my mind for running out on me."

After Renee stomped out of the café, customers whistled and clapped.

Jenna shook her head and put money on the table for the two coffees.

When she rose to leave, Foster joined her, and they went outside. "You're Paisley's hero of the month, Jenna. What was that all about?"

"She and her friend had an argument, and she thought the friend was in the women's restroom, so she made sure her friend didn't miss one minute of her performance."

"Thanks for coming so quickly," Foster said.

"You're welcome." Jenna smiled as she climbed into her car.

After she started the engine, she called Morgan. "Morgan, I think Renee is unhinged. She made quite a scene in the café, and I don't want her to do the same at the inn."

"I could cancel her room key card, so if she shows up before you do, she won't be able to slip in, or I can watch for her."

"Watch for her, and I'll be there as soon as I can; maybe one of us will have a sudden inspiration in the meantime."

"I almost forgot. Darlene said to tell you our old friend Georgia from the Georgia Bureau of Investigation is in Sophia's room along with a guy she didn't know. You work on the inspiration, and I'll hold down the fort." Morgan chuckled as she hung up.

As Jenna headed toward the inn, Jenna narrowed her eyes. *I'm really confused by what Renee told me. She jumped from one topic to the next, and I was never sure who she was talking about from one sentence to the next.*

When she arrived at the inn, she exhaled. *Renee's car isn't here.*

She parked next to the cottage and smiled. *I almost forgot I live here.*

Ethan strode to her car and opened her door. As she climbed out, he asked, "Where did you go?"

"I went into town."

She glanced at his face. *He's frustrated with trying to talk to me.*

Jenna exhaled. "Foster called me because Renee had a loud argument with her friend in the café. She thought her friend had gone into the women's restroom, so she continued the fight at full volume, so her friend could hear her."

Ethan took her arm as they strolled together toward the inn. He snorted. "The friend gave her the slip."

"Exactly. I checked the women's restroom, and no one was there."

"Did that slow her down?"

"No, she went on a different rant then stormed out. Paisley is my kind of town. Everyone applauded when she left."

Ethan chuckled. "I'm sorry I wasn't there."

"What about you?" she asked.

"Shane and I were questioning some of Morgan's design choices. He's going to talk to her after lunch."

"That doesn't sound good; he's going solo?"

"We didn't want it to look like we were ganging up on her."

"Why don't you include me? Then she won't feel so targeted."

Ethan stopped. "Give me a second."

He held onto her and sent a one-handed text.

Jenna frowned at her hand. *I can't hold a phone and text with one hand. Maybe I should practice.*

"I told Shane if he included you, I'd be there too."

Ethan's phone buzzed. "And he said okay."

Jenna giggled. "Good choice."

"Can we talk about my mustache? Do I shave it?"

"No, don't shave it, but we do still have to talk. I don't know how we will find a good time, but right now isn't it."

Jenna felt his arm stiffen, and the wall returned.

"Something else we have to talk about is the wall," Jenna said.

"What wall?'" Ethan's voice was flat, with no expression.

"You stiffened up when I said now wasn't a good time. It's like a wall between us."

Ethan rolled his neck to loosen the muscles. "Like the mustache wall."

"You're right."

"We need some uninterruptible time."

When they stopped at the back door, Jenna put her hand on his cheek, then touched the tip of his mustache with her fingertips.

He put his arms around her and hugged her. After he released her, he said, "You're hard to talk to because you aren't interested in or even any better at small talk than I am."

Jenna smiled. "How was your day?"

Ethan's grin lit up his face. "Fine. How was your day?"

"Fine." Jenna laughed, and Ethan joined in.

"I'll see you later." He whistled as he strolled away.

"For the design war, right? I'll be ready," Jenna said.

Ethan raised his hand and waved.

Jenna smiled as she hurried into the inn. When she went into the kitchen, Katy greeted her.

Darlene was stirring a sauce on the stove. "Change in menu, Boss Lady. We'll have chicken enchiladas with a tossed green salad. Our dessert is key lime pie."

"People have been raving about our talented chef. They will be pushing to get into line for room reservations after lunch."

"That's the goal. Miss Georgia left to pick up some kind of investigator equipment. She'll be back; she said her new partner, Clint, was still upstairs. I told her I'd have lunch for them when she got back." Darlene turned back to her sauce.

When Jenna sat down at her desk, she logged into each of the ten groups. *I need a second monitor.*

Jenna mumbled, "There are definitely two people. Each hook, the Angel Girls, tugs at members' heartstrings then reels them in for the collector to dive in and complete the deal. Hooks are fragile, so the members want to save them. The collectors are quick and matter of fact, and the members are grateful for someone who takes action. I can see how automation helps, and there are definitely two voices. I wonder what would happen if I jumped in as a collector?"

Should I clear that with Sergio? She sent him a text. "I'm going to poke a sleeping bear."

CHAPTER FOURTEEN

Jenna checked the groups until she found one that was collecting money for a terrified child who had been kidnapped but had a plan to run away.

Beansy jumped in. "I can get her a first class plane ticket on an employee discount, so there will be extra money for food and clothes. Don't send money anywhere yet. I'll have a ticket and a secure place set up by the end of the day."

A few minutes later, her phone rang.

Sergio said, "Holy smokes. I saw what you just did. You caught me off guard. Antique Five will lose their mind. What are our next steps?"

"Wait for the response from Antique Five who probably hasn't seen it yet."

"Do you think the collector is one of the Orion Tech executives, and the hook is Renee? But she's so flamboyant."

"She's very calculating, dramatic, and focused on herself, which is what she needs to impersonate an Angel Girl. She could even have run her scripts through AI to give them the appropriate emotional tone. Assuming everything is being managed on the Orion Tech servers, the collector has to be a senior level technical person because of the access."

Sergio exhaled. "That's Fred or Nicci."

"Could someone be blackmailing Fred?"

Jenna frowned. "Or Nicci."

"Or me, but I can vouch for Nicci. I guess you'll have to trust me because I still have access to the Orion Tech servers. I'm going to see if I can find a bear to poke too."

"You ask me to trust you, and in the next breath you tell me you have access to the Orion Tech servers." Jenna chuckled.

Jenna heard his smile in his voice. "So? You don't appreciate the irony of all this? We're two professionals leaning on each other like we've been partners for years. I don't have any other choice if I want to keep up with you. What's your excuse?"

"You're getting old, partner. We shook hands."

Sergio's tone became somber. "That we did. I'll find a big stick. Let me know if you see any reactions." Sergio hung up.

Jenna stared at her computer, refreshed her screen a few times, and then rose and stretched her back. Katy stretched and yawned.

"I need to walk away from it for a few minutes," Jenna said. "Let's go bother Darlene."

When they strolled into the kitchen, Darlene glanced at her. "Morgan and Wendy are in the laundry room doing an inventory of cleaning supplies. I'm still missing two platters. Are you available to check the dining room?"

Jenna nodded.

When she slipped into the dining room, Orion was speaking. Everyone was listening intently and taking notes. While she listened, Jenna quietly gathered the two platters and a few plates then brushed crumbs on the sideboard onto the platter and picked up a few crumpled napkins. She glanced at the cups and peered into the coffee machine.

Before she opened the dining room door, she heard several phones beep, then Orion said, "Let's take a break, and then we'll jump to questions."

Jenna went into the kitchen and dropped off the platters then returned to the dining room with a small tray of clean coffee cups. While she gathered the dirty cups that had been left on the sideboard, Nicci joined her.

"How's your day?" Nicci asked.

"More or less routine. Sounds like the meeting's going well."

"It is. This has been a great opportunity to get everyone together. Did you have more paperwork for me to sign?"

"I sure do. Thank you for the reminder. Come with me to the office, and we'll take care of it."

After they were in the office, Nicci asked, "I know you heard all the alerts on the phones. Part of our test system that we haven't used in ages had a failure. I didn't think it was a big deal, but Orion was highly agitated when he glanced at his phone and immediately called for a break.

He and Fred went outside. It must be more than just the test system because we had a break ten minutes ago. I have to get back before I'm missed."

When Jenna opened the door to the dining room, it was still empty.

"Good," Nicci said. "I'll join the line for the restroom. Everyone else is outside or in the living room."

Sergio found his big stick.

Jenna sent a text to Sergio. "Failure alert for an old test system at OTI. O and F went outside."

Sergio replied, "Thanks. Seems like an extreme reaction to an old test system."

Before Jenna reached the door to go to the kitchen, her phone rang. She exhaled. *Renee. I should let it roll over to voice mail.*

She strolled to her desk and answered as she sat down.

"Jenna, I can't find Isabelle anywhere. I've called her phone, and it immediately drops. Did she return to the Peach Blossom Retreat or call you?"

"I haven't heard from her. There are a lot of low signal places she could be. I understand the signal at the peach orchard isn't that great. Didn't she say something about going on the tour? Maybe she went there after all. I'm sure you'll hear from her later."

"A problem came up with something. You know, with my publisher. Isabelle wouldn't know anything, but it's just odd I can't find her. So, nobody has called for me there? Orion hasn't asked where I am?"

"I haven't seen Orion. Morgan is responsible for their meeting, but she's in a staff meeting right now. I'll ask her if anyone has been trying to find you after her meeting is over."

"You aren't much help at all. It's a wonder your business stays open." Renee hung up.

Jenna smiled. *Does that make me a successful incompetent?*

Jenna sent Sergio a text. "Renee called me. Call when you can."

Her phone rang. When she answered, Sergio asked, "What did she say?"

"She was agitated because she couldn't find her friend, Isabelle, but when she asked if Orion had asked about her, I was positive that was the real reason she called."

Sergio chuckled. "Her friend, Isabelle? Isabelle is Orion's admin assistant. Orion or Fred must have called her to keep Renee busy for the day. If I didn't dislike Renee so much, I'd say that was a dirty trick, but under the circumstances, it was probably the nicest thing they could have done. As far as I know, Renee doesn't have any friends."

"Sounds like we've poked the bears. Now what?"

"Lure them out of the cave?"

"I think you're on to something. What is it they want?"

"To stay hidden in the cave, but maybe the cave is falling in. Is there any way someone who is working on the test server can discover it was hacked?" Jenna asked.

"Let me get this straight. You are asking a cyber security professional to inject an amateurish hack."

"Is that too hard?"

Sergio burst out laughing. "I'll just toss in an old-fashioned bug, and we can wait for the fireworks."

"Is there any possibility of someone innocent being blamed and fired?"

"Maybe Nicci, if she's lucky, but that's just wishful thinking on my part because I'd love for her to leave Orion Tech Industries; other than her, no one. Let me know when you see results."

After she hung up, Katy whined.

"You're right. It is time for a walk. Let's go."

"Where's Morgan?" Jenna asked Darlene when she and Katy went into the kitchen.

"Right here." Morgan rose from behind the counter with a screw driver in her hand. "The screw on the lower cabinet was coming loose, and it was driving me nuts."

"Lunch will be ready to serve in thirty minutes," Darlene said.

"Katy and I are going for a walk. We'll be back in plenty of time for me to help serve."

When Jenna and Katy went out the back door, a squirrel scampered across the yard, and Katy raced after it. A split second before Katy reached it, the squirrel leaped to a tree branch and stared at Katy as it chattered at her. Katy gazed up at the squirrel, daring it to slip as it jumped from its branch to another tree branch on a different tree.

Jenna's phone rang. *Sergio so soon?*

"What are you doing?" he asked.

"Katy and I just stepped out back. We're thinking about a walk. Why?"

"Fred's technology team is digging into the test server. I know that team; it won't take them long to discover the back door and the IP addresses you and Bobbie used. Are you still logged into any groups?"

"No, I've logged out and turned off my computer."

"Good; I'm going to wipe out you, Bobbie, and me from the server and close the back door so it is seamless. I'll leave all the Angel Girls and collectors, but with the back door closed and a critical piece of the server corrupted, they'll have no access to any of the groups."

Jenna frowned. *Sergio must have created the back door access to the test server when he left Orion Tech Industries. I wonder why.*

"Won't they be suspicious?" she asked.

"Of course, but of what? It's an old server, and old servers have failures."

"I meant suspicious about the back door."

"They won't find a trace of it. The good news is whoever set up the server as access for Angel Girls and the collector didn't know we were already there, and now there's no trace of us."

"Isn't that a strange coincidence they picked the same test server?"

"Not if they've been at Orion Technical Industries for a while. That test server was never touched. I gotta go." Sergio hung up.

"I am really confused, Katy, about the old test server and why both Sergio and whoever set up the scam would use the same server. Has Sergio been gathering data about the scam? Why didn't he just say so? Let's head back; my head hurts."

When Jenna and Katy went into the kitchen, Morgan said, "You're just in time. After we serve lunch, can you take over? I have to go into town for a quick errand, but I won't be too long."

"If you have to leave earlier, I can take care of lunch."

Morgan shook her head. "Serving lunch won't take that long, and my errand isn't urgent."

Jenna opened the door to the dining room a few inches. Nicci had moved to a table toward the back, and a man Jenna didn't recognize was speaking. Nicci's brow was furrowed, and she was biting her thumbnail. When Nicci glanced at Jenna, her face brightened; she tiptoed to the door and joined Jenna.

Jenna whispered, "Lunch is ready. When can we serve it?"

Nicci smiled. "You can serve it now; our financial officer doesn't break for anything except food. Watch."

Nicci cleared her throat, and the financial officer stopped mid-sentence and stared at her.

"Our lunch is hot and ready. After you wrap up, we can eat."

The speaker's face brightened. "In conclusion, see me after lunch if you have any questions."

Jenna and Morgan rolled out the utility carts. While Jenna set up the plates, silverware, and salad with salad dressings at one end of the sideboard, Morgan set up the chafing dish buffet and then returned with the steaming pan of chicken enchiladas.

Jenna checked the level of the sweet tea then refilled the ice bin; Morgan carried out a tray with dessert forks and plates of key lime pie and lined them up on the smaller sideboard.

After they returned to the kitchen, Jenna said, "They're set; you can go anytime, Morgan."

"Thanks; I won't be long."

When she left, Darlene asked, "Where is Morgan going?"

"Into town."

Darlene smiled. "It's about time."

Jenna cocked her head. "For what?"

"I'm not supposed to know."

Jenna frowned. *Everybody has a secret.*

"Would you mind stepping into the dining room so I can introduce you?"

"I don't do that," Darlene growled.

"I know you don't, but I heard a guest call you Chef DeeDee, and I'm positive Chef DeeDee would smile and wave."

Darlene stared at Jenna. "Chef DeeDee?"

"Sounds classy, doesn't it?"

Darlene fluffed her hair. "Should I leave my apron on?"

"Of course."

When they stepped into the dining room, a woman said, "Ooo, it's Chef DeeDee."

She rose and applauded, and the rest of the room joined her.

Darlene smiled and waved then quickly retreated into the kitchen.

Jenna stayed and thanked everyone on Darlene's behalf.

When she joined Darlene in the kitchen, Darlene wiped her eyes and then cleared her throat. "Thank you, Jenna."

"They really enjoyed your food; thank you for letting them show you how much they appreciate your cooking."

Jenna returned to the dining room with the cart and quickly cleared the dishes. After she rolled the utility cart into the kitchen, Darlene growled, "I can take it from here."

Jenna smiled as she went into her office to read her email. When she heard a car turn in the visitor parking lot, she furrowed her brow. "That's not Morgan. She wouldn't park in the visitors' lot."

Jenna peered out the window and rolled her eyes as Renee stormed up the path from the lot to the inn. When she heard Renee come inside and stomp up the stairs, she sighed. *I hope she doesn't get into an argument with anyone.*

A few minutes later, Jenna's phone buzzed a text from Renee.

"I want to check out immediately. I'm at the registration desk and no one is here. Typical of your service."

Jenna shrugged. *At least she's leaving.*

Jenna strolled to the registration desk while Renee glared at her and tapped her foot.

Renee sniffed then looked down her nose at Jenna. "I have a reservation at the new hotel on the other side of town. This inn is just too cutesy for me. I will include that in my review along with details of the lack of service."

"I'm sorry to hear that," Jenna said.

Renee slammed her room key on the counter. "I'll bet you are. I can break you." She hissed through her teeth.

"I've closed out your room. Do you want a receipt?" Jenna asked.

"Yes, and I'll take my refund in cash."

Jenna brought up Renee's room and issued a refund. "Our refund policy required twenty-four hours' notice, but I'll be happy to make an exception for you. I've refunded the credit card."

Renee snorted. "I didn't pay for the room with my card. I want my refund in cash. Immediately."

Renee glowered and held out her hand.

"We don't keep cash on hand, Renee. I've already refunded the remaining of your reservation."

"I knew you would find a way to cheat me." Renee snatched her suitcase off the counter and jostled her sunglasses that dangled by the ear piece on the strap of her purse as rushed to the front door.

Jenna beat her to the door and opened it so Renee could leave. When Renee elbowed Jenna to move out of her way, her sunglasses clattered t to the floor. As she pushed past Jenna, Renee inadvertently kicked her sunglasses and sent them skittering across the foyer.

"Wait," Jenna said.

Renee snorted. "You've kept me waiting long enough. You can talk to my lawyer."

Renee stormed down the path, jumped into her car, and sped down the driveway before Jenna could explain.

"That was one dramatic exit, wasn't it, Katy? I'll mail her sunglasses to her."

Jenna sighed as she bent over to pick up Renee's sunglasses. When she touched them, she dropped to her knees.

"I can't see," she gasped as she clutched the sunglasses in one hand and groped for the nearby table with the other. Katy whined and nudged her. She found Katy and wrapped her arms around her.

While she fought to control her breathing, she dropped the sunglasses then stared at Katy. "I can see."

She continued to hug Katy as she slowly scanned the room.

"It wasn't just black." Jenna shuddered. "Light just didn't exist."

"Where are the sunglasses?" Jenna's heart pounded as panic tightened her chest.

Katy licked Jenna's arm, and Jenna inhaled then exhaled. "Now, I'm scaring myself. The sunglasses can't hurt me, can they?"

Jenna peered under the table. "There they are. They can just stay there for now."

Jenna rose to her feet. "Let's go to the office."

When Jenna opened the kitchen door and Darlene wasn't there, she glanced at the clock. "Darlene went home. That's good."

She sat at her desk and put her head down. "That terrified me, Katy."

Her phone buzzed a text. "This better not be Renee."

She read the text from Ethan. "The only way we'll have coffee time is if we just make time. How about now?"

Jenna put her elbows on her desk and held her head. "He couldn't have picked a worse time. What do I say, Katy?"

She stared at her phone. *Whatever I say, he'll take it wrong.*

Finally she texted, "Later is better."

Morgan burst into the office. "Was I gone too long?"

I was so focused on waiting for a response from Ethan that I didn't hear her car.

"Not at all, but you missed Renee's theatrical exit. She canceled the rest of her reservation in a huff and left."

"She asked for a refund, didn't she?" Morgan rolled her eyes.

"That's only half of her audacity. She wanted her refund in cash. I refunded the credit card, which was not hers."

"Hence, the flounce," Morgan said.

"Exactly."

Morgan turned on her computer. "I'll take a quick peek at the system to see what we have."

While Morgan was on her computer, Jenna sighed in relief when her phone buzzed. *Oh good. He's not upset with me.*

The text was from Nicci. "Can you come to the dining room? We're wrapping up, and Orion has a few words to say on our behalf."

Jenna's heart sunk then she exhaled as she responded. "On my way!"

She went into the dining room through the kitchen door with Morgan and Katy on her heels.

When she opened the door, Orion stood in the front of the room.

He beamed. "Jenna, we have had an extremely productive meeting, thanks to you and your staff. The atmosphere of your beautiful inn is calming and inspiring, and we loved Chef DeeDee's delicious food."

"Go into the dining room; you're in my way," Morgan hissed.

When she stepped into the room, Morgan hurried to sit next to Nicci.

Katy stayed at Jenna's side.

"Nicci, would you do the honors?" Orion asked.

She strode to the front then motioned for Jenna to join her. Jenna glared at Morgan then smiled as she strolled to the front and stood next to Nicci.

Nicci smiled. "As a company, we take pride in our technical skills, but our best skill is knowing when to call in the experts. With Morgan's help, we reached out to a local history expert for advice. He found a pair of kerosene lamps that were owned by the Wyndham family in the mid-1920s."

Nicci set the kerosene lamps on the empty table in front of her. "I'll read the note from our expert."

She pulled out a note from her pocket. "The matching pair of oil lamps are amethyst glass, which give them their pale lavender color. Their ruffled top chimneys are the originals. They were a wedding gift to Henry and Nettie Wyndham in 1920."

Jenna gaped at the lamps. "They are beautiful. You can't imagine how much this means to me." A tear slipped down her face. "Thank you so much. They belong in the living room on the mantel."

Nicci brushed away a tear. "I think so too."

Orion said, "We're excited we could be the catalysts to bring you the lamps that obviously belong here. Thank you again for your hospitality."

After everyone left except Nicci, Morgan asked, "Can we take the lamps to the living room?"

Jenna smiled as she picked up one with two hands; Morgan carried the other one.

After they placed the lamps on the mantel, Morgan and Nicci stepped back, but Jenna sat in her yellow chair and smiled at Nettie's portrait. The sunlight streaming into the window brightened Nettie's face, and the portrait seemed to return Jenna's smile.

"Is she happy?" Morgan whispered.

"Very," Jenna replied.

Nicci rose from the sofa and stepped back to stare at the portrait. "She's smiling."

Jenna nodded.

As Nicci turned to leave the living room, Jenna said, "Nicci, Renee checked out this afternoon."

Nicci's eyes brightened. "Really? Why?"

Jenna smiled. "Because of my terrible service."

Nicci tilted her head. "Did she ask for a refund?"

Morgan chuckled. "That was my first question too. She asked for a cash refund, but the mean Boss Lady had already refunded the room to the credit card on record."

Nicci laughed. "That is the best terrible service I've ever heard of."

"I think we'll still end up with a full house this weekend. I have to get back to work." Morgan left.

After Morgan left, Nicci asked, "Did Renee say where she was going?"

"She said she had a reservation for a room at the new hotel on the other side of town, but she doesn't have the best history for being acquainted with the truth, so no telling." Jenna shrugged.

"I'm going to tell Sergio we can take the walk to the peach orchard. We'll see you at happy hour."

"Thanks again for the lamps. They're perfect."

"I'm so pleased you love them. Orion gave me a blank check, and Morgan gave me the idea. I waved my hands, and it all happened. Foster is amazing, isn't he? I agree; they are perfect." Nicci grinned.

Jenna walked into the kitchen and sent a text to Ethan. "Are you available for coffee before or after happy hour?"

She stared at her phone.

"Let's go home, Katy. I wouldn't mind a little down time before happy hour."

After they were in the cottage, Jenna turned on her gas fireplace to take off the chill. She pulled off her boots and sat in her green chair.

Jenna leaned back and closed her eyes. She didn't realize she'd dozed off until the buzz of her phone startled her awake.

Chapter Fifteen

Jenna blinked to refocus her still-sleepy blurry eyes. *Ethan.*

She read his text. "Where are you?"

She replied, "At home."

"Make the coffee; I'll be right there."

Jenna stood in front of the coffee maker as it sighed and gurgled. "I suppose it won't finish any faster if I watch it."

She walked away and stood at the front door. "This is worse, Katy."

Jenna paced until she received another text. *The sheriff?*

She shook her head as she read, "Where are you?"

"Why is everybody asking me that? Am I that unpredictable?" She exhaled. "I suppose it's a valid question, Katy."

She replied, "At home."

"I'll be there in five minutes."

Before she replied, Katy whined, and there was a knock on her door.

She opened the door and smiled. "It's nice to see you. The coffee's almost done, and the sheriff's on his way."

Ethan returned her smile. "Typical day with us these days, isn't it?"

Jenna nodded as she gazed at him. *He said us.*

She frowned. *It's just a word.*

Ethan held up a small sack. "Don't tell Darlene, but I picked up chocolate covered ice cream bars."

"I love chocolate covered ice cream bars. I'll put them in the freezer, and we can have them after the sheriff leaves."

Katy whined.

Ethan peered out the window. "The sheriff's here. Should I step outside?"

"I'd like for you to stay." Jenna opened the door, and the sheriff strolled inside. He nodded at Ethan.

"I have fresh coffee; would you care for some?" Jenna asked.

"I won't be here that long, but can we sit down?"

After the three of them were seated at the kitchen table, the sheriff said, "This is public information, or at least will be within the hour. I thought Renee Sabot was staying here at the inn."

"She was until earlier today when she checked out."

The sheriff nodded. "Wasn't that earlier than expected? Why did she leave?"

"She was paid through the weekend and said she was checking out because my service was terrible. She insisted on a refund, which I gave her."

Ethan snorted. "Absurd."

"I have to agree with Ethan," the sheriff said. "So, did that satisfy her?"

"No, I refunded the credit card that was used to pay for her room; she wanted a cash refund because the credit card was not hers. She left when I refused to give her a cash refund."

"Did she say where she was going?"

"She told me she had a reservation at the new hotel."

"Renee reserved their best suite on the third floor with a balcony. Not long after she checked in, she fell from the balcony and didn't survive the fall."

Jenna felt the panic closing in. "Could she see?"

The sheriff narrowed his eyes. "Why?"

"She couldn't see, could she?" Jenna hyperventilated, and the room spun and turned black.

"Jenna." Ethan was kneeling next to her with his arm around her as he patted her face with a damp cloth. "You're okay honey; I'm right here."

Jenna relaxed then gazed at the sheriff as she exhaled. "Renee dropped her sunglasses before she left the inn. I tried to tell her, but she was too angry to listen."

Jenna reached for Ethan's hand. "When I picked up her sunglasses, I couldn't see." She shuddered from the memory then clutched Ethan's hand and continued, "until I dropped them."

"Where are they now?" the sheriff asked gently.

"They landed under the small table in the foyer; I assume they're still there. I was afraid to touch them even with my foot."

The sheriff shook his head and exhaled. "She had a pink bandana tied over her eyes."

Jenna shuddered. "I tried, but I couldn't stop her."

"Is Darlene at the inn? I'll take the sunglasses with me." the sheriff said.

Jenna shook her head. "Morgan is. I'll send her a text."

Her hand trembled as she reached for her phone.

"I'll text her," Ethan said.

After his phone buzzed a reply, Ethan said, "She'll open the back door, Sheriff."

"Thanks. I'll let Morgan know someone from the GBI will be here later to examine Renee's room."

After the sheriff left, Ethan's phone buzzed with a second text. He furrowed his brow as he read, then smirked. "This is from Shane. He and Morgan had the design war without us. Guess who won?"

Jenna furrowed her brow. "They came to a mutually beneficial compromise."

Ethan chuckled. "Actually, Shane said he won. He told her he's not a designer, and Morgan agreed."

"I can believe it." Jenna smiled as she leaned forward, but the pamphlet she'd put in her back pocket caught on the chair and fell to the floor. After she picked it up, Ethan poured coffee while she read it.

Ethan put their cups on the table. "Is that the furniture pamphlet from Bobbie that Shane gave you on Monday?"

Jenna slowly sat down as she examined the pamphlet. "I've been moving it from spot to spot all week. The furniture is nice, but it's too contemporary for me."

Jenna turned to the middle of the pamphlet. "Woah."

"What?" Ethan rested his hand on her shoulder as he leaned closer to look at the pamphlet.

"Right here." Jenna pointed. "Who put the squeeze on Daffodil?"

"What does that mean?"

Jenna picked up her cup and sipped her coffee.

After Ethan joined her, Jenna said, "Somebody was blackmailing Nicci."

Ethan gaped at her. "What? I think I need some background."

"I think you do too. We'll have to postpone the mustache talk."

Ethan crossed his arms. "Oh."

"Let the wall go, Ethan, or I can't talk about Daffodil."

Ethan snorted. "I'm supposed to give up the mustache for daffodils." His mouth twitched. "I don't know why I'm saying this, but go ahead."

Jenna smiled. "Thank you."

She told him about Pink Lady, Daffodil, Beansy, and the Angel Girl and Knit One scam.

After she told him about Sergio, he asked, "Are you sure Sergio is a good cop, not a bad cop?"

"I'm positive. I think Renee was the Angel Girls, and someone at Orion Tech was the Knit Ones. Everything points to Fred Haas."

"What do you mean?"

"He's the Chief Technology Officer at Orion Technical Industries. He's technically strong and at a level in the company that he would have access to any of the systems. But I don't think he is the Knit Ones because when we shook hands, I got the impression he is all business. Of course, maybe he considers the scam part of his business model." Jenna rubbed her forehead. "I hadn't thought about that before."

"Who else would have access like Fred?"

"Nicci and Sergio. Nicci is hiding something, and Bobbie said someone was blackmailing her, and from what Renee said, maybe it was her, but wouldn't Sergio know about it?"

"Do you think Nicci is Knit One?" Ethan asked.

"Not at all, but now I've dismissed the only three possibilities unless there's another person like Sergio at the company. Maybe Orion kept up his skills, or I can ask Nicci who replaced Sergio. I should ask her about what Renee was sending her."

Ethan's phone buzzed a text. He exhaled after he read it. "Terrell has run into a problem at the Peach Pit. What did you name it?"

"Peachy Suite."

"Yeah, that."

"You need to go, don't you?"

Ethan furrowed his brow and squirmed.

Jenna quickly rose from her chair and gave him a sweet, open mouth kiss. "It's okay; we'll get together later."

Ethan rose from his chair and returned her kiss. When he released her, he smiled.

As he strode to the door and left, Jenna smiled. *There's that cute swagger again.*

Jenna's phone buzzed a text from Nicci. "Did you hear about Renee? I'm at the hotel and in a bind. Come quick. I have to turn off my phone now."

"I have to go, Katy. Do you want to go or stay here?"

Katy closed her eyes.

"I don't blame you; it's been a busy day." Jenna put on her coat but didn't zip it. "Ethan said his range partner moved away; maybe that's where we should go for our next coffee meetup so both of us can get away from work."

When she drove past the visitors' parking lot, the only vehicle in the lot was Sergio's truck.

As she headed toward town, Jenna frowned. *Why didn't Nicci ask Sergio for help?*

She pulled over onto the shoulder and called Ethan. "I'm on my way to the new hotel. I got a text from Nicci asking for help."

"As I get back to my truck, I'll be on the road."

"I didn't mean to bother you; I just wanted you to know where I was. There's no need for you to come."

Ethan chuckled. "I hear you."

"Okay, we'll race."

Jenna pulled back onto the highway and sped away.

Jenna slowed to the speed limit as she drove through the town of Paisley. *I forgot about the bypass. I wonder if that would have been faster.*

She cleared the city limits and picked up her speed. When she reached the hotel, Jenna cruised the front parking lot for Nicci's car.

After she reached the last row, Ethan pulled into the lot and waited for her at the end of the row.

She stopped next to his car, and they lowered their windows.

"Why are we here?" he asked.

Jenna read Nicci's text to him.

"I don't know why she didn't text Sergio. I'll text him."

Jenna sent the text. "Where's Nicci?"

Sergio replied immediately. "I thought she was with you. Where are you?"

"The hotel where Renee fell. Nicci texted she was here."

"I'll be right there."

Jenna handed her phone to Ethan.

He narrowed his eyes as he returned her phone. "We should leave."

"There's a parking lot in the back; let's check it first, then we can leave."

"I still think we should leave, but give me a minute. I'll go first and park away from the building, so I'll have your back."

Jenna nodded. *Everything seems off to me.*

"I'll text the sheriff."

She sent the sheriff a text. "Nicci Dubois sent me a text asking for help. Ethan and I are at the new hotel. Something seems off."

The sheriff replied, "On my way. Clint might be closer. Wait for us."

"Do we leave now?" Ethan asked.

"I want to check the back parking lot."

"Let me get in place first." Ethan pulled away slowly.

Jenna nodded. *Just another guest trying to find the perfect parking spot. Well done.*

Ethan called. "Nicci's car is in the middle of the second row. It's empty. A man is sitting in two cars away in the third row. I'm parked in the fifth row behind Nicci's car. I can sit here while you watch the exit until the sheriff shows up."

Jenna shuddered. *That will take too long.*

"I'll be careful." Jenna hung up.

When Jenna rounded the corner, she crept past the first three rows then parked in the fourth row on the end. She glanced at Ethan who stood next to his car while he watched the man who sat in the third row.

She locked her car and grabbed her phone from her back pocket to carry in her left hand as she strode purposely toward the hotel's back entrance.

When she neared the first row, a familiar voice called out, "Hey, Jenna."

Orion.

When she paused, she heard a soft thump from the second row. *Nicci?*

She glanced at Orion as he rushed toward her.

"Jenna, I thought that was you. Did Nicci text you too?"

Slick, Orion.

Jenna peered at her phone then tapped 'record' on her screen with her thumb as she lowered it. "My phone's been off. Is Nicci here too? I have a meeting with a GBI agent who wants to talk to me about Renee. Do you know Clint? Do you think he wants to talk to all of us?"

"I didn't see a GBI cruiser when I pulled in." Orion paused.

"He's probably parked in front. I didn't notice."

"When is your meeting?" Orion continued toward Jenna.

"Now; what about you?"

"He must be running late." Orion stopped when he was five yards from Jenna and glanced toward the building while he clenched his right hand then rubbed his fingertips with his thumb.

"You're the last thorn in my side, Jenna. I couldn't believe an old woman was tracking me in those groups. That was an embarrassment."

"An old woman? Where was she getting her information?"

Orion snorted. "You aren't as smart as everyone thinks, are you? Where do you think? Angel Girl had to brag."

"What about Sophia?"

"Sophia got too nosy and uncovered Renee's work, which I admit wouldn't have been too hard. Renee was sharp at one time, but she got sloppy. It was her idea to blackmail Nicci, which might have worked if Renee had known the meaning of finesse." Orion's chuckle was hollow and sarcastic.

"Where's Nicci?"

"Close enough to get the point she'd better cooperate if she doesn't want to end up like you, the old woman, Sophia, and Renee."

"Doesn't it seem odd to you that you can't seem to get along with women?" Jenna eased her right hand to her hip.

She watched as Ethan slowly moved closer to her.

"Women love me; enough talk," Orion growled.

"Hey, Orion!" Ethan shouted as Orion pulled out his pistol and aimed at Jenna.

Orion, Jenna, and Ethan fired simultaneously.

Orion staggered then his pistol clattered on the pavement as he collapsed.

Jenna's hand was shaking as she set her pistol on the pavement. She stopped recording on her phone.

Ethan raced to her and grabbed her close. Jenna leaned against his chest.

A GBI cruiser sped into the parking lot and slammed to a stop next to the first row.

Jenna exhaled. "It's Clint."

Ethan tenderly brushed her hair away from her face with his fingertips. "I can't believe you're on a first name basis with every lawman in at least two counties."

Clint strode to them. "Give me a quick rundown."

"I recorded most of it. Orion West confessed to murdering Bobbie Moore, Sophia Baker, and Renee Sabot. He intended to murder me. I recorded him," Jenna said.

Clint raised his eyebrows. "On your phone? Has anyone checked Orion West?"

"No," Ethan said.

Jenna straightened her back. "Nicci."

"Where is she?" Ethan asked.

The thumps became louder and more frequent. "She's locked in her car's trunk."

"Ambulance is already on the way," Clint said. "I'll check Orion West and see if he has the keys for her car."

Jenna tugged on Ethan's sleeve. "Nicci's car."

He kept his arm around her as they strode to Nicci's car. Ethan pulled on the driver's door handle, and the door opened.

Ethan snorted. "How did you know the keys would be on the seat?"

"Look at her key ring. It has keys, a tiny flashlight, a small hand sanitizer, and a squishy ball. It would be easy to find in a purse, but impossible to stick into a pants pocket."

Ethan pressed the button to open the trunk, and it flew open as an ambulance, a truck, a sheriff's cruiser, and other law enforcement vehicles swarmed the parking lot.

As Jenna rushed to open the trunk wider, Sergio slammed to a stop behind Nicci's car. He jumped out of his truck as the trunk flew open, and Nicci blinked at the sudden brightness.

Sergio reached past Jenna and carefully pulled away the pink tape from her mouth before he cut the pink tape binding her hands and feet.

When he lifted her out of the trunk, Nicci said, "Nice work, Jenna."

"You're going to have a doozy of a black eye tomorrow, honey," Sergio said. "Do you want the ambulance crew to check you?"

"No." Nicci cleared her throat. "He spoofed Jenna's phone and sent me a text that I thought was from Jenna asking for my help. He sucker-punched me then taped me up and threw me into the back of my car."

"He sent me a similar text that I thought was from you," Jenna said. "Orion said Renee was blackmailing you. Was that true?"

Nicci glanced at Sergio.

Sergio frowned. "What is it?"

"After you left, Orion fabricated evidence that showed you were siphoning money out of Orion Tech Industries. He was a very sadistic man. He must have given the evidence to Renee who decided she was supposed to force me to quit. Orion made it very clear to me that if I tried to leave, he'd leak that and more, and Sergio's career in law enforcement would be over. Fred and I were quietly replacing the so-called evidence against Sergio with benign numbers, but Orion became suspicious after Renee told him Pink Lady was hiding Sergio."

"Why would she say that?" Jenna bit her lip. "Sophia told me Renee was dangerous."

Nicci gazed at Sergio. "Could you extend our room for another week, Jenna?"

Jenna smiled. "Of course."

Jenna glanced at Clint who stood near her car. He motioned for Jenna and Ethan to join him and the sheriff.

Clint gazed at Jenna. "Orion had a fatal wound to the temple and one in his heart. His gun was fired. Where did his shot go?"

"When he aimed at Jenna, I shouted at him. He glanced at me when he pulled the trigger, so his shot went wild. The three shots were at the same time and almost sounded like one," Ethan said.

"Can you send me that recording, Jenna?" Clint asked.

She nodded, and with Clint's help, Jenna sent him the recording.

"You could give your statements now, or I could follow you to the inn and take them there," the sheriff said.

"I can give my statement now," Jenna said.

After the sheriff took their statements, he said, "If I think of anything else, I'll call you. Good work, Jenna. Please don't do this anymore."

"Are you okay with driving, honey?" Ethan asked. "We could pick up your car tomorrow."

Jenna narrowed her eyes. "I don't want to leave it here."

"I'll follow you."

CHAPTER SIXTEEN

After they parked at the inn, Ethan put his arm around Jenna. "Cottage or the inn?"

"Let's go to the inn. It's almost happy hour, and I can help Morgan with serving. After happy hour, the four of us can talk."

"I have a better idea. Let's tell Morgan and Shane what happened then go to the cottage to relax. I need to talk about my wall."

When they went into the kitchen, Morgan was at the counter, reading the instructions for happy hour. "Where have you been? You look exhausted."

"Sit for a minute."

After Jenna and Ethan told them about Orion and his confession, Morgan said, "I can take care of happy hour, Jenna. Why don't you take the night off?"

"You don't have to do that," Jenna said.

"I'll help her," Shane said.

"Give me a second, and I'll pack up your share of happy hour," Morgan said.

"Let them do something nice for you, Jenna." Ethan put his arm around her shoulder.

"Three against one isn't fair." Jenna rolled her eyes.

Shane snorted. "Whatever it takes."

Morgan filled a sack with appetizers, bread, cheese, and slices of cheesecake.

"Thank you for everything," Jenna said.

After they were in the cottage, Ethan said, "I feel more comfortable talking while I'm working. Can I show off my culinary skills by fixing you a plate of appetizers?"

"Sure. I'll take care of the drinks. Do you want coffee, hot tea, sweet tea, or water to drink?"

"I'll have sweet tea. Morgan's housewarming gift to you was a bottle of wine. Would you care for a glass of wine?"

"I'll have sweet tea too."

While Jenna put their drinks on the table, Ethan fixed their plates.

After they sat down, Ethan gazed at her. "I told you my wife died in a crash when a drug addict hit her head on. That wasn't quite true. My wife did die in a head-on crash, but she was the addict, and she killed a young family. She had all her things packed in her car's trunk. I didn't know it until later when I found an angry note at home; she was leaving me for her supplier. The doctors told me addicts are masters at hiding their habit, but I was devastated because I never saw it. I was certain I failed her because if I'd paid attention, I could have helped her.

That's the wall you've talked about. I never wanted to be in the position of failing someone again."

Jenna put her hand on his and felt his pain. She grimaced. "I'm so sorry. It's a terrible scar, isn't it?"

"You're right; that's exactly what it is. I'm healing slowly, but there may always be a scar."

"Let me tell you about your mustache. I absolutely love it, but I didn't want to. Tom and I had been together since we were in second grade. When we were married, he had a mustache, but he shaved before he went into the military. He continued to be clean shaven until he came home on leave with a scruffy beard and a straggly mustache before he left on his last tour. Tom didn't quite look like himself, but worse than that, he didn't act like himself at all. He was cynical and suspicious. When he accused me of having a boyfriend, I was heartbroken. We were barely speaking by the end of his two-week leave, and that was the last time I saw him alive. I blamed all our problems on that mustache."

"So, where do we go from here?" Ethan asked.

Jenna traced his mustache with her finger. "Without our walls and with your mustache unless you want to shave; it's your choice."

"That's a great start."

"But we still have a lot of work to do."

"I know, and all the time we need; isn't it great?" Ethan leaned close and kissed her.

Did you enjoy Jenna's story?

Leave a review with your favorite bookseller and with
Barrett Book Shop!
Next to read:
JENNA ROSS THRILLER, BOOK 3
Fall 2025
Check BARRETT BOOK SHOP for other Judith A.
Barrett books to read!
BarrettBookShop.com
Browse, shop, read, enjoy!

SUBSCRIBE AND SAVE
Join the eNewsletter mailing list and become the
first to know about book specials and read unpublished
stories and exciting news!
SUBCRIBE to her Newsletter via her website
www.judithabarrett.com/newsletter

More About the Author

Judith A. Barrett, award-winning author, lives on a farm in Georgia with her husband, two dogs, and chickens. She writes series for her readers: thriller, romantic and cozy mysteries, historical fiction, and post-apocalyptic science fiction novels. Stories with a twist: not your typical characters from not your typical author!

Her motto: *You keep reading; I'll keep writing!*

When she isn't writing, Judith is meeting readers at arts and crafts fairs, working on farm chores, hiking or camping with her husband and dogs, or rocking on her front porch while she watches the sunset and plans the next plot twist in the book she is writing.

Website   judithabarrett.com

VIP Readers   judithabarrett.com/newsletter

Exclusive Discounts and Sales barrettbookshop.com

Not into emails, even though Judith's story-focused newsletters are interesting, Not-Your-Typical newsletters? Follow Judith on Barrett Book Shop, Her

Blog on her website: The Latest Twist, Bookbub, or your favorite bookseller for news of her latest release!

Let's keep in touch!

Find your next book(s) and buy direct from the author at the Barrett Book Shop!

www.ingramcontent.com/pod-product-compliance
Lightning Source LLC
Chambersburg PA
CBHW020843020726
47497CB00005B/1238